VERY NEARLY DEAD

A K REYNOLDS

BLOODHOUND
— BOOKS —

Print ISBN 978-1-912986-64-4

For Melinda

HERE AND NOW

A lamp post brought my car to a halt. If not for the seatbelt I would've been hurled through the windscreen. My reflexes contributed to my survival. Some instinct made me jam on the brakes as I careered out of control. Once the car was stationary I sat in the darkness, my heart pumping wildly. That was when the boy's face came back to me, wide-eyed and open-mouthed, as did the sound his body had made when my car ploughed into him.

Oh my God, Jaz, what have you done? I thought.

I turned off the ignition and put on the handbrake, then felt at a loss as to what to do next.

'Hold it together,' I muttered, looking around to assess the situation. My car was at a slant because the two nearside wheels were on the pavement and the other two were on the road. I took a deep breath, told myself I had to check how the boy was, unfastened my seatbelt, and climbed out. My head was spinning and everything had an unreal nightmarish quality. I prayed to God I'd wake up in bed and all would be back to normal, but deep down I knew that however nightmarish this all felt, it was actually happening. Things swung dizzily in and out of focus and I wondered if I'd been concussed, or if

I'd done something I shouldn't – something I didn't want to think about.

I walked around the other side of the vehicle to get a better view of my victim. He'd been thrown off the bonnet and landed on the pavement. I should have been in a blind panic but I wasn't. Shaken up and distressed, yes; blind panic, no. That's how I knew I was drunk. It was a revelation which filled me with dread. I'd sober up quickly, once the enormity of what I'd done sank in.

With a shock I realised I knew the boy lying on the ground. He was a former client of mine called Sean Price, and was only sixteen years old. I'd got him off charges of possession of a controlled drug, and intention to supply a controlled drug. He'd grown a beard since I'd last seen him, and his thin whiskery features made him look like a dead rat, but surely he wasn't dead. His eyes were open, unseeing, but there had to be life behind them. I bent down to examine him. I'm no medical expert, I'm a solicitor. Still, I thought I'd be able to reassure myself the boy was at least breathing.

He wasn't.

What next, then?

My stomach made an involuntary movement, a sort of flip, as I assessed the future.

My specialist area was criminal law. I was a defence solicitor. It wasn't too hard for me to work out what the consequences of my actions would be, even in the inebriated and overwrought state I'd somehow gotten myself into. I didn't have to look anything up because I'd dealt with this sort of thing for my clients many times. It was second nature to me, so much so that I was able to recite the penalties while crouching over the body. (I now accepted *he* was no longer a boy, *it* was a *body*.)

There would be: a prison sentence of up to fourteen years, a fine which could be unlimited, a two-year minimum driving ban, and eleven penalty points on my driving licence. Plus, I could expect to be struck off the roll of solicitors and face disciplinary action from the Solicitors Regulation Authority. In the grand scheme of things, however, all the penalties, other than the prison sentence, would amount to no more than a slap on the wrist.

I said it out loud, 'Fourteen years.'

It seemed an unfeasibly long time. Then I considered the possibility of time off for good behaviour, parole, and so on, and reckoned I might get away with only serving seven years. But even seven was a long time behind bars. Too long for me, even though I was still, just, in my early thirties, with most of my life ahead of me, as long as I didn't somehow throw it away.

I didn't want to go to prison. That said, I was just coming home from one. I'd been out on a call to a police station cell dispensing advice to a new client. It was my night for doing the call-outs, a part of the job I loathed. The worst thing about my role, as I very quickly found out, is that they were all guilty. I hadn't, to the best of my knowledge, ever defended an innocent man or woman. But it was my job to get them acquitted irrespective of guilt.

I'd been very successful at getting acquittals. I was good at playing the game with the Crown Prosecution Service lawyers. That was the part of the job I liked, the intellectual aspect where you use your knowledge and skills to get one over on the opposition. But when I thought about the people I was using my skills to help, it could be depressing, which is probably why my drinking had increased over the years.

Or maybe it was for another reason – the secret I harboured. The one I'd buried deep within my soul and which every single day since the day of its interment had hammered on the sides of its coffin demanding to be exhumed.

Whatever the reason, I'd started drinking at every opportunity I could, and I knew that this very evening after leaving the police station, I'd called in at O'Shaughnessy's. The new client had been depressingly guilty, as usual, and I'd gotten him off the hook, as usual. Then on the way home, feeling angry with the world for what I was forced to do for a living, I'd noticed the bright lights in O'Shaughnessy's piercing the cold night air. The interior looked warm and inviting in the way that only a good pub at night can. Naturally I'd pulled into the car park and ventured inside for a swift, morale-boosting drink.

I'd just had one so far as I knew, a half of weak pale ale to help me feel at peace with myself before going home.

But did I remember it right? Had I stopped for just one, or had I drunk more than one? I must've done, given the way I was feeling. And now I was facing a charge of causing death by dangerous driving while under the influence of drink. I wondered if my forensic legal defence skills were good enough to get myself acquitted, and decided they weren't. There was too much of a weight of evidence against me – the dent in the front grill, the body, DNA evidence linking the body to my vehicle, and my blood alcohol content.

I got back in my car and reversed it half a yard then I climbed out and inspected the lamp post. It was obvious it'd been hit by a vehicle. What's more, you could tell it'd been a blue vehicle.

I went back to the boy. There was what looked like a bloodstain on the pavement next to his head. It made me shudder, both because I'm squeamish, and because it seemed to speak volumes about the severity of the crime I'd just committed. The skid marks on the road also gave me pause. No doubt the police had some kind of tyre analyst who'd be able to prove those skid marks were made by tyres which matched mine.

Potentially the most damning evidence of all was the witness, if he or she had indeed been a witness. It was impossible to say for certain, but I thought I remembered a car behind me as I turned onto Fosby Street, the street on which I'd just had my accident.

Witness or no witness, it was a near certainty I was going to lose my liberty and my job. In addition, my home would go. The fine the court would impose would see to that, and if it didn't, I'd lose my home anyway, because I wouldn't be able to keep up the mortgage payments from a prison cell.

My imprisonment would be a bitter pill for my parents to swallow. I couldn't bear to think how they'd take it. Neither of them would be keen to spend the next fourteen years, or even the next seven, visiting me every week in HM Prison Holloway or wherever I ended up.

For the first time I thought to look around and take in my surroundings. I'd had my accident on Fosby Street. It was off the beaten track, being a shortcut I often took to get home. To one side of it there was a wall to stop pedestrians falling into a steep railway cutting. To the other, a derelict warehouse which, according to a poster, was to be sold at auction. Further along the street there were rows of shabby terraced houses. All of them had the curtains and blinds drawn. It seemed that none of the occupants had heard anything, or, if they had, they'd chosen to ignore it.

Like most London streets this one was jammed with parked cars. I scrutinised them to check whether any were occupied. I couldn't see any car with a driver in it, although rather worryingly one had the lights on.

I had to decide what to do about my victim.

I knew what I ought to do. I had a duty to turn myself in. If I did turn myself in, my life would be ruined and the lives of my parents would be, too. Then there was my younger brother. I adored him and he'd always looked up to me. It'd be impossibly hard for him to hear the news that his big sister had become a criminal.

I took a deep breath and steeled myself for the upset I was going to cause myself, and my nearest and dearest, and got my mobile out of my bag to call the police.

Then I thought, *What am I doing? This boy's life is finished. If I turn myself in, I'll end another life – my own. Four lives, if you include my close family members. What's the point of that?*

I looked at the car parked down the street with the lights on. I couldn't tell what kind of a car it was. But did it matter? It was enough there was a car parked nearby that might have a witness in it, one who would've had a grandstand view of events. I now noticed the engine was running. More than likely there was someone in it. Perhaps I didn't have a choice in the matter. Perhaps I had to call the police because there had been a witness. The driver of the car might have called the police already, might even have given them the registration number of my own car.

The other car started moving. It came slowly towards me. My skin prickled and I stiffened with fear. I was in the headlights, paralysed like a rabbit.

The car turned and disappeared down a side street.

Tuesday evening at 11.30pm is a cold, dark, quiet time in January, even in London, at least on the outskirts in a side street like this one was. The curtains of all the houses were still drawn. I didn't seem to have attracted any attention.

A gentle rain began to fall. I put my mobile back in my bag and looked around. There were no cameras which might have recorded what I'd just done. The witness driving the car, if witness he was, didn't seem interested in me. Given the area I was in, he was probably a drug dealer who had business to attend to. A hit-and-run incident wouldn't be of concern to him unless the victim had been one of his pushers, which apparently Price wasn't.

I decided to take a chance on getting away with my dark deed, got in my car, and drove off as quickly as I dared. It wasn't that quick, because I stuck conscientiously to the speed limit. The last thing I needed was to be flagged down by a copper for speeding.

Another incentive for driving slowly was the fact I could barely drive in a straight line. Whatever I'd drunk in O'Shaughnessy's was beginning to hit home harder than ever, and I felt myself nodding off at the wheel again. It was all I could do to keep my eyes open. If I'd driven any faster, I might well have wrapped my vehicle around another lamp post on the way home.

Fosby Street was only a five-minute drive from where I lived, two miles or so, but those two miles made all the difference. The difference between life and death, you could say.

Usually I park my car on the drive or on the road outside my house, depending on how lazy I'm feeling, but for once I put it carefully away in the garage. The world couldn't be allowed to know it'd been in an accident. That might attract the unwanted attention of the local constabulary. I climbed awkwardly from my car, my co-ordination shot because of whatever I'd consumed earlier in the evening, and pulled the garage door down, plunging the interior into near darkness. The only illumination came from a window at the side which let in the glow from a nearby streetlight. I waited a moment or two for my eyes to become accustomed to the conditions before locking the garage door. I let myself out by the side entrance, my breath misting in the cold night air, walked the two yards separating me from my house, and went indoors.

The first thing I did when I got inside was pour a large glass of red wine. The second thing I did was tip it down the sink. It wasn't difficult to throw it away, even for me, a lush. Killing Sean Price had changed me. If there's one thing which is guaranteed to make you think seriously about your alcohol problem, it's killing someone in a drink driving accident. Not that I'm recommending it as the way forward if you drink too much.

Even though I was stressed out I was desperate for my bed. Waves of fatigue were rolling over me. Climbing upstairs cost me as much effort as the ascent of the upper reaches of Everest must have cost Hilary and Tensing. I staggered into my bedroom fully intending to get undressed and put my jammies on, but instead I pulled back the duvet and collapsed onto the sheet beneath it. The night had been so emotionally draining I hadn't the energy to do anything more than pull the duvet half-over my prostrate form and lie there, consumed with worry. Sleep, which soon came, should've provided deliverance, but it didn't. My nightmares saw to that. The land of nod was no more relaxing than being awake had been, so it was something of a relief when I opened my eyes. What I found when I did was unusual and a little perturbing. The lights were on and the curtains open.

Shit. Just how much loopy juice had I drunk last night? I rolled over thinking I'd sleep some more, then remembered it was a weekday and I needed to go to work. What time was it? A glance at the bedside clock told me it was 9am. Christ, why had I not heard the alarm? Had it not gone off? Or had I been so spark out I hadn't heard it? Anyway there was no time to waste. I had to get weaving.

As I climbed from under the covers I noticed I was fully clothed. Then the recollection of the events of the previous evening hit me like a sledgehammer on the frontal lobes. I saw a boy's twisted face, felt the two thuds of my car making contact first with flesh, then with a concrete lamp post, and to this horrible cocktail my memory added a third ingredient: a squeal of tyres. Was all that for real? Had I actually killed a young man?

My stomach felt like it was dropping through the bedroom floor.

It wasn't a bad dream. I had actually done it.

Oh my God.

I'd killed Sean Price and compounded the offence by fleeing from the scene of the crime. I was toast.

What should I do?

I knew I wasn't going to work. That was one decision which came easily. I needed to stay at home so I could take whatever action was necessary to extricate myself from the mess I'd gotten myself in.

Even if I'd forced myself into the office I wouldn't have been able to do anything useful. My hands were shaking and I had no focus, other than for the dead boy. I could focus on him all right. I couldn't stop focussing on him.

I stood up on legs which were weak but steady at least, not the way I remembered them being the last time I'd used them, rubbery and unreliable. Then I went to the bathroom and brushed my teeth. It was my usual routine and I found it strangely comforting. It made me feel marginally more in control of events.

I went downstairs and had a coffee, all the while wondering whether to turn myself in. No doubt about it, if I did turn myself in and made a clean breast of everything, I'd get a shorter sentence than if I waited for the police to come and get me. But I'd made things look bad by running away from my handiwork.

My other option was to sit tight and hope the police would never come for me.

I rehearsed the arguments in my head like I'd done the night of the accident: no-one in the houses on Fosby Street appeared to have seen me, and the only witness, the one driving the car that'd disappeared up a side street, hadn't seemed interested in what I'd done. There were no cameras in the vicinity. If all the evidence the police had was paint on a lamp post, and skid marks on a tarmac road, then maybe I was in the clear.

So, in summary, I had two choices.

One: make a clean breast of it and suffer the consequences – losing everything and spending at least the next seven years in jail. Or two: take a chance on not being caught.

If I got away with it, there would be no consequences. If I didn't, I'd be in a bigger mess than ever.

I thought of my life on hold for seven years or more while I served out a prison sentence, and the horror on my parents' faces (which was probably the most persuasive image I could call to mind). Then I felt a pang of guilt and not just for the boy. It occurred to me for the first time that he, too, had parents, and they would be in bits by now, having had news of his death.

Would it comfort them if I came forward and confessed? Would they be understanding, or hate me forever? I suspected they'd hate me forever and derive little comfort from knowing who had done for their boy. But it would likely please them knowing she was locked up and off the streets, unable to do the same thing to anybody else's young son.

I pictured the disappointment on my little brother's face if he was told I'd been charged with drink driving. I was something of a heroine to him. His opinion of me, and our relationship, would both change drastically if that happened, and not for the better.

Having considered all these issues I decided to put me and my needs first.

In other words, I staked my future on a roll of the dice. I was gambling I'd get away with my crime. Having taken the decision, I forced myself to go to the garage and turn on the light. There was work to do.

I hadn't looked at the car since parking it there the night before and I needed to know how bad, that is, how incriminating, the damage was.

Plus, I was hoping against hope this was all some kind of a delusion, a mad nightmare I'd woken up from, and when I inspected my car I'd find nothing amiss. I'd had nightmares before which had seemed all too real. Why couldn't this be one of them?

When I inspected my car my heart sank. A wedge-shaped vertical dent down the front from the grill to the bumper was what sank it. The dent confirmed I'd crashed into something the previous night.

How much of the damage had been caused by the boy and how much by the lamp post was anybody's guess. It could have been all down to the lamp post, but what if it was? There was a depression on top of the bonnet which spoke of a body landing on it before being hurled off at speed.

Paint was missing from the edges of the dent. It reminded me there would be traces of paint on the body and on the lamp post which could be used to identify the manufacture of the car which had mown the boy down, and possibly the age of the car, too.

Was that blood near the dent? I didn't know. Whatever it was, I set to work on it with a cloth and a bottle of Demon Clean to get rid of it. I felt like Lady Macbeth.

The car was going to be a problem. Driving around in it would be like wearing a sign saying: 'Arrest me – I'm the one who mowed the dead boy down'.

On the other hand, I couldn't very well drive to a body shop and get it fixed. If anything would get me arrested, that would. It wouldn't be long before everyone in London, especially body shop owners, knew of the boy who'd been run over and left for dead in a hit-and-run incident. The body shop would report me to the police, and that would be it. Probably even now, the police were sending messages to all the car repair shops in London, telling them to look out for a car with a dent in the front, and report it when it came in for repair. They'd no doubt use the paint on the boy's body to narrow down the search to certain makes and models of cars. It didn't bode well.

Not that I knew whether alerting body repair shops to accidents was police procedure. It probably wasn't. They were likely too busy to take such measures. Still, in my paranoid world, it was a possibility I had to consider.

There was something else, too. All those cameras they had everywhere these days. There weren't any on the street where I had collided with the boy, but there might have been some in neighbouring streets. The police would be able to work out the approximate time of death of the boy, analyse the video footage from those cameras, and come up with the answer that it was an Audi which had done for him. The paint would narrow it down to a blue Audi. I could only hope that those cameras hadn't picked up my registration number. If they had, I was as good as arrested and charged.

I finished my cleaning and wondered if I could face breakfast. I couldn't. It made me feel sick, even though I was desperately hungry, far more so than was usual for me.

What should I do next? I needed to think.

The answer came to me surprisingly quickly: I had to drive a long way off, up to Yorkshire, maybe even Scotland, to get the bodywork fixed. So far north people weren't going to know about the incident I'd been involved in. The death of a boy in London in a hit-and-run incident wouldn't register there. They had their own dead boys to worry about.

I was still well over the limit. I must have been. I felt groggy and out of sorts. I could only hope I wouldn't make a driving error which would get me pulled up by an officer in a squad car. No reason to think I would. It hadn't happened to me yet. Mind you, this would be only the second time in my life I'd ever driven with too much alcohol in my system. The first time had been when I'd run over Sean Price. Prior to that, I'd always taken great care to never drive after drinking. I'd taken public transport to work and used taxis when I had to – an expensive remedy but one which I could now see had been well worthwhile. If only I'd paid for a taxi to take me home from O'Shaughnessy's, I wouldn't be in this mess.

I was definitely going to get off the sauce, now I'd seen the damage it could cause.

My hands were trembling. Not excessively, but I could see the tremors, and if I could see them, other people could too. Hopefully, if anyone noticed, they'd assume I was the nervy type, and not that I was an alcoholic.

I opened the garage door, reversed the car onto the drive, and shut the door again. Then I had a thought. At some point in the future, if I was investigated by the police, they'd check my mobile phone records and work out I'd gone to an out-of-town body shop the day after Sean Price had been killed. I was about to switch it off when I noticed I had messages so I dialled 234 to listen to them.

A mechanical voice with a distinctly female tone to it said, 'You have two new messages. First new message. Message received Wednesday, 24 January, at 11.30am: "Hi, Jasmine, it's Camilla. It's not like you to take time off work without ringing in. Hope you're not ill. Give me a call if you can to let me know how you are. See you."'

Camilla was my secretary at Womack and Brewer LLP, the firm of solicitors I worked for. It was odd my mobile said I'd received her call at 11.30am; it'd only just gone 10am. I put it down to a malfunction and listened to the next message.

The mechanical voice spoke again, 'Second new message, message received Thursday, 25 January, at 9.50am.'

I clicked it off.

Thursday, 25 January, at 9.50am?

That was impossible. It was only Wednesday the twenty-fourth of January. My mobile phone was definitely playing up. Or was it? What if it really was the twenty-fifth? I looked at the display. The small text beneath the time stated, 'Thur 25 January'.

I went indoors and checked the display on my iPad, which confirmed it was the twenty-fifth.

My head swirled.

I'd gone to bed on Tuesday the twenty-third of January.

I'd woken up on Thursday the twenty-fifth of January.

What had happened to Wednesday the twenty-fourth? It was as if it'd never existed.

Somehow I was missing a day. My memory was playing tricks on me – either that, or my devices were giving me the wrong information.

I was about to close the iPad when I noticed an alert telling me I'd had a message from Kylie. I couldn't ignore Kylie, even though my circumstances were desperate, so I read her message.

School reunion soon. Are you coming? And do you want to meet up for a coffee sometime? Love, Kylie xx

Christ, the school reunion. I'd forgotten it was coming up. There was a group of people who'd gone to the same school as me and who took it on themselves to make sure we had one every year. I hated the reunions, but I always went. I had to, because if I didn't, people would come looking for me, to make sure I was still keeping my mouth shut. If I wasn't, they'd shut it for me – permanently. It was never overtly stated that this was on the agenda, but I knew it was, as did the rest of the small group of people I'd associated with at school.

None of us trusted any of the others to keep our mouths shut. We'd all kept schtum for eighteen years, but still we worried someone might crack, and we'd be brought to justice and sent down for a very long time. So we all attended the reunions to make sure everyone was on-message. At all other times I made a point of not having anything to do with the rest of them as I was desperate to forget the past and put it behind me.

It was pretty much understood that Seth, in particular, would be annoyed if any of us didn't show up to a reunion – and no-one wanted to get on the wrong side of Seth.

I didn't want to meet with Kylie, even though we'd been good friends back in the day. As a result of the crime we were all covering up I'd gone off a number of people, including her. I wanted to tell her I couldn't meet her and wouldn't go to the reunion – but in the interests of survival, I messaged back.

Yes, I'm coming to the reunion. And coffee sounds good. How about next Tuesday lunchtime? xx

She replied:

Tuesday fine. TNQ at 12.30? xx

Then, just to be absolutely sure of the date, I switched the television on and tuned in to a news channel. That confirmed it was the twenty-fifth of January. I was definitely missing a day.

What was going on?

I replayed in my head as best I could my actions over the previous couple of days.

I'd gone to work as usual on Monday, done the same on Tuesday, got home, sat in front of the TV in the evening, and received a telephone call about a suspected criminal who needed the advice of a lawyer. He was being held in the Crystal Palace nick. I drove over there, advised him, went to O'Shaughnessy's where I remembered having only drunk a half of session beer, then I'd got in my car. While driving under the influence of what must've been a lot more drink than I remembered having, I'd had my accident, left the scene of the crime, got home, and collapsed into bed. Then I'd got up – on Thursday instead of Wednesday.

Was it possible I'd been up and about on Wednesday, done stuff, and forgotten everything about it? Maybe it was. I'd had blackouts in my time, but they were the sort of blackouts where I'd lost an evening. Never before had I lost an entire day.

The room spun as I tried to come to terms with the idea.

There was another possibility. I could have slept from about 11.50pm on Tuesday to 9am on Thursday, fully thirty-three hours.

I hoped to God that was the explanation – because if it wasn't, then the alternative was that I'd had one of my blackouts covering a longer and more sustained period than ever before. The thought of what I might have got up to while so totally out of control made me shudder. I might have fatally compromised my plan to evade justice.

My chest heaved and I began to hyperventilate. Then I told myself: *breathe deeply and get a grip, Jasmine, you're going to get through this.* Forcing myself to slow my respiration, I managed to calm down.

What should I do, now I'd had this revelation on top of everything else? There was only one course of action which made any sense. Carry on with my planned bodywork repairs, and hope for the best. I switched off my mobile, returned to my car, and headed for the M1, taking a circuitous route to avoid the roads I'd been driving on the previous night. The dehydration I was feeling coupled with sweat erupting from my every pore told me I was unfit to drive. I was over the limit, and my nerves felt barely capable of transmitting messages to my extremities. Nevertheless, I somehow made the car head in the direction I wanted, at the correct speed, without attracting the attention of the law.

As I drove up the M1 I realised I was spookily tired, and that trying to get any further than Luton would be to risk falling asleep at the wheel, so I pulled off at Junction 11 and found a back street with tin sheds and brick sheds either side of it, each of them home to some sort of motor-related business. I say back street; it wasn't even a street. It was a narrow dirt track.

One of them specialised in 'Re-sprays, Panel-Beating etc.' It looked like the place for me. It felt safer than a big corporate repair place would've done. I reasoned the corporate establishments would be more likely to ask awkward questions.

A small metal sign proclaimed: Jack Davis, prop. Est. 1998. It was a one-man show. It would be ideal.

Jack's business was housed in a red-brick shed with an open front. The wind was whipping through it. I wondered how it could be possible to work in there without getting frostbite. I was cold even though I was wrapped up in my parka.

Jack was inside, wearing blue overalls and a protective mask, and was busy spraying black paint on a black BMW with blacked-out windows. It looked like the kind of car your average drug dealer would drive, which told me I'd come to the right place. I hung around patting my hands together to keep them warm until he noticed me.

'Mr Davis,' I said. 'I've got a job for you.'

He pushed the clear plastic visor of his mask up from his face. He had lines between his eyebrows and more lines running from his nose past the downturned corners of his mouth, suggesting anxiety. That made me feel guilty, and put me off him, but by then I felt committed to getting a quote at least.

'Let the dog see the rabbit,' he said, frowning at me. I got the impression he didn't smile much.

I gestured in the direction of my car which was parked only a few yards from where he'd been working, and wondered whether I'd wasted my time coming all the way up here, and whether I could've risked having the job done in London. Then I reassured myself it was better to err on the side of caution – if, indeed, Jack Davis, prop., Est. 1998, represented caution.

'There's a couple of dents in my car,' I told him, pointing at them, one after the other, quite unnecessarily.

He gave me his trademark frown, the lines between his black eyebrows deepening. 'I can see that. What caused them?'

I pondered saying something like *what business is it of yours?* And decided against it. A friendly approach would be better, as there was a chance it would get him onside. 'I'm not sure.'

He looked at me with his downturned mouth, and I noticed his eyes for the first time. They were the sort of grey-blue eyes which wouldn't take any shit from anyone.

'How can you not be sure? It's your car, isn't it?'

Of all the body shop owners in Luton to choose from, I had to choose the stroppy one, the one who wanted to know things I wasn't willing to discuss. I felt a growing unease. Where was this line of questioning going? Why didn't he just offer his professional opinion on fixing it and give me a quote?

'Yes, it's my car,' I said.

I was playing for time. I needed a better answer, an excuse for not knowing what had caused the damage, and a plausible one at that, if he made the point I thought he might make next, which he did.

'It looks like you hit some*thing* or some*one* with your car. You hit them pretty badly too, by the looks of things.'

Christ on a bike – what was he wanting me to tell him? The name of my victim?

He gave me an unflinching stare with those grey-blue don't-take-any-shit-from-the-likes-of-you eyes, and I wondered whether I should stare right back, but I'd heard liars do that to convince people they're not lying, and thought Jack Davis might've heard the same thing, so I didn't. At the same time, I couldn't look away too quickly, because liars do that, too. I had to hold his gaze for just long enough to look like I was telling the truth, then slowly let it go. It was a fine line between staring for too long and not long enough.

'I had it stolen the other day by a couple of joyriders,' I told him, looking him in the eye. I glanced casually back in the direction of the damaged bonnet. 'I don't know what they got up to in it.'

I didn't know where the story came from, but felt relieved I'd thought of it.

He nodded and ran his fingers through his greying hair. 'It happens a lot,' he said. 'Joyriders love causing accidents. I repair too many cars damaged by joyriders.'

'I can imagine.'

He gave me another of his penetrating looks. 'It must've shaken you up, having your car taken and crashed.'

'Why do you say that?'

'You look like you're still worrying about it.'

I realised he was staring at my hands, which were betraying my feelings and self-consciously thrust them into my pockets. Not that it did any good – he'd already noticed they were trembling. What he didn't know was they were doing it from withdrawal symptoms as well as worry.

'How much will it be? And how soon can you do it?'

He took a pace back, looking the car up and down, and did the whistling thing through his teeth tradesmen do to let you know the job you've asked of them is so big and so difficult that it's unreasonable of you to have asked them to do it at all.

'Have you had the mechanicals checked out?' he asked.

'No, but it drives okay.'

'You ought to get it looked at by a mechanic. You never know what damage might have been done under the bonnet.'

'I'll get it sorted after you've got the accident damage to the body fixed. How much will it be?'

He pursed his lips and walked around my car, delaying his reply to let me know he was giving the matter an awful lot of thought. When he'd walked a full circle, he scratched his head a couple of times, pursed his lips again, and said, 'Parts, labour, paint, sundries, hmmm, fifteen hundred pounds in total.'

It was my turn to whistle through my teeth.

I wondered whether I should get a few more quotes, but decided not to. In the general scheme of things, speed was more important than economy.

'How soon can you do it?'

'Next week at the earliest.'

'I need it for tonight.'

'No can do.'

'What if I pay you extra to jump the queue?'

The expression on his face told me he thought I was unhinged. 'I could get it done for tomorrow lunchtime if you were to pay me a couple of grand for it,' he said. 'Cash,' he added.

'Can't you do it sooner?'

'Nope, sorry. These things take time.'

'All right, I'll go with that. I don't want to go see my customers with my car in a state. It'd create the wrong impression.'

I don't know why I offered him an explanation for wanting the job doing quickly. And I don't know whether he believed it.

'You'll need this,' I said, handing him the key to the vehicle. 'By the way, I forgot my mobile. Could you possibly order a taxi to take me to the railway station?'

He turned up one corner of his mouth and disappeared indoors, if his brick shed could possibly be described as indoors. He emerged a minute later.

'On its way. Best get back to work.'

He donned his mask and got back to his paint job while I stood shivering on the dirt track, waiting for the taxi. The wind got up and blew a discarded takeaway carton into a puddle next to me. The taxi arrived so I got inside, noticing Davis looking at me. I gave him a friendly wave through the window as I departed. He waved back, which surprised me.

I caught the train to London and disembarked at Kings Cross, picked up a copy of the *Evening Standard* on the platform, and boarded a train headed for Crystal Palace. It's a journey I normally enjoy, but there was no enjoyment in it that day, only concern, as I scoured the newspaper, firstly to confirm again it really was the twenty-fifth of January and not the twenty-fourth, and secondly for information about my hit-and-run victim. There was none. I didn't know whether to feel relief or puzzlement, and decided on the former.

When I got home I read it again cover to cover, to make sure I hadn't missed anything. I hadn't. There wasn't so much as a sentence about Sean Price in it.

I called my bank and arranged to make a cash withdrawal of £2,000 to pay Jack Davis. It occurred to me it'd be tricky explaining the withdrawal to the police if they ended up investigating me, then I put it to the back of my mind. I couldn't afford to worry about detail. I had to concentrate on the big picture – concealing the damage to the car.

Afterwards I switched on the television hoping to catch some news about Sean Price's death, and hoping at the same time not to. I wanted to know how the investigation was going, and preferably to hear it was going badly, due to a lack of leads.

There was no mention of anything to do with a dead boy on the television news, and nothing on the local radio station, so I checked the internet. There was nothing there, either.

The news of his death didn't seem to have broken, which was odd. It gave me the troubling idea I might have moved his body during my blackout. I put it to the back of my mind where it kept company with other troubling ideas.

My stomach rumbled and I realised I was hungry. I forced down a couple of hastily made sandwiches while considering the threats I faced. It occurred to me the police might make door-to-door enquiries in the area. But then again, they probably wouldn't. They were understaffed, as Doug, a copper at the Crystal Palace nick, was always telling me. They had other things to cope with. Paperwork mainly, he said. They spent more time on that than they did on keeping our streets safe, according to Doug. It was something I'd always deplored in the past. Not anymore. I now applauded the fact they were too bogged down with paperwork to carry out their job effectively.

When I'd eaten, I called my secretary. 'Camilla,' I said. 'It's Jaz. How are you?'

I had to begin the conversation with small talk. Camilla might have been my secretary, but I also thought of her as a friend.

'I'm fine, Jaz, how are you? And where have you been? You're not sounding your usual self.'

'I'm not. Please cancel all my appointments this week. And please pass on a message to Brewer. I've got flu. I'm really ill. I can barely stand up. I would've rung in yesterday to let you and him know, but I was so poorly I didn't feel able to do even that much.'

I didn't have to put on a special poorly voice to convince her. It was genuinely croaky because I was upset.

'You sound dreadful. I'll tell Brewer right away. He had a bit of a grumble about you not ringing in yesterday, and another one this morning.'

'Thank you.'

'You poor thing, I hope you get better soon. Don't worry about your files. If anything urgent comes up, I'll take care of it, and if I'm out of my depth I'll discuss it with Stephen.'

Stephen was the partner in charge of the criminal law department at Womack and Brewer.

'Thanks, Cam. It's very good of you. I'll have to lie down now. I'll be back at work as soon as I can. Bye.'

'Bye, Jaz.'

That would buy me some time at work. Things were falling into place.

The afternoon stretched ahead of me. How could I fill it in such a way that I wouldn't make myself more worried and paranoid than ever? I felt a desperate urge to go back to the scene of my crime, and check if there was crime scene tape around it, but managed to dismiss the crazy idea. Instead, I stayed indoors and watched daytime television, while resisting the voice in my head which was telling me I should drink a couple of bottles of red wine. *Go on, why don't you,* it was saying. *You know you'll feel a lot better if you do.*

My first Alcoholics Anonymous meeting was scheduled for 7pm that evening. I had to attend, because if I didn't, I was going to take the advice the voice in my head was giving me, sooner rather than later. At 6.45pm I put on my parka with the hood up and walked to the local church hall where the meeting was being held. It was an unpleasant, ugly stone box with fluorescent lights dangling from the ceiling. The harsh light they gave off made me feel bilious. Beneath them, in the middle of the room, there was a semicircle of uncomfortable metal-and-plastic chairs. A couple of people were sitting in those chairs when I entered. Their veined noses and puffy cheeks told me they were heavy drinkers, so I assumed they were members of the AA and occupied one of the chairs.

Thank God, I thought, *that I don't yet look like those two. I hope I never will.*

The chairs filled and I counted twelve of us in the semicircle when the meeting began. There were four empty chairs, so I assumed they'd been expecting sixteen and four had fallen off the wagon.

Five of us were women, six were men, and one appeared to be transgender – man-to-woman. The men all looked as if they'd done something they shouldn't and been caught doing it. The women and transgender person looked as if they couldn't believe that it had come to this.

As a newcomer I had to introduce myself and tell my story. It was a big ask for me, because my mind was too busy fretting about the boy I'd run over to focus on storytelling. Nevertheless, I came up with something. 'Hello, my name is Jasmine Black, and I'm an alcoholic. I'm trying to think about how and when my drinking went wrong. I began in my teens. I had a group of friends and we used to buy bottles of White Lightning and drink them in Crystal Palace Park, and smoke a few joints, just for fun. Then something happened, and I began drinking to escape.

'For most of my twenties it was like that. In the last couple of years it's got worse. I'm a solicitor, and a couple of years ago, I got someone off who was a murderer. I was sure he did it, but I raised enough doubts to convince the jury to let him off. Over the years, I've got a lot of other people off, too – criminals who were all guilty.

'Being congratulated by wife beaters and rapists and the like for helping them, and getting them off, didn't sit well with me.

'At the end of each case I drank to get over the feeling I'd done a mischief to the victim and family of the victim. I'd remember seeing them in court every day of the trial, the victim and her parents, husband, and sometimes her children, too. I had to act as if I didn't care about them, but I couldn't help caring. It might be time for me to quit my job as well as the drink. Thanks for listening.'

When I mentioned quitting my job, I surprised myself. It hadn't occurred to me before. The last thing I wanted to do, or so I thought, was give up the career I'd so carefully been building for myself, and which I'd proved I was good at. The impulse to give it up must have been a subconscious one, bubbling away under the surface, possibly for years. Now it was out in the open I wondered if I'd dare act on it.

The other attendees clapped, then it was someone else's turn to give a speech. At the end of the meeting I was given a buddy to help me mend my ways. It would be his job to counsel me, and help me stay on the wagon. He was a middle-aged man called Bernie with a lined face and hangdog expression.

It was only day one, but I felt as if I'd made progress. Still, I couldn't feel too pleased with myself. I had the sword of Damocles hanging over my head and there was no telling when it would drop. It was hard not to spend all my time feeling as if my world was about to implode.

I got home and drank a cup of camomile tea in the hope it would calm me a little. Every time I had nothing else to think about, I heard a squeal of tyres, imagined a young boy's face twisted in fear, and felt those two horrible impacts of my car hitting first flesh, then concrete.

I spent what was left of the evening feeling anxious and watching TV, then turned in. Even though my head was buzzing with paranoia I was able to sleep, because fatigue caught up with me. I didn't sleep too well, though.

The next day – Friday 26 January – I got up early, went straight to my bank, withdrew the £2,000 in cash I needed to pay Jack Davis for the repairs to my car, and headed up to Luton.

'Good as new,' Jack said, when he showed me his handiwork. I inspected it carefully and had to admit he was right. Then I counted out the cash into the rather greasy palm of his hand.

'Thanks,' he said. 'Drive carefully.'

'I always do.'

'Beware of joyriders.' He said it with a smile, the only smile I'd ever seen him make.

I gave him a thin smile in return, got in my car, and drove back to Crystal Palace.

I left the car out on the drive, as I thought it might seem suspicious if the police made house-to-house enquiries and some neighbour, trying to be helpful, said, 'There's a woman down the street drives a blue Audi and she used to park it outside all the time, but now she hides it away in her garage.'

That was unlikely – the police had bigger fish to fry. But, I told myself, you can't be too careful – not in this situation.

I was still officially ill, and I planned to go on being ill for at least another week. It would take that long to get myself into a good enough frame of mind to cope with work. When I did, I'd have to give some thought to handing in my notice, but that was something which would have to come further down the line. Quitting my job would be stressful, and I had a pile of stress on my plate already, far too much to digest at one sitting. I couldn't face heaping any more on it. And before I could even think about work, I needed to know what was going on with the police investigation, if there was one.

Perhaps there was a bundle of papers at the bottom of a lot of other bundles on an overworked constable's desk. Maybe that was why I hadn't heard anything. It didn't make me feel any safer. Once my victim's bundle reached the top of the overworked constable's pile, I'd be under investigation. Then they'd get me.

I just about managed to sleep that night, but it was a fitful kind of slumber, very far removed from the sleep of the just, and I woke up early the next morning.

Most unexpectedly, I was in a reasonable frame of mind.

Jaz, I said to myself, somewhat optimistically, *I've just thought of something. You know how you've missed a day? That could mean a lot of things. It could mean the accident involving the boy never happened. Sure, you ran into a lamp post, but you might have imagined the bit about the boy. After all, there hasn't been any news about a boy being knocked down on Fosby Street.*

When the thought hit me, I was once again seized by a desire to return to the scene of my crime and investigate what'd gone on. So strong was the impulse I wondered if I had the gall to take a walk down Fosby Street, and decided I had. I put on my coat and took a stroll.

The scene of the accident was only two miles away from mine, but what a difference those two miles made. I lived in an area where the houses were in good condition because they were lived in by owner-occupiers. The boy had been run over on a street with houses which were more-or-less identical to the ones on mine, but most had overgrown gardens and looked in need of repair, because they'd been converted into multiple-occupation rentals for young people on low incomes.

I walked past the lamp post I'd crashed into, and gave it a furtive glance. There were blue marks on it. On the pavement nearby there was a stain, hardly noticeable, probably something you'd only see if you set out to look for it, as I had. I was convinced it was a blood stain, the blood of Sean Price. I hadn't imagined it, then. I had indeed killed someone, and my own life would never be the same again. There was ample evidence that someone had run over someone else. Plus there had been a body. Why weren't the police onto it?

I hurried to the end of the road and took a different route home. On the way my mobile phone rang. Without thinking, I swiped the screen. It was Camilla. I cupped my hand around my face, hoping to supress the traffic noise.

'Hi, Jaz, how are you doing?' she asked.

'Badly. I'm still in bed.'

A particularly noisy car drove past. It must've had exhaust problems. I coughed loudly several times.

'Is there anything I can do for you? Some shopping perhaps?' That was typical of Camilla. She was very considerate, but the last thing I needed was a visit from a work colleague.

'No, thanks for offering though. You'll have to let me be now, Cam. I'm so tired.'

'Okay, take it easy. Promise me you'll give me a call if you need anything.'

'I promise. Bye, Cam.'

'See you, Jaz.'

I did feel genuinely ill, just not with flu, and I'm sure it showed in my voice. I was coming down with a bad bout of anxiety. I decided I should do something about it. I took a detour to the eight-till-late to buy a bottle of fresh orange juice. The walk would do me good, I told myself, and so would the juice.

I got to the shop, picked a bottle from the fridge, and went to the till, which was near the door. While I'd been doing my shopping a woman had come in, and she appeared behind me with a basket of shopping. I paid for my juice. As I did so, I heard her say to the proprietor, 'Did you hear about the hit-and-run the other night?'

That was enough for me. I panicked and fled, or at least walked very quickly, back home.

I told myself I had to get into a good frame of mind so that I could get back to work and do the things I normally did. Then, as I could hardly bear to sit still, I took a walk through Crystal Palace Park and somehow whiled away the afternoon and evening.

On Saturday 27 January I woke up early. Everything was as it should be. I hadn't crashed my car, hadn't been driving while under the influence of drink, and hadn't killed anyone. I was happy, or at least as happy as I usually was when I got up at the weekend. It was a state of affairs which lasted for about half a second before I remembered the accident. In an instant I went from moderately pleased with myself to near suicidal.

I got out of bed with difficulty because the depression which hit me made me want to lie down feeling sorry for myself. With an effort of will, I forced myself to go to the bathroom. Once there, I performed my morning ablution rituals in an attempt to bring some normality back into my life. While showering, I experienced a hot flush and felt as though I was going through the menopause even though that was, hopefully, still many years away. When I'd done with my hot flush I began to think more clearly.

Three days had gone by since my accident. No-one could now prove I'd been drunk at the time. The charge of driving while under the influence of drink was no longer a threat to my liberty. What, then, did I have to fear?

I reasoned it out: if and when the body was examined, it might be possible to link it to me by the traces of paint it would have on it. A forensic examination of my car would reveal the recent repair. There was, of course, the possibility of a witness in the other car which had been parked up the road.

Rather than facing a charge of causing death while driving under the influence of drink, I'd face the slightly lesser charge of causing death by dangerous driving. The tariff for that could range from two years to fourteen in custody, depending on the gravity of the offence. The gravity would no doubt be near the maximum because of my failure to come forward and confess when I'd done it. Better news than the sentence for the offence aggravated by drinking, but hardly reassuring.

Once I was up and dressed, I got on my PC and searched for news of unidentified bodies in Crystal Palace in January 2018. There hadn't been any.

I thought I must've made a mistake, so I did all the searches again with different search terms, but still nothing came up. The body of the boy had not only not been identified, it hadn't even been noticed.

But someone had found his body, because it wasn't still there. And if someone had found his body, there was no excuse for not reporting it to the police. And no excuse for the police failing to investigate the matter. There was probably no excuse for me not already residing in HM Prison Holloway.

Unless, that is, he is still alive.

If so, there would have been no report of a death, but certainly, you would think, there would have been some mention of the crippled victim of a road traffic accident – perhaps a story about an unidentified someone who was in a coma at the local hospital. But when I checked, there was nothing. This was odd, because I had no doubt that my road traffic accident had been newsworthy, at least in the locality.

I went out and bought a cheap pay-as-you-go mobile and telephoned the hospitals which would have been involved in the boy's care if he'd been admitted to a hospital. I told them I was trying to find my brother Sean Price. They all informed me they had no records of any Sean Price being admitted.

What could it mean?

What had happened to him?

I didn't know. Maybe I'd never know. But for now, I decided to accept I'd had some kind of a lucky break.

It meant I didn't have to feel so paranoid anymore, and could go about my business as if everything was normal. Apart, that is, from the images which forced themselves into my thoughts every time I let them, especially at night when all I wanted to do was sleep.

Kylie was waiting for me by the door to TNQ when we met the following Tuesday, on 30 January. It was a year since we'd last seen each other, and she looked better than I remembered. She had perfect blonde hair, the face of a model, and a gym-honed body. What's more, she was wearing a no-expense-spared trouser suit.

In contrast, I was – am – mousy-haired, averagely good-looking if you discount my modest but growing tummy, and I'd bought my clothes from the Oxfam shop round the corner. (Desperate times called for desperate measures – it was this kind of cost-cutting which enabled me to make my exorbitant mortgage payments.)

'Jaz, how are you?' She grinned, showing me a set of perfectly even teeth so white they gleamed in the unseasonal sunshine.

'Things are good,' I lied.

She pushed open the door and I followed her inside. The place was bustling with office workers taking their lunch breaks and pensioners doing their level best to kill the remaining time they had before death, but even so we managed to find a table by the window. We both picked up a menu and I felt myself wince when I saw the prices.

'How's work?' she asked.

'Going from strength-to-strength,' I said, with as much conviction as I could muster.

'Are you still helping small-time crooks to prosper?'

Ouch. She couldn't have known what a sore point that was with me.

'They're not all crooks,' I replied, with a touch of desperation in my voice.

She raised her eyebrows. I say eyebrows; they were actually thin lines pencilled onto her smooth forehead.

'That's not what I've been hearing. How's the bid for partnership going?'

It wasn't going at all well. Success in the legal profession had had the opposite effect on me to what it should've done. I'd been ambitious and enthusiastic when I'd started out, but with each trial I'd won my enthusiasm had suffered, and when I'd won the murder trial it'd been broken like a butterfly caught in an avalanche. After that, my indifferent attitude towards my work meant I'd become last in line for any promotion which might be going, behind even the office cat.

I paused for a moment to give myself time to think up a convincing lie. There was no way I was going to tell Kylie the truth – I wanted to sound positive, upbeat, and in control of my life. 'You don't get to be a partner right away, you know. You have to make your mark – but I have, and the powers-that-be are making all the right noises.'

She narrowed her immaculately made-up eyes. She wanted to be sure I wasn't going to have some kind of breakdown, and spill the grimy beans about our shared dark past. I suppose I could have been projecting my own motives onto Kylie – I was, after all, watching her closely for the same reason.

A waitress came over to our table. Kylie pointed at a couple of items on the menu.

'I'll have the goat's cheese tart with a salad, a portion of mixed beans, and a slice of pumpernickel bread, please.' She glanced in my direction and smiled. 'What are you having, Jaz?'

Christ, I thought, *we'll be going Dutch and that little lot will cost me.* It's something of a myth that lawyers earn buckets of money. Some are very well paid, and some eke out a comfortable living. Those among us who work for small firms in criminal law generally aren't paid too well. When we aspire to have big mortgages, as I had done, our resources are limited.

'Chicken salad for me, please,' I said. It was one of the cheaper items on the menu.

'Watching your weight?' Kylie asked.

'I happen to like salad and chicken.'

'Would you care for drinks?' the waitress asked.

'Sparkling Evian, please,' said Kylie.

'Café Americano for me, no milk, no sugar, no biscuit on the side,' I said, and the waitress hurried off to get our orders. I tried to relax, but was already feeling uncomfortable at the thought of how much I was going to be stung for the meal.

'So, how's business?' Kylie asked.

'Brisk,' I said, nodding with conviction. 'The criminal classes are always at it, and I get a lot of repeat business. Sad to say that no sooner do I get a felon off the hook than he commits another crime and the process starts all over again.'

I didn't mention that in spite of my healthy caseload I was struggling to make ends meet. 'Are you still in the interior design business?' I asked.

'Yes,' she said. 'It's great. One of my designs was featured in *Interiors Today* magazine.'

'Very impressive. You've come a long way since giving up your acting career.'

'I suppose I have. I was never going to make it big in that line of work but it got me a lot of useful contacts. How's Robert?'

Ouch. I'd been expecting the question, but even so it hurt. Still, in a way I was glad she'd asked it. I needed practice at dealing with it before the reunion. I gave her my rehearsed answer, 'He's history. We decided to go our separate ways.'

'I'm sorry to hear it.' She looked and sounded genuine, which annoyed me. The thing I hate above all else is people feeling sorry for me.

'Don't be. I'm much happier now he's out of my life.'

'Oh, like that is it?'

'Yes, it's like that.'

'Any new romantic interests?'

'No.'

I felt loserish admitting to that. But then, I was a loser. I'd gotten divorced from my husband, was in a dead-end job – yes, on the surface it looked glamorous, but believe me, being a solicitor doing criminal law in a small firm with no prospects of promotion is as dead an end as you will find – I had no children, the biological clock was ticking ever more loudly, and I had no boyfriend or prospect of one. I wanted a boyfriend as that would help with passing myself off as normal. But I knew I could never be normal, because I harboured a terrible secret – the same secret Kylie was keeping.

We finished our food and split the bill. I paid for my share on the one credit card I had which wasn't maxed out.

We left and said our goodbyes to each other.

'See you on Saturday the third of March,' said Kylie as she disappeared down the street. She said it in a friendly enough way, but she was probably making a point.

'Yes, see you Saturday the third of March.'

We parted company, without either of us having even once mentioned the mammoth in the room, loudly trumpeting to get our attention.

As I made my way home, I thought about the coming reunion.

It would be worse than the previous ones had been, if that was possible. In addition to the usual paranoia I'd be going through because of the incident from my schooldays, I'd be worrying about the Sean Price business catching up with me, and I'd have to explain to people why my husband wasn't with me, then I'd have to explain why I hadn't gotten myself a boyfriend yet. Everyone else would be in couples and I'd be the only singleton, standing out because she didn't have anyone. All that explaining, all that pretending to be happy I'd have to do, putting on a brave face and a fake smile, and trying to convince Seth and the others I wasn't a liability, it made me exhausted just thinking about it.

A week went by, and I returned to work on Monday 5 February feeling as if a nuclear warhead was going to go off at any second and destroy everything I valued, leaving no trace of my life. But by the time two weeks had gone by, I'd begun to feel I'd gotten away with it.

After three weeks I felt I ought to go out and celebrate my good luck. Celebration to me could only mean one thing, so on Friday 23 February, after I finished work, I took myself to The Angel cocktail bar. The words of the AA meeting I'd had the night before should've been ringing in my ears, but if they were, I ignored them. I bought myself a gin and tonic and took up a place by the window to watch the world go by. It was a peaceful world once again, one I no longer had to fear quite so much. I raised my glass.

'Cheers,' I whispered so as not to let on to the few other customers in the place I was talking to myself. 'You've come through your crisis, Jaz, and you're out the other end.'

Then I whispered, 'You reckoned that killing the boy shook you up so much you'd never drink again. It didn't take you long to forget about him, did it?'

Feeling I ought to show more respect, I took a sip of my drink and raised the glass a second time. 'Here's to Sean Price,' I said quietly. 'May he rest in peace, and may his parents find peace too.'

Then I took another sip, put down the glass, and stared out the window.

The street was bustling and amongst the crowds of shoppers, office workers, and revellers, I noticed a young man. He was well-dressed and purposeful, swinging his arms like a soldier on parade as he made his way down Thomas Street.

His face was all too familiar.

It was Tony, a boy from my distant and troubled past.

My skin prickled with the sort of adrenaline fear I get when I'm in my car and someone cuts in front of me on the motorway, leaving no margin for error. My hands began to tremble. Then I realised I'd been mistaken. It wasn't Tony, just someone who resembled him. Soon his back was disappearing amongst the evening drinking crowd, and I should have relaxed, but didn't. That face had dredged up long-supressed memories which turned me into a nervous wreck.

I picked up my glass, the ice clinking because of my shaking hand, took a big gulp, then another, and my first drink was gone. I'd planned on nursing it for a while, long enough at least to read a few stories in the newspaper I'd bought on my way here, but my nerves had put paid to that plan.

I went to the bar and got another gin and tonic, a double, then returned to my seat still thinking about Tony. He'd be thirty-four now, and no doubt would look very different if he was still alive. But he wasn't. He was definitely dead, and I couldn't stop thinking about him, wishing he was still around, and, all-too-often, imagining he was.

I took a few deep breaths, got a grip on myself, and read the rest of the newspaper I'd bought on my way to the cocktail bar. Then I knocked back enough drinks to bury my guilt-ridden past for good. Or so I hoped.

I don't know what time I got home, or how I got there, or pretty much anything else I did that night. Next morning – Saturday – I woke up with the fluey feeling you get when you've had too many and stayed in bed for longer than you should. Finally, I got up to have a pee, and after that there didn't seem to be any point in getting back under the duvet, because I knew I wasn't going to be able to sleep. I wrapped myself in my white towelling dressing gown, padded downstairs in bare feet, and switched the electric kettle on.

I like to grind my own coffee but I was feeling too delicate to operate the grinder. Instead, I made a large mug of instant coffee which I took to the front room, and deposited on an occasional table. When I got there I opened my iPad to find a message from Kylie reminding me that the reunion was coming up on 3 March.

I shut the iPad and lazily pointed the remote at my TV, pressing the buttons until I got *Sky News* on the screen. When I'd done that, I barely listened to the young male newscaster telling me about the events of the day. I only had it on to stop me from noticing too clearly that I was a thirty-plus-year-old loser who lived alone, had no boyfriend, and seemingly no prospect of getting one, and who had been involved in two killings. It was what the telly was for, at least in my house.

As I drank my coffee, I wondered what fresh hell would be waiting for me at this year's reunion.

On Friday 2 March I got out of bed and worked out how long I had left before I'd be compelled to meet with my former associates at the school reunion and pretend it was a normal meeting of normal friends. There was a day-and-a-half to go. Yet another message from Kylie confirmed the fact that I had approximately thirty-six more paranoia-filled hours to get through, after which I'd have another year's respite until the next one. Or would I? It was likely I'd spend the entire year – indeed, the rest of my life – being tormented by what I'd done to Sean Price, in addition to being tormented by the mess I'd gotten involved in during my teens.

The walls seemed to be closing in on me. I decided I couldn't go to work, not in the state I was in, so I rang in sick.

What a life I was leading, if you could call it a life. It was devoid of meaningful relationships and maintained by liberal doses of alcohol. Alcohol was the medicine I used to hold it all together. It was also the poison that might ultimately blow it apart.

With all the stress I'd been going through I didn't think I could face up to my former associates for an entire evening. There was a horrible chance I'd get myself wasted and say something I shouldn't.

That's the thing with secrets. You bottle them up as best you can but you better make damned sure the seal on the bottle is good and tight, because they spend all their time struggling to get out. They can be strong and determined little buggers, secrets.

How many times had I been with a friend, especially when drunk, and desperately wanted to say, 'You know that thing with so-and-so? Well, this is really what happened.'

But telling the truth wasn't an option, not to anyone. It could get me killed.

So I just had to keep schtum, the way I had done for eighteen years. The trouble was, I was weakening. I could feel it.

At first it'd been easy, in a way, to keep my mouth shut. Fear took care of that. But it had to win a fierce battle for control of my mind with guilt to get its way. That was just the first battle in a long war of attrition. Ever since, guilt had been gnawing at me, and my resistance had been worn down.

Sooner or later I was going to spill my guts, I was sure of it. And what would happen to me then?

God alone knew.

I had to go to the reunion. If I didn't, they'd come looking for me. They'd corner me after work in the car park or some other dark place to question me, to make sure I was still on-message. If it went as well as it possibly could, it'd still be an ordeal. And it might not go well. Failing to be at the reunion could raise doubts about me. They might decide to take me out because that'd be – as far as they were concerned – good risk management. In the very worst-case scenario, they'd torture me first. Or Seth would, at any rate, and maybe he'd get one of the others to help. I wasn't sure the rest of them would have any stomach for it.

Anyway, it'd be better to avoid the risk by showing up at the reunion, acting normal, and going home.

But I knew it wasn't so simple.

It was hard keeping quiet about things even while I was sober these days, and every time I got myself into a state I opened my mouth and was barely able to control what came out of it.

Which reminded me: I'd lost a day. I'd had one of my blackouts, the worst ever – and I'd had some bad ones in my time. The whole of Wednesday 24 January had been erased from my mind. What had I done on that Wednesday? Where had I been, what had I said, and who had I said it to?

I racked my brains but all I could see were the same images over and over again: a young boy's twisted face, and then, another young boy's twisted face – one from long ago, all of eighteen years since.

It was only 10am and those memories made me want to reach for a drink right away but I forced myself to put the kettle on instead.

'Keep calm, Jaz,' I said. 'There has to be a way out of this.'

But deep down I knew there was no way out. Deep down I knew the best I could hope for was to negotiate the living hell I was in without getting arrested and banged up, or, worse still, being tortured and killed by a criminal gang.

The kettle steamed and clicked off so I spooned some instant coffee into a mug and poured boiling water on it, followed by a little cold water to cool it down. As I sat at the kitchen table drinking my coffee I realised I wouldn't be able to get through the school reunion. The stress I was already dealing with on any given day was too much for me. There was no way I'd be able to take on any extra. And attending the reunion would involve a lot of extra. Way too much for me to deal with.

But I couldn't afford to miss it.

Torture and death didn't sit at all well with me, especially if I was going to be the victim.

So what now? Go on the run? Was it an option?

I'd have to give up my house and all I'd built up. And if I did, they'd probably track down my mum, dad, and brother, and torture them to get information out of them – or maybe just for fun. Because that's what this stuff was for at least one of them – Seth – fun.

No, I couldn't run. I couldn't afford to put my family in peril. I had to face up to it on my own.

What if I went with someone to the reunion? What if I had company? That'd help me. If someone went with me, I'd have a psychological crutch to lean on, and I wouldn't fall down. Robert, my ex, had served the purpose wonderfully well during our courtship and marriage. It was too bad I'd fucked things up with him. I needed him. In the end, he hadn't needed me.

There was a knock at the door which derailed my train of thought – a loud copper's knock. I jumped from my seat, nearly spilling my coffee, while rehearsing in my head the way I was going to play it.

You're going to be surprised there's a policeman calling on you, Jaz, as surprised as any innocent person would be.

My heart was pumping wildly as I opened the front door. When I saw a delivery driver standing on my doorstep I relaxed.

'Sign here, please,' he said, holding up one of those devices which takes an electronic signature. I took the plastic wand and signed the screen with a shaking hand.

'Sorry, it doesn't look like my signature,' I said.

'None of them ever do,' he replied, handing over a long, narrow parcel.

I went to the kitchen with it, trying to remember what I'd ordered online. I only ever order books as a rule. This was no book – it was about two foot long, three inches by three inches in cross-section, and weighed eight or nine pounds.

I couldn't remember ordering anything online recently. Not a book, nothing. I checked the label on the package to make sure it was for me. It was – the name on the label was Jasmine Black, and it was my address, too.

Could it be I'd ordered something during a recent blackout and hadn't noticed? Was it possible I'd got up to some drunken semi-comatose activity which included going berserk with my credit card online? I hoped not, because I could ill-afford such ventures.

Another possibility: someone had bought it for me. I quickly dismissed that one. I had no friends who'd buy me presents. Not one. Well, maybe one or two, but only on my birthday and at Christmas. No-one would just spontaneously buy me something.

So the answer had to be that I'd ordered it myself.

I put the package on the table and got the scissors from the kitchen drawer. The thing was so well wrapped I'd rip off my fingernails if I attempted to open it without the aid of a tool of some kind.

I cut through the tape at one end and prised open a cardboard flap. There was a small amount of polystyrene padding which I removed. Then I was able to tip up the parcel and allow the contents to just slide out onto the table.

What appeared was a tubular object, smooth and black with a dull sheen, tapering towards one end which had grips on it. A piece of paper came out with it, which bore the words: 'Self-Defence Baseball Bat'.

I put my hand to my mouth and stepped back, feeling so faint I almost collapsed to the floor. With my heart pumping I retreated until I'd backed up against the worktop and could retreat no more.

Had I really sent myself this object then forgotten I'd done it? It was just about possible. I'd once been out with a group of friends on a session and remembered nothing that had happened after 9pm, but my friends assured me I hadn't gone home until 2am the following morning. What's more, when I'd gotten out of bed the next day, I'd found an open packet of battered cod on the worktop, with one piece of cod in it. The other had been put under the grill in an unsuccessful attempt to cook it. There was a trail of discarded clothes – my own – leading from the kitchen to the bottom of the stairs.

So I'd got home, tried to cook myself a meal, then undressed and taken myself to bed – and I had no recollection of any of it.

So, yes, it was possible I'd ordered the item myself and forgotten what I'd done. Or was it? Cooking yourself a meal is one thing; ordering a product online is quite another. I grabbed my iPad, clicked on my E-mail app, and inserted the search term 'Baseball'. An E-mail appeared from Amazon. My hands began to shake. I opened the E-mail. It began with the words 'Thank you for shopping with us'. Casting my eyes down the body copy, I saw an image of a baseball bat. What was this? Some kind of guilt trip being imposed on me by my subconscious mind?

Maybe.

But there was another possibility I didn't want to think about.

Someone had hacked into my Amazon account and was fucking with me.

It would've been nice to have been able to talk about it with a trusted friend, but what could I tell anyone who wasn't in on the secret?

'Hey, someone sent me a baseball bat today, and it might have been me. How weird is that?'

That wouldn't make me feel any better at all. The only way I'd feel better is if I discussed it with Kylie or someone else from the group – but to do so would be to invite the Grim Reaper to come knocking at my door, and however bad I felt, I wasn't minded to do that.

So I put the baseball bat in a cupboard and put the cardboard wrapping in my recycling bin, and the polystyrene in the general waste bin. As bad a lush as I was, I was still capable of respecting the planet – at least some of the time.

I looked at the clock. It was 10.20am. I felt as if four hours had gone by since putting the kettle on, but only twenty minutes had passed. That's what happens when you can't relax and you feel as if your life is about to implode any moment.

I got dressed and went to the gym, where, as usual, I made a few half-hearted and futile attempts to rid myself of the blip my tummy had acquired. While I didn't achieve any fat loss to speak of, the physical exertion had the benefit of briefly keeping my mind off things. But immediately I stopped exercising and went to the shower, sweaty and aching, my mind stubbornly returned to everything which was bad about my life. It was as if I was determined to torture myself.

How I wished I could arrange blackouts to order which would rid me of all my worst, most painful memories, so I could start out with a clean slate.

I envied other people who didn't have the sort of personal history I had.

They were blessed with slates so clean you could store a surgeon's scalpel on them. They had untroubled consciences and led blameless lives. They didn't fear every knock at the door, every school reunion, every relationship they'd ever had way back when.

After leaving the gym I headed for the shops and browsed shelves full of stuff I didn't need or want just to kill time. Then I dropped into Waterstones, sat in one of their armchairs, and buried myself in a book, forcing myself to concentrate on the text. It transported me to another world, and before I knew it an hour had passed. The story made me feel marginally better, at least while I was involved in it, because the heroine was in even more of a pickle than I was.

I bought the book – a lengthy psychological thriller – and headed home to finish it. On my way I took a short cut through the park where I saw two men sitting on a wooden bench next to the path. A woman walked over a rolling grass lawn to join them. They all looked to be about thirty, but had the lined and seamed faces of seventy-year-old lifelong smokers.

The woman spoke to the two men, but she wasn't looking at them.

She was looking in the direction of one of the park entrances, near which a young man was loitering, trying his best to look intimidating.

'He isn't geared up yet. He's waiting for some. It'll be about half an hour,' the woman said.

I hurried past them and took a different exit to the one I'd planned on taking to avoid the youth. This was all too much for me – it brought back too many memories. I emerged from the park and walked the remaining distance through the streets to my house. The route took me past the local eight-till-late. I decided it wouldn't hurt to buy myself a bottle of red. When I scanned the wine shelf, I realised that what I wanted – needed – was two bottles of red. I emerged from the shop with three bottles.

Back home I curled up on my sofa with the book in my hand, an occasional table next to me, and a full glass of red on the table with an open bottle next to it.

Just so long as I immersed myself in my book and drank red wine I was able to keep the hostile world at bay.

But all too soon I finished it – and the bottle of red – and it was only 4pm. Bad thoughts started crowding in again. What next could I do to kill time?

I started dwelling on the damned school reunion.

You can't go, Jaz, you'll never get through it. But you can't afford to blob, either. What can you do? Who can you get to come with you, and help you make it through the evening in a sober enough state to keep your lip buttoned?

Robert? We were divorced, but on good terms, kind of. He pitied me – which I found hurtful and offensive. But out of pity he might just be willing to help me. But what if he had a girlfriend? How would she feel about him gallivanting to a school reunion with his former wife? Surely that would be the stuff of her nightmares.

Sustained by Dutch courage, I picked up my mobile and called him.

'Jaz?' he said when he picked up. He sounded puzzled. His

eyebrows would be knitting together forming lines on his forehead – a facial expression to which he often resorted, when taken unawares by something.

'Yes,' I said, injecting a degree of cheeriness in my voice which bore no relation whatsoever to the way I felt, 'it's me. How are you keeping, Robert?'

'Um, I'm keeping well, thank you. But – er – I'm right in the middle of something.'

'Oh,' I said, wondering how I should broach the difficult subject of needing his help. Then I decided to just pile into it. No point in beating ineffectually about the bush. 'Look, I've got something to ask you.'

He didn't reply, but I heard him say – in a muffled voice, as if he was covering his mobile with his hand – 'It's my ex.' Then there was a pause followed by his quiet voice again: 'I don't know what she bloody well wants.' Finally, in his normal voice he said: 'What's that?'

'You know the school reunion I go to every year?'

'Yes. What about it?' Even though he only replied with these four words, they were enough to convey the suspicion he must've been feeling. Then he added: 'Have you been drinking?'

I briefly considered lying but decided it wouldn't wash. He must've asked about it because I'd slurred a few words or something.

'I've only had two glasses of red wine.'

'You sound like you've had more than two. You need to get your drinking habit under control, Jaz.'

I shuffled uneasily on the sofa.

'I am doing. Look, I need your help.'

'What kind of help?'

'I need someone to go to the reunion with.'

'Jaz, with the best will in the world, that's impossible. I'm in another relationship, and even if I wasn't, we both need to move on.'

Deep down I still had feelings for him and regretted the fact we'd split up. It'd all been my fault. My moodiness and snappiness brought on by drink and guilt had proved too much for him, although he did find me funny and entertaining when I wasn't being a stroppy cow.

'All right, Robert,' I said with a sob. 'Bye.'

'Sorry I can't help you, Jaz. Bye.'

So that was that then. I had no escort to go to the reunion with, no-one to support me in my time of need. I poured another glass of wine, wondering if there was any other man I could dredge up from my past to help me. No-one sprang to mind through the alcohol-fuelled fog I was rapidly descending into. What about one of my women friends? I couldn't help but think that'd be even more weird and desperate than my call to Robert had been. I could imagine the conversation, 'Wendy, would you come to my school reunion with me, please? I've no-one to go with.'

'But I never went to your school.' Nervous shuffling at the surreal nature of the request. 'I wouldn't know anyone there apart from you. What would I even talk about with them?'

So that was out. It had to be a man I went with – because taking your partner along was acceptable. Taking anyone else would be, well, just weird, because everyone knew I wasn't lesbian or bi.

Then I had an idea. Why not get a new boyfriend who'd accompany me to the reunion? Yes, meet someone new. Why not? I needed a boyfriend. I hadn't had one in a quite a while, and I was missing all it entailed. The excitement of getting to know a special person, the settling-in period when you find out what he's really like, and finally the comfortable period when you just enjoy having him around, even when all you're doing is watching television together. I needed that, because I wanted company in the evenings, wanted to talk about the mundane details of my life with someone other than friends and work colleagues. Regrettably, I could never discuss the important stuff with anyone.

Anyway, if I got myself a new boyfriend, I could kill two birds with one stone. I'd have someone to accompany me to the reunion, and afterwards he'd be available to talk to now and again when I needed company. When I thought about it, I was missing an awful lot of shared experiences – for instance going on a walk with a partner, or going to a pub, or watching TV while enjoying a bottle of wine.

Wine – that reminded me I needed more, so I went to the kitchen, opened another bottle, and took it to the front room. Then I opened my iPad and checked out the internet dating sites I'd browsed about a million times before. I'd sworn off them more than once. Friends had told me I ought to persevere – they always had examples of people who'd met via these sites and were now happily married. When I protested that I never met anyone suitable, they always came back with, 'You have to keep at it. So-and-so had twenty-five dates before she met the right man.'

So-and-so had a lot more patience than me, obviously. After only five disastrous dates I'd given up on meeting anyone via the internet and decided to rely on real life. Unfortunately, real life had proved equally unreliable as a means of hooking up with someone who'd make a good long-term partner.

Anyway, it was time to give the internet another chance, because it was the only opportunity I was likely to get of landing someone in time for the reunion.

I poured myself another glass – a generous one – and selected a site to post my details on: Elite Dates. ('Meet your ideal mate – the one who'll share intimate moments with you, as well as your interests, ambitions, and values.')

Then I set about creating a profile. The photo I chose was one in which I had my hair up to show off a pair of huge dangly earrings. My cunningly-applied make-up gave me cheekbones I didn't actually have. My made-up face looked quite attractive, I decided, as I took another sip of my wine. The photo had been taken at a party when I'd been wearing a red vest-top, faded torn jeans and heels. The jeans were close fitting so my blip was visible – but it didn't look as bad as I always imagined it to be. This prompted me to get off the sofa and examine myself in the full-length mirror I have at the bottom of the stairs. The blip, I decided, wasn't so prominent after all. I must have body dysmorphia sometimes.

Next, I had to compose some flattering but plausible descriptive text to accompany the profile. I told prospective dates I was a young solicitor ('young' – it wasn't too much of a stretch, given I was thirty-four) interested in reading, long walks, socialising, live music, festivals, and food. I was vivacious and outgoing – an extrovert with a love of culture, both pop and the deeper stuff.

When I read it back to myself, I said, 'What's not to like, Jaz?'

Then I hit the post button and awaited developments. They were not long in coming. Soon enough I had a bizarre procession of freaks lined up in my inbox, every one of them desperate to get his perverted hands on me. Among them was a man who was potentially not a freak and might even be eminently suitable – a medic at the local hospital. He was thirty-five, five-eleven, fashionably bearded and behind the facial hair I could see he had a pleasingly sculpted face. He liked most of the things I did, plus he was a triathlete. God alone knew how he managed to fit that in.

Things had to move fast with this medic if he was to accompany me to the reunion.

I took a sip of wine and messaged him:

I'm at a loose end tonight how about you?

He replied immediately.

I am too as it happens. Do you fancy meeting up?

I glugged down more wine.

Sounds like a good idea. Where and when?

How about Westow House at eight? Have a drink there and go for a meal afterwards?

Sounds good to me.

OK see you then.

It was 6pm. I had time to finish the bottle, plan my outfit, and take a leisurely bath to get in the right frame of mind before going out. I poured another glass, and another – the final one. Then I gathered my strength and hauled myself upstairs, staggering halfway up them and nearly falling back down.

Watch yourself, Jaz, take it easy.

45

I got to the bathroom, turned on the bath taps and went to my bedroom to choose my outfit.

The medic had seen a picture of me in jeans, so that's what I decided to wear for our date, with heels like in the photo, and a tasteful GAP T-shirt. I laid them out on my bed and returned to the bathroom, lit a few scented candles and had a good long soak.

The wine and the prospect of meeting someone new was almost enough to take my mind off my woes – almost.

After my bath I put on my dressing gown, put up my hair as best I could, and applied my make-up. It wasn't quite as good as usual due to the effects of the drink, but I made a passable job of it.

Finally, I got dressed and checked myself out in the mirror. The effect was sexy but not provocative and tarty. By now it was 7.45pm, so I ordered an Uber which arrived within minutes, and by 8pm I was entering the doors of the Westhow.

Dr Nicely Handsome – his name was Simon – spotted me immediately, and came to my side.

'Hello, Jasmine,' he said, and for a moment looked as though he didn't know whether to shake my hand or kiss my cheek. I leaned forward and proffered the side of my face. He took the hint and our cheeks brushed, then we headed for the bar. Somehow I got there in a straight line. He turned to me. 'Have you been out somewhere already?'

Either he'd smelled the drink on my breath, or I was a little unco-ordinated. I decided to brass it out. 'No, what makes you think that?'

'It's just – never mind – what would you like to drink?'

'I'll have a glass of red wine, please.'

'Small, medium or large?'

'Might as well make it a large. Merlot, please.'

His brow furrowed. 'Oh-kay.' He waved a twenty-pound note in the air until one of the barmen noticed us and came over. 'A pint of Yankee Steam Ale, please, and a large glass of merlot.'

The barman set the drinks in front of us and Simon paid. 'Shall we grab a seat somewhere?' he asked.

'Sure,' I said, and we found an empty table.

'Well done, Jaz, you're holding it together really well,' I told myself.

'What's that?' said Simon.

'Nothing,' I said quickly. 'I didn't say anything.'

'I could've sworn you did.'

I made a mental note to try harder not to talk to myself out loud when in company. 'Nope,' I insisted, shaking my head. 'I said nothing. Nada. Rien. Niente.'

There was an awkward silence.

Come on, Jaz, I said, without, of course, moving my lips or anything. *Get this conversation going.* Then I took a slurp of merlot and asked, 'What kind of music do you like?' It's one of my go-to questions whenever I meet someone new. It gets almost everyone talking. And if someone happens to not like music, that's good too. It tells me to run a mile and never have anything to do with the freak again.

Simon looked relieved, probably because I'd gotten us past the awkward moment, and maybe also because I was talking to him, rather than to myself.

'Music, let me see. Rock mainly, but I'll listen to pretty much anything when it's live. Jazz, Funk, Blues, you name it.'

After that the evening took on the quality of looking through a kaleidoscope. The pieces were all milling around, and as soon as they turned into a pattern I thought I recognised they tumbled into a different pattern, and I couldn't keep track.

Then, all of a sudden, the evening was gone, and I was in bed feeling dehydrated with a horrible taste in my mouth. I threw off the covers. Daylight was coming in through the curtains.

I needed a pee and got out of bed. Then I saw I was fully dressed. What was going on? I'd worry about that later. The urge to go was desperate. After I'd been to the loo I drank some water, fragments of the night before bubbling up from the recesses of my mind. I vaguely remembered drinks in the Westhow and food in an Italian place with a medic called Simon who insisted on being called Si. How I'd gotten home I didn't know.

My head was pounding and in spite of the water I still felt dry. I needed coffee. As I made my way downstairs my head began to spin. When I got to the bottom of the stairs I heard the clink of crockery in the kitchen. There was an intruder in my house. I stopped dead, thought about tiptoeing back up and calling the police on my mobile. Then I thought, *Don't be daft, Jaz, an intruder wouldn't take time out from burgling you to make a coffee. It's got to be Simon in the kitchen.*

I pushed open the kitchen door and saw Simon sitting at my table, head down, staring at the screen of his mobile phone, with a steaming mug in front of him. He looked up when he heard me come in. The expression on his face told me he wasn't too pleased to see me. 'You've surfaced at last,' he said.

'What time is it?'

'Nine. I've taken the liberty of making myself breakfast. I hope you don't mind.'

'Not at all.'

The kettle had just been boiled and there was enough hot water left in it for me to make myself a mug of coffee.

'What happened last night?' I asked. There was no point in pretending I remembered it. I didn't, and he'd catch me out easily enough if I tried to lie about it.

'You got very drunk and I ordered a taxi and got you home.'

Oh dear. As I'd feared, I hadn't made a good impression. There was another issue I was curious about. 'Did we have sex?'

'That was never on the cards. I only came home with you to make sure you didn't have alcohol poisoning. You threw up as soon as we got here. I slept on the sofa and checked on you now and again to make sure you were okay.'

Exactly what you'd expect from a medic.

I'd woken up feeling oddly calm because all the drink had made me feel so ill I forgot to feel stressed. As I sipped my coffee, my current desperate circumstances came back to me. I'd killed a boy, was worried I might have my collar felt by the police, had a dark secret buried in my past which might sink me and a lot of others, there was a school reunion to go to tonight to meet people I never wanted to see again – but I had to see them, or they'd come after me. And I remembered why I'd met up with Simon in the first place: I wanted to meet someone who'd be willing to go to the reunion with me. Thinking about it, that'd never been a plausible aim in the time-frame I had available. In the cold light of the morning, it seemed positively outlandish I could ever have thought it possible. Nevertheless, I was so desperate I decided to see if I could pull it off.

'Simon?'

'Yes.'

'I've got a favour to ask you.'

He pressed the button on the side of his mobile, put it in his pocket, and met my eyes with his own. 'What's that then?'

'I've got a social event tonight and I need someone to go with. I'd feel like a loser if I went on my own. Will you come with me?'

He shook his head. 'Sorry, no. You're not my type. I like you, but you've got a drink problem. Seriously, you need help. And you need to be careful when you go on dates with strangers. I could have been a rapist or murderer for all you knew, but you didn't take any precautions. I've ordered an Uber and I'll be going now. Take care of yourself, Jaz.'

He stood up and awkwardly brushed my cheek with his before leaving.

And that was it.

I was on my own. I'd blown it. Mind you, it might've been mission impossible. Who else could I ask? I racked my brains. What about Bernie, my counsellor from the AA? No, he wouldn't be any good. In the unlikely event he agreed, he wouldn't want me drinking – and I'd need to drink something to get through the evening. I wanted someone to make sure I didn't drink too much, not stop me altogether.

I showered, worked myself up into a lather, took a walk through the park, and before I knew it, it was time to get my glad rags on and go. I changed into a pair of faded jeans with a low-cut sleeveless navy top and a couple of bangles adorning one of my wrists. Naturally I wore heels as they gave me a feeling of power, God knows why, maybe the fact I stood taller in them was the reason. Somewhat unimaginatively, I wore my hair up again and chose a different pair of dangly silver earrings. I thought gold was vulgar, and even if I was going to my doom, I wanted to do it tastefully.

The reunion was held in the function room at the Selhurst Park Conference Centre, part of Crystal Palace Football Club. That was just as well, because the event was difficult for me to stomach, and if they'd had it at St Benedict's – our old school – it would've been intolerable.

I checked my make-up for the final time, ordered an Uber which would be ten minutes in coming, opened my last bottle of red wine with trembling hands, poured a measure which must've been 300 ml at least, and tried to pretend to myself I was taking modest sips of it, but the truth must've been different because the glass was empty by the time my taxi arrived. I began the journey to the conference centre with jangling nerves but by the time I got there I was feeling just a tiny bit drunk, and that had a calming effect.

The conference centre was a huge red brick and grey metal structure tacked on to the end of the football stadium. The club had done its best to make it look inviting at night, by placing an array of outdoor lights strategically around the exterior, but nothing could conceal the fact it was essentially a large, ill-shaped box of a building.

A burly security guy wearing a dark suit stood in front of the door. He had a shaven head and a threatening bruiser's face. I was willing to bet that beneath the suit, his body was covered in unsightly tattoos. I had clients who looked like him. He gave me a hard stare when I arrived, then checked a list when I gave him my name. He allowed himself a half-smile as he waved me inside. It occurred to me he should've checked my ID, but then, it was only a school reunion, so why go to such lengths? Who was going to crash it, and why? It wasn't as if it was Glastonbury or anything. There was probably no need for any security at all. The drinks weren't free. We all had to pay for our own. The only benefit anyone would get from crashing the place was the enjoyment of the room in the company of people they didn't know, most of whom they wouldn't want to know.

I checked-in my jacket – a black number with the cuffs rolled up – and made my way into the room where we were having our party.

It always amazed me that year after year, so many of my former school friends showed up to the event. There must have been nearly the whole of my year there – which amounted to about three hundred former pupils. The place was heaving. But here's the thing: only half-a-dozen of us had a compelling reason to show up. The rest – people like Beth and Adele – were doing it because they actually wanted to.

I walked among them, giving a cheery wave here, a grin and a nod there, and even the occasional girly giggle – which was larding it on a bit thick, to be honest. Soon I heard a familiar voice, 'Jaz, great to see you! We haven't been in touch since last year.'

It was Emma, who might've been a nice person and worth knowing, but I was on a mission.

'Oh, hi, Emma. I'll be with you in a minute. Please excuse me.'

My objective was dead ahead – it was the bar – and I wasn't going to be side-tracked for anybody. I was going to get there as quick as possible, and order a large glass of red wine. I upped my pace, pushing people to one side in my eagerness to reach the bar. One or two of them gave me dirty looks, but so what? If only they'd known how badly I needed a drink, they wouldn't have been standing in my way. The whole crowd of them would've parted just like the Red Sea did for Moses and his tribe of Israelites as they fled from the Egyptian army.

A cartoon image of a grinning shark got in my way. Its mouth was wide open displaying a sinister set of teeth. I blinked and focussed. The image was on a colourful tie, the tie being worn by a tall, thickset guy wearing a navy pin-striped suit and white shirt.

I was in such a hurry I didn't bother looking up at his face, I just tried to push past him, but he stuck out his arm to stop me. I was about to get cross when I looked up and recognised him. It was Seth Delaney. He was the last person on earth I needed to annoy. No-one crossed Seth Delaney. No-one in their right mind, anyway.

I guess a lot of women would have found him handsome. He had chiselled movie-star looks and black hair cut in an extreme version of a short back and sides cut, with the hair on the top of his head left flamboyantly and incongruously long. My heart beat faster when I recognised him – a whole lot faster – but that wasn't because I fancied him. No, I was feeling my flesh crawl.

'As I live and breathe, it's Jasmine Black,' he said with a grin every bit as sinister as the one on the shark adorning his tie. 'Here, let me look at you.'

I gave him an anorexic smile. He put his hands on my shoulders, staring at me with an unblinking gaze. Although he was always amiable, Seth scared me more than anyone I'd ever met. I'd seen what he was capable of, but that wasn't the reason. It was because, in spite of his charm, there was something dead at the back of his eyes.

'You're still the same sweet, attractive girl I knew at school, Jasmine,' he said, kissing me on the cheek. 'You and I could have been an item, don't you think? I think so, anyway.' He lowered his voice and leaned in close so that I was the only person who could hear his next line: 'If not for Tony.'

The mention of Tony made me shudder, as he knew it would.

He enjoyed fucking with my head like this. It occurred to me he might be responsible for the baseball bat, but I wasn't about to ask him if he'd sent it. If it hadn't been him, he'd ask me a load of questions about it, and then, if he thought there was the tiniest chance I was going to say something incriminating about our past to someone outside of our group, he'd end my life. I didn't doubt that.

His hands continued to rest on my shoulders while he looked at my face, enjoying the deep discomfort I was trying vainly to conceal. I wanted to wriggle free of him but knew it'd be a mistake to do anything which could be interpreted as hostile, so I pliantly allowed him to keep his hands where they were. At least he wasn't groping me, small comfort that it was. I wondered what I'd do if he did, and decided I'd have to stop him and hope it didn't lead to anything too unpleasant.

'I tell you what,' he said, his dead eyes showing no emotion even though he was grinning, 'I'll buy you a drink.'

It was, as they used to say in the old movies about the Mafia, an offer I couldn't refuse.

He turned to face the same direction as me and put one hand in the small of my back, pushing me gently in the direction I'd been heading – the bar. Didn't he realise I needed no encouragement to get there? The people ahead of us parted to make way for him, even those who didn't know what he was, or what he was capable of. They saw him as Seth the charismatic and important schoolboy-turned-successful businessman, that was all. If they'd known the truth, they'd have done more than make way for him – they would've fled in terror from the reunion.

Everyone we passed looked his way and said, 'Hi, Seth,' or 'Great to see you, Seth,' or 'Buy you a drink, Seth.'

A woman called Kimberley was watching me and Seth, her eyes narrowed beneath a crown of overdone hair. Her eyelids were so weighed down with mascara she could hardly keep them open. Standing there in a too tight lime-green top, she looked envious, even though she was with her husband. She would've swapped places with me in an instant, naïve fool that she was. She fancied Seth like mad and rumours were rife she cheated on her hubby.

We got to the bar and Seth made eye contact with a barman who hurried to serve him, leaving a disgruntled customer to get attended to by someone else.

'What would you like, Jaz?' Seth said, his shark's gaze penetrating deep into my soul.

'Red wine, please,' I replied in as even a voice as I could.

He got my wine and a tonic water for himself. Seth rarely drank and when he did, he didn't do it to excess.

'So, what's been happening in your life, Jaz?' he asked.

It was an innocent enough question but it set my nerves on edge. A lot had been happening, none of which I wanted to talk about. I'd run over a young boy and killed him, and was worried that any day now the police were going to call round and question me, maybe even arrest me for it. I'd become an alcoholic and was attending AA meetings – but was drinking like a sailor on leave this evening. So how sincere was my commitment to getting on the wagon? I'd gotten myself drunk and lost a day – a whole thirty-three hours for Christ's sake – and couldn't account for it. The thought of what I might have said and who I might have said it to during my lost hours was worrying the hell out of me. And finally, I'd received a baseball bat through the post. Someone, I was increasingly sure, had ordered it online for me. That was nice of them, wasn't it? A touching reminder of a past I shared with Seth, Kylie and a handful of others. Who'd sent it and why?

A wave of paranoia hit me. Supposing Seth had sent it, it might have been a test of some kind. He might've been trying to find out how honest I was with him. If I told him about it, that could mean I'd passed his test. But if I didn't, it could be a fail and it might carry consequences – fatal ones.

I had to buy myself time and think this through, decide what the best course of action would be. Fess up or keep schtum.

'Could we talk later, Seth? I need to circulate.'

He put his hand beneath my chin and pushed it up, forcing me to look into his eyes. His irises were so dark they blended into his pupils, adding to the shark-like effect of his unflinching stare.

'You can circulate after you've answered my question,' he said.

I knitted my eyebrows.

'Oh, okay. What's been happening in my life, let me see. I've been working all hours defending people from criminal charges, successfully as it happens, and I've been off work with a bout of flu which might have been brought on by overwork. That's about it, really.'

'No boyfriend?'

'No boyfriend.'

He pulled his lips back from his teeth, this being his idea of a smile. 'Maybe we should get together.'

'The moment has passed, Seth. We had our chance years ago, remember?'

He moved his hand from under my chin. 'So we did – but no harm in testing the water.'

I felt my features twist into a frown. 'That water is very cold. So cold it's beyond icy.'

He threw his head back. 'Ha, I'm just fucking with you, Jaz. Don't get so uptight.'

I felt my frown getting worse. 'You don't know the effect you have on people, Seth. You ought to be more considerate.'

'Oh, but I do. They like me.'

Right on cue, Kylie appeared by his side and touched his arm.

She was wearing a slinky red dress which showed off every one of her curves. You didn't have to look too carefully to see the line her panties made across her pert butt, or to tell she was wearing a black bra. I was pretty sure those provocative things hadn't happened by accident.

'Seth, it's great to see you,' she said. It looked like she meant it. The events in our teens hadn't put her off him, nor had his colourful career. Quite the opposite, in fact. She revelled in his company, loved playing the part of – what? – a gangster's moll? Was that what she was? I sometimes wondered.

She turned to me. 'Jaz, you're looking good.'

This was no more than a brief aside, as she immediately focussed all her attention back on Seth, standing right in front of him, and rather closer than I would have thought normal for a mere friend.

Her dress was too short and too revealing for my liking, but she did have a good body and great legs, I'll give her that, and her tummy was in better shape than mine. No doubt most of the men in the room fancied her.

Kylie and Seth exchanged fond cheek kisses, then Seth put his hands on her hips and they stared into each other's eyes.

'Kylie, it's great to see you, too. Drink?'

She looked as if she wanted the moment to last forever. I remembered her copping off with Seth at school, and had observed her latching on to him at previous reunions, but I hadn't realised till then she still felt that way about him. She was making it obvious. If she wasn't his moll, that's what she aspired to be. And now everyone knew, or at least suspected. While Seth was distracted with her, I took the opportunity to slip away with my glass of red, pushing my way through the crowds to a corner where I stood on my own watching everyone enjoy the event.

My wine seemed to evaporate at high speed in spite of my best attempts to make it last. On the plus side, my wine consumption and the fact I was no longer speaking to Seth meant my nerves were settling a bit. Just so long as I kept my mind off bad things, I was able to remain relatively calm. The problem was, I had so many bad things to think about that no sooner had I suppressed one of them then another would come bubbling to the surface.

A man waved at me and made his way to my corner. It was Charlie Duggan, carrying a tumbler of whiskey with ice. He was a big man like Seth, and, like Seth, he'd gone to the lengths of wearing a suit for the school reunion. It was charcoal grey, and he'd teamed it up with a light grey shirt and sober tie. He'd combed his mop of dark hair into a neat parting, which somehow made it more obvious he was greying at the temples. His round face was lined with troubles.

He extended his hand to shake mine, changed his mind, and opened his arms instead. We hugged, and I felt him pulling me close as if I was a long-lost friend. In a sense I was. If things had panned out differently, I could've seen me and Charlie spending time together, maybe even becoming an item. Apart from me, Charlie was the most gentle of the group that'd been involved in the incident all those years ago. I suspected the rest of them didn't know what 'gentle' was – but they were capable of making a good pretence of it when the need arose.

We let each other go, and he examined my face – while I examined his. What were we both looking for? Reassurance, I think, that our mutual secret was safe, but possibly something more.

'How are you keeping, Jaz?' he asked. He was smiling, but it was just a mouth-smile. The corners of his mouth moved up into a U-shape, but his eyes refused to join in the celebration.

'Oh, same as usual, pretty good.' I did my best to inject some sincerity into those words.

'I'm not,' he replied, 'and I don't believe you are.'

I threw back the last of my wine, about a third of a 250 ml glass, in one gulp. 'What do you mean?'

'Well, your eyes are darting about, and you have a nervous tic.'

A tic? What was he on about? Then I realised the corner of one of my eyes was twitching. I rubbed it, which didn't do any good. It continued to twitch.

'Oh that,' I said, putting on the bravest face I could about it, 'that's nothing.'

He attempted another smile which was just as unsuccessful as his first attempt. 'We ought to face the truth. You and I haven't had a proper conversation since, well, you know when. We really ought to, because then we could move on.'

My stomach began to slowly turn. 'A proper conversation? About what?'

I thought he'd drop it but he wouldn't.

'You know what.'

'Seth wouldn't like it.'

That was true, but it wasn't the only reason I said it. The truth was, I didn't want to discuss the part of our shared past Charlie wanted to talk about. I'd buried it as deep as I could, and wanted it to stay buried. If I were to dig it up and carry out a post-mortem on it, it'd make me ill.

'Seth wouldn't have to know.'

I needed an excuse to extricate myself from the situation. I held up my wine glass. 'Please excuse me, Charlie, I need a top-up,' I said, glancing towards the bar.

Charlie knocked back the remains of his whiskey. 'So do I,' he replied. 'I'm coming with you.'

Great. He was going to stick with me in the hope he'd be able to buttonhole me on the one subject we had to avoid, in this room at any rate, to ensure our future survival.

I set off, vaguely aware of him following close behind me. When I got to the bar I turned my head and saw him standing beside me.

'What do you want? I'll get it,' he said.

I pretended I hadn't heard and hoped he'd give up on me and go talk to someone else about the past.

'What do you want – I'll get it,' he repeated, a little louder this time.

There was nothing for it but to give in gracefully – I couldn't spend the entire evening running away from Charlie. I could only hope he wouldn't bend my ear too forcibly on the subject of our shared past. If he did, I'd need more than another glass of red to get through it. An extra-large pack of Valium might not be enough.

'A red wine, please, Charlie,' I said. 'Make it a big one.'

He got my drink and a large whiskey for himself then he leaned close to me, and spoke sotto voce, so that only I could hear him, 'We do need to talk,' he said.

Seth was at the other end of the bar with a group of admirers. He must've had some sort of sixth sense, because he glanced in our direction while Charlie was whispering in my ear, and his dead eyes briefly focussed on us, while his grin wavered just a little. Did he suspect something was amiss?

'Not now, Charlie,' I said, hoping my voice wasn't giving away too much of the alarm I felt at the prospect of Seth knowing what was on the cards. Then I looked around wondering whether anyone else had noticed anything odd about the way Charlie was talking to me. Probably not. Only a small group of people knew we were privy to confidential information which ought never to be discussed. Everyone else here had come to catch up with former school friends, or show off how successful they'd been since leaving St Benedict's.

'It's been eighteen years,' he said, taking a sip of his whiskey. More than a sip.

'What do you expect me to do about it?'

'Be a human being, for God's sake. Act like you care.'

I'd misjudged Charlie. I'd assumed I was the one with the biggest conscience out of the lot of us. I was wrong. Charlie was the one who felt the guilt the most.

There was no telling how deep the shit would be that Charlie would land us in if he aired his feelings in this room of all rooms. My stomach turned more quickly. I took a hefty slurp of wine to calm it down. The last thing I could afford to do was act like I cared. If I did, I might have to talk about it. And if I talked, even just to Charlie, I might get myself killed. If I talked to anyone else, I might get myself locked up for a crime which had taken place a long time ago.

'I do care, Charlie, but I can't talk about it. You know that.'

'Yes, I know it. But I can't carry on like this. The guilt is killing me. I've got to bare my soul to someone, and the only person I can think of is you.'

It made perfect sense. It also made me realise Charlie had become a liability – a bigger liability even than me. I could only hope – for his sake as well as mine – that he kept a lid on things. I drank more wine. It seemed to be my only answer to every problem. Then I surreptitiously looked at Seth. He was staring at me and Charlie with his cold dead eyes. I knew that look. I'd seen it before. It'd scared me way back when, and it scared me now.

'Don't spill your guts, Charlie,' I whispered. 'Not to me, not to anyone. If you do and word gets back to Seth–'

'You wouldn't tell Seth.'

'No, I wouldn't. But you don't want to get into any bad habits. They could kill you.'

'What sort of bad habits?'

It was Seth. He'd stolen up and caught me unawares. And what I'd thought of as a whisper must've been louder than that for him to have heard me. What else had he heard?

'Drinking too much,' I said. 'You can have too much of a good thing.'

Seth looked at my glass and raised his eyebrows. 'I'm not sure you're qualified to give that advice,' he said. 'And I'm not sure I believe you. You two better behave yourselves – or I might have to have a quiet word.'

I've never seen the blood drain from anybody's face as quickly as it did from Charlie's. His hand trembled so much the ice clinked in his glass. Seth looked at me with a shark-like grin on his face. 'You ought to get your nervous tic seen to,' he said.

I self-consciously rubbed my eye again, while he walked away, laughing.

'Fuck,' said Charlie.

'Yes,' I said. 'Fuck. Better not even talk about talking about it from now on.'

He downed his whiskey in one and ordered another. 'I'm cracking up,' he said, not quietly. Heads turned. Fortunately, Seth was out of earshot and had his back to us.

'For fuck's sake, Charlie, do us both a favour and shut your mouth.'

He reached into his jacket pocket, pulled out an e-cig, and took a long draw from it. He sighed in a satisfied way as a white mist left his mouth and swirled around his face.

'That's better,' he said. 'I'm trying to give up smoking, but this is almost as good. It hits the spot.'

'You're not allowed to use those in here,' I told him, pointing to a sign behind the bar. 'We better find a seat somewhere quiet where you won't be noticed.'

I led the way through the people crowding round the bar area to the tables and chairs at the back of the room. Soon I found an empty table and we both grabbed a seat at it. Charlie hung his jacket over the back of his seat. There were dark sweat patches under his armpits and a sheen of sweat covered his face.

'I've been keeping things to myself all this time,' Charlie mumbled drunkenly, loosening his tie. 'But you know something? The game's up.'

Because he was mumbling and no-one was nearby, I was pretty confident he hadn't been overheard. All the same I felt the nervous tic in my eyelid getting worse.

'What?'

He loosened his tie some more and drank some more whiskey. He must've ordered a triple because his glass still looked rather full.

'The game's up,' he repeated.

'Shut the fuck up, Charlie.'

He unbuttoned his shirtsleeves and rolled them up to the elbow as if to show he meant business. He picked up his glass and finished his whiskey in one determined gulp. 'You want to know how I know the game's up?' he asked.

The tic got so bad it began to affect my vision. It made Charlie's face quiver when I looked at him through the eye with the tic in it. I pointed to it.

'Can't you see what you're doing to me? Stop it, Charlie!'

He put both hands on the table and looked down. For a moment I thought he was embarrassed then I thought he might be doing that because he was drunk and drugged-up.

He raised his head slowly, as if it was taking a supreme effort. 'You need to know something,' he said.

I leaned closer to him and whispered urgently, 'Not if it's about the past I don't.'

He spoke out loud, little caring who heard. 'It'sh only a matter of time before we'll all be behind barsh.'

Drunk though I was, his words pierced my brain like arrows.

What could this mean? Was Charlie on the verge of cracking up and handing himself in? Or had someone else told him they were ratting us all out to the police?

He picked up his empty glass, held it up to his face and looked at it as if searching for answers. Then he put the glass back on the table.

'Need anosher drink,' he said, getting to his feet. He staggered backwards but managed to stop himself from falling over. 'Closhe,' he said.

Then he took a couple more steps, in the right direction this time, and collapsed face down on the floor. He made no attempt to get up. He didn't even move. He just lay there face down, like a statue fallen off its pedestal. Inebriated though I was, I knew something was very wrong. I went to his side, dropped to my knees, got my hands beneath him and rolled him onto his back. Then I put my face close to his and said, 'Charlie, Charlie, are you okay?' he didn't respond. I raised my head. People were giving us concerned glances. 'Help me someone! This is serious!' I shouted.

A small crowd soon gathered round us. I heard a calm voice speaking with authority. 'Let me through, I'm a doctor.'

I recognised him as Raymond Wells, someone who, in my teens, I'd considered to be nice enough but a sad loser type. It turned out he was one of those rare St Benedict's success stories – like me, if you could call being a lush successful.

He got to work on Charlie, feeling the pulse in his neck then giving him CPR. Someone else standing over him desperately pressed the keys on his mobile and made an urgent call. I heard him shouting the word 'Ambulance!' to make himself heard above the music still booming from the speakers.

'Is there a defibrillator on the premises?' Wells shouted.

'I'll find out,' someone said – it was Seth. He went to quiz the bar manager and returned a few seconds later.

'Sorry, no,' he said.

Wells continued the CPR for a few more minutes then stopped. 'I'm sorry,' he said. 'It's no use. He's dead. Charlie is dead.'

Charlie, dead? I couldn't believe it. I still saw Raymond Wells as the sad loser I'd known at school and thought he must've got it wrong. I put my hand on his shoulder and shook him.

'Charlie can't be dead. You've got to give him more treatment,' I said.

'Sorry,' he said, getting to his feet. 'There's nothing more I can do. There's nothing anyone can do, other than God.'

I'd been feeling a bit sick and now I felt sicker than ever. My eyes began to well up so much I had to wipe the tears from them with the back of my hand.

'How?' I asked. 'How did he die?'

'That'll be a job for the coroner to work out,' said Wells. 'You'll have to let me go. I need a drink.'

I couldn't blame him for wanting refreshment. I needed a drink too. But it would've felt disrespectful to leap right up and neck a glass of red, while Charlie was lying on the floor on his own, even if he was dead, so I knelt next to him, wondering whether he'd died of a heart attack or a stroke. I imagined that with all the stress he'd been going through, either was likely. Then I wondered if he might have overdosed on something. Charlie didn't take recreational drugs as far as I knew, but things might have changed. Or his doctor could've prescribed anti-depressants, and if Charlie had been having a particularly bad day, he might've taken more than he was meant to.

The music suddenly stopped. The DJ had realised something was amiss. Seth went over to him and they exchanged words then the DJ gave Seth a mic.

'Ladies and gentlemen,' said Seth. 'There's been an unfortunate incident. I regret to tell you that one of our colleagues has passed away. Charles Duggan, known to everyone here simply as "Charlie". He was respected and liked by everyone who knew him. Out of respect for Charlie, we're not playing any more music tonight. Please don't go home, as the police have been called, and they may want to interview you.'

He gave the mic back to the DJ, walked over to me, took me by the hand, and led or dragged me to the bar, I'm not sure which.

'Let's get you another drink,' he said, his features immobile as those of a Botox user.

It was another of those offers I couldn't refuse. 'Red wine, please.' My sick stomach would just have to cope.

There must have been some sort of telepathy going on, because our gang from our schooldays all congregated in the same spot.

'You need something stronger. I'll get you a brandy.' He leaned across the bar. 'Two double brandies, please.' He noticed Kylie and the rest had joined us. 'Make that six double brandies.'

He handed them round and raised his glass. 'To Charlie,' he said.

We all raised our own glasses and chorused, 'To Charlie!'

I began to well up again. Seth noticed and gave me a couple of tissues. After I'd mopped my eyes and gotten over my fit of sobbing, we told each other what an all-round great person Charlie was, although all of us knew there'd been something lurking in his background which raised a lot of damning questions. It raised those same damning questions about the rest of us, but of course we never mentioned that.

Kylie drank her brandy looking as if she couldn't care less about Charlie's death but was making an effort to pretend she did. As I glanced around, I realised she was pretty representative. Charlie and me must've been the only normal people in that group of ours. The rest of them were dead inside.

Before long, Seth was back to his shark-like self, laughing and joking as if nothing had happened.

Out of the corner of my eye I noticed a couple of paramedics walking through the hall towards Charlie's corpse, and, following in their wake, a couple of policemen.

2

WAY BACK WHEN

S t Benedict's was a huge brick building housing upwards of a thousand pupils. It had a central block four storeys high, attached to which were smaller blocks containing the school hall, gym, and changing rooms. To the rear there were muddy games pitches, and to the front a series of bleak playgrounds. It was surrounded by a high wall, creating an overall impression similar to that of the jail at Wormwood Scrubs. The look of the place filled me with dread, as did its reputation.

It was the last place I wanted to go. I'd been perfectly happy at the Dickens Academy, but my parents had moved and I had no option other than to transfer to St Benedict's.

It didn't help that I was wearing hand-me-downs. The way I was dressed was the stuff of nightmares for a girl of my age. My grey skirt was faded, my blouse was at least two sizes too big, and my grubby school tie was frayed at the ends. Everybody else had school uniforms which fitted them perfectly and were new, or newish. The other pupils looked me up and down, taking in the way I was dressed and passing judgement on me. So, on my first day, I kept a low profile. It helped that the teacher didn't make too much of a fuss when she introduced me to the class.

I sat at the back and talked to no-one, but kept my eyes open and tried to work out who I should associate with. I wanted to get in with someone who'd be my ticket to social acceptance, and I reckoned if I couldn't do that, the next best thing was to not be noticed.

I slunk from class-to-class, friendless and alone, wondering if I dared speak to someone and hoping someone would speak to me. It was a forlorn hope. My skirt was too long. It made me look like a freak, as did the rest of my outfit. So the chances of anyone talking to me – anyone who was cool, that is – were slim.

A boy looked at me as I made my way down a corridor between lessons. I tried a shy smile and he sneered. I immediately looked away, wondering if this was an indication of how life would be from now on.

During the first break I went to the school toilets and ensconced myself in a cubicle. I rolled up the waist of my skirt a few times as best I could to make it the same length as those worn by the other girls. When there was no-one else in the toilet and it was safe to check myself out in the mirror, I devoted a minute or two to examining the way I looked to see whether I could possibly cut the mustard at the new school.

The procedure with the skirt had made me slightly less freaky. I had that going for me at least. But my hair was mousy and haphazard, my face was bereft of make-up, and my uniform was lumpen and shapeless. Even my shoes were all wrong. They were clunky and embarrassingly brown, instead of the black they should have been. I couldn't see anyone cool wanting to hang out with me.

When lunchtime came I got my school dinner and took it to the end of a table at the back of the dining hall. I sat on my own, eating it glumly, occasionally raising my eyes to look around from under my overlong fringe. I soon enough identified the cool girls of my year: the three of them were sitting together a few yards from me. I was too insignificant for them to pay any attention to me, so I could spy on them without being noticed.

They wore their skirts and ties ridiculously short, and their hair and make-up were done to perfection. Seeing their made-up faces made me feel naked and inferior. What's more, I now realised I'd gotten my tie all wrong. I'd tied it with the wide bit hanging down long to the waistline of my skirt. It should've been done so that it dangled about three inches below my collar. I made a mental note to fix it after lunch, and wondered whether I'd ever be able to make new friends in this vast prison of a school I found myself in.

As I shoved a forkful of shepherd's pie into my mouth, I heard a female voice. 'Mind if I sit here?'

'No,' I mumbled without looking up. 'Go ahead.'

She sat opposite me, and I sized her up. Mousey hair like mine, a face which looked geekily intelligent, but far from attractive, and she was bespectacled and overweight. In other words, she was a disappointment to anyone seeking social acceptance in a new school.

'I haven't seen you before,' she said. She had an odd accent, like a pirate. 'Is this your first day?'

I nodded, wondering whether it was wise to get involved with this girl. It might in some ways be worse than being on my own. If she proved to be unpopular, as was likely the case, my fate would be sealed. I'd never get in with the cool crowd, or even with the semi-cools.

'I've been here a couple of weeks now,' she said. 'My parents moved over from Cornwall.' That explained her odd way of talking.

I nodded again. I didn't want to give her too much encouragement. Then I thought, maybe I was taking the wrong approach. People probably saw me as a freak. I didn't want to burn my bridges with this girl. She might be my only possibility of having a friend. 'Why?' I asked.

'Because my dad got a new job. It's meant I've had to get used to a new school. Neither of them thought of that.'

Having finished half my shepherd's pie I tucked into some veg, wondering how to respond, or indeed whether to respond. After a moment's consideration I swallowed a lump of cabbage and replied, 'Neither of them?'

'My mum and dad. They only ever think of themselves.'

She ate her meal in record time then another girl appeared by her side.

'I'm going to the shop. Are you coming, Adele?' she asked.

'Obs,' my new acquaintance replied.

She stood up and left me with the words, 'Got to go. Might see you later.'

So the invitation to go to the shop wasn't extended to me. I'd thought of Adele as a potential burden, but her friend clearly thought of me in the same way. It could mean I needed Adele more than she needed me. Maybe I was up myself and needed taking down a peg or two.

I finished my dinner and wolfed down a sponge pudding with gloopy custard. The afternoon would've dragged had I not been thinking about Joshua. The thought of seeing him kept me going.

When I got home my mother was cradling him in her arms. I held out my own arms hoping she'd pass him to me, but instead she turned away, clutching him tightly to her massive breast.

'He's my son,' she said firmly in her coarse way. 'And I'm going to look after him.'

She sat down in an armchair and unbuttoned the top of her crimplene blouse, exposing one of her giant tits. The sight was so disgusting I felt sick and had to turn away. Moments later Joshua was hanging from it. I stared at them both, wondering whether what was going on was altogether healthy. My mother must have read my mind, because her face darkened.

'What are you bloody well gawping at?' she demanded. She sounded like one of those horrible girls who're always trying to pick fights with you.

'Nothing,' I said. 'I was just wondering what you were doing.'

'I'm nursing him,' she explained, though it was hardly an explanation, at least not to me.

'I didn't know he needed nursing,' I said, in the most faux-innocent voice I could muster. 'When did he fall ill?'

She detected the note of sarcasm in my voice and rose up from her chair, Joshua still in her arms. 'You cheeky little bitch,' she said. 'I'll fucking well leather you.'

I took a nervous step back. My mother was a big woman and I was, and still am, slightly built, and only five foot nothing. She juggled Joshua to free her beefy right arm from its job of supporting him and used it to wallop me on the side of my head. The blow was so fierce that my ears rang for hours afterwards. Throughout the drama, Joshua never once took his mouth from the end of her tit. In fact, he gurgled away quite happily as I reeled sideways and fell sprawling onto the sofa. My mother sat down with a look of contentment on her flabby face while Joshua continued his guzzling.

As I lay there I thought of telling her my secret. I knew if I did it would pay her back for all she'd done to me. More, it would destroy her. The secret bubbled up into my mouth and struggled to get out – but I kept it in. For all of my mother's faults, I didn't have it in me to do that to her. My secret would just have to stay with me, eating me up inside like a colony of termites.

Once I would have burst into tears when my mother hit me, but by that age – I was sixteen at the time – I suffered in silence. I'd determined not to give her the satisfaction of knowing she could hurt me. I fled upstairs to my tiny bedroom and threw myself onto my bed. Then I shut my eyes and began to conjure up images of my Golden Age – the period when I'd gone to the Dickens Academy, Joshua didn't exist, and my parents both loved me. But it hurt me to think of a time without Josh, so I soon gave up and did my homework.

Later, when my mum put him to bed, she said to me, 'Keep quiet and let him get his sleep. He needs it. Don't go pestering him. Have you got that?'

I felt tears welling up in the corners of my eyes but managed to hold them back as I nodded agreement.

When the coast was clear I sneaked into Joshua's room, picked him up out of his cot, and carried him around. He seemed to enjoy it.

But after a while he howled, so I quickly put him back down and raced into my own room before the Sasquatch thundered upstairs to comfort him.

I might have been tempted to let him suck at my own breast, but for the fact that I'd seen my mother feeding him, and the image was gross enough to put me off breastfeeding for life. I hoped Joshua would one day share my negative feelings about breastfeeding, but he never seemed to tire of my mother's sour milk.

The next day I sat in the same place as before, at the back of the class, with only myself for company. The three cool girls were nearby. I didn't bother looking at them. There was no point, as I had no chance of joining their group. What level of social group would I sink to, I wondered – Adele's? It seemed I wasn't wanted there. Was there one lower than hers? If so, I might be better off as a sad loner. But sad loners get picked on, especially at places like St Benedict's. I wondered how long it would be before I attracted the bullies.

There would be a period of grace, no doubt, as I was a new girl. Once that'd ended I could expect no mercy. People were already giving me looks of the type I remembered giving myself to girls I didn't much care for. It was only my second day, but already I felt the pressure mounting to become part of a social group, especially during breaks, when I stood out and felt more alone than ever.

It wasn't until the afternoon that I realised there was another loner in the class – Kylie. I'd been so wrapped up in my own woes I hadn't noticed her. Even if I had, I would've steered well clear – she wasn't the type to get me accepted into any set I wanted to be a part of.

I'd heard her in the dinner queue, 'I'd like the fish and chips, please, with parsley sauce,' she'd said to the dinner lady.

Those few words betrayed the fact she was different to everyone else. She spoke in a plummy accent. The cool set were just behind her.

One of them pulled her face into a horrid expression and repeated what Kylie had just said in a mock posh way. All three of them had laughed out loud while Kylie reddened.

By the afternoon of day three I was desperate, and ready to lower my sights. So when Kylie said, 'Hi, how do you like your new school?' I wondered what it would be like hanging out with her. Not good, I imagined. She'd get the piss taken out of her a lot of the time, and she didn't seem the type to stand up for herself. As her friend I'd have to devote a good deal of energy to bolstering her spirits when she'd been picked on. She might make things worse for me, or she might make things better. It was a fifty–fifty call. I decided to take a risk on her, and was more forthcoming than I had been with Adele.

'It's crap,' I whispered, 'and full of plebs. I used to go to the Dickens Academy. That was all right.'

She leant in close to me. 'I know what you mean. I've been here a week and I still haven't made any friends.'

So we had something in common. It didn't surprise me. Kylie would struggle to find friends here. She looked okay – she wasn't overweight or anything – and she wasn't dressed in hand-me-downs – her uniform was brand new. But the fact she was well-spoken and clearly from a good background made her ill-equipped for life at St Benedict's.

After the lesson we walked together to the next class, talking quietly about our dismay at the kind of school we'd been sent to. I heard one of the cool girls behind us mocking the way Kylie talked. I turned my head and saw which one it was. Her blonde hair was clipped up in a funny sort of quiff at the front, and she had streaks. I'd seen women in their twenties doing that recently. I'd never have worn my hair that way, even if everyone else was doing it. I thought it was ridiculous.

She saw me glance at her. 'What are you fucking looking at?' she said.

Nice.

Me and Kylie both glanced at each other and ignored her.

The next day when we left school together, Kylie's mum was near the school gates. 'I've heard all about you,' she said. 'You're Kylie's new friend.'

'Mum,' said Kylie, squirming with embarrassment.

'Would you like to come to our house to eat one evening after school?'

I thought about my own terrifying mum and my taciturn dad who said very little. While I didn't much care for the ordeal of spending time with my parents, I wanted to go home every evening to see Joshua. After much consideration I said, 'That would be nice.' Then, turning to Kylie, I added, 'If it's all right by you.'

'Yes,' she said. 'I'd love you to come to our place to eat.'

'How about tomorrow?' her mum said.

'I'm looking forward to it.'

Usually I walked home, but the next day Kylie's mum picked us both up in her car, a Volkswagen Polo, and took us back to their house, which was rather nicer than the home I was used to. It was a big semi, tastefully decorated. The kitchen table had two places set at it with fancy place mats and other decorations.

'My mum doesn't usually go to such lengths,' Kylie said. 'She's pushed the boat out for you.'

We had home-made spaghetti bolognaise. This seemed exotic compared to the food I was used to at home, which was always chips with something. Afterwards we went upstairs to Kylie's bedroom and listened to music. She had a sound system and TV in her room, as well as a bookshelf. I had books and little else.

It turned out she'd read a lot of the same stuff as me – *The Secret Club* series and *The Hyde Park Abomination* and so on, so we had a lot to talk about. She was also funny, but you'd never have guessed when we were at school. We became firm friends, but our friendship had a sell-by date we weren't aware of at the time.

It wasn't long before the cool girls started picking on us quite openly. Their ringleader with the odd hairstyle – Beth – was the worst. She was always mimicking Kylie's posh accent. Then she'd look at me and say, 'Isn't it time your mum got you some clothes that fit properly?'

It was mean to pick on me because of my clothes, but that's how some girls are.

One evening when me and Kylie were leaving school together, the cool girls were just behind us making comments and laughing. They didn't stop till we were well beyond the school gates. They did the same thing next day.

When we were alone together in her bedroom, Kylie sat on the floor, hugged her knees, and began to cry. 'They've upset me now,' she said, sounding like a little girl only four years old. 'They've upset me a lot.'

Mr Atkinson, the PE teacher, was very much in favour of girls doing the same sports the boys did, so he had us playing cricket during the games lesson. The ball came to me when someone was running between the stumps and I had to throw it hard at the stumps to get the batter out. I must have misaimed it because it hit Beth hard in the mouth. I apologised right away, but even so she cried. Her teeth didn't look right, her mouth bled, her cheeks got all puffy, and she had to go home. Later I learnt she'd had to visit the dentist to get her teeth fixed.

But after that she stopped saying things about us. It meant we were able to relax a bit and be ourselves, and Kylie became more confident and said funny things at school as well as at home. She became popular, and a bit mean with it. We were walking past Beth one time and Kylie sucked her lips over her teeth like a toothless old crone and leered at her. I grabbed Kylie's arm and pulled her away.

'What did you do that for?' she said.

'We shouldn't go out of our way to be nasty,' I replied. 'What goes around comes around.'

Little did I know we were destined to get mixed up in something nastier than either of us would ever have believed possible.

People thought I was hard because I'd thrown the cricket ball which had hit Beth in the mouth. All of a sudden we were the cool ones, and people wanted to be with us. But we were very selective. We allowed a few hangers-on to talk to us now and again, but it was really just me and Kylie, a team of two.

I suppose it was being cool which got us noticed by Seth. He had a reputation for being hard and for being the coolest boy in the school. He was good-looking in a sinister kind of way, dark hair swept to one side, an evil grin often playing on his lips. He had a gang of followers and they were pretty much feared throughout the school.

One day he was slouching against the wall at the back of the bike sheds, cigarette dangling from his thin lips. He looked like a big grinning shark with a cig in its mouth.

Me and Kylie were walking past, having a giggle.

'Hey,' he said.

We stopped to look at him. His friends – four other boys, and a girl – stared at us.

'Are you the girl who threw the cricket ball?'

I nodded. 'Yeah.'

'Nice one. Want a smoke?'

Kylie's eyes widened and I think she might have looked at me and shaken her head very subtly, but I said, 'Okay.'

I'd never smoked before and knew it was meant to be bad for you, but I wanted to try it, especially if it meant I could hang around with Seth and his gang. I walked over to him as casually as I could, and Kylie, with some show of reluctance, followed me.

'What's the matter?' he asked her. 'I don't bite.'

She gave him a wan smile. He took a packet of cigarettes from the pocket of his blazer and handed us both one. We put them in our mouths where they dangled, unfamiliar and clumsy.

'Either of you smoked before?'

We shook our heads in unison.

'Okay, I'll light them, and you take a breath and suck when I do.'

He took a lighter from his pocket. It was a silver zippo with a grinning cartoon shark on the side. He flipped open the top, spun the ratchet, and a flame appeared which he waved beneath the ends of our cigarettes, first mine, then Kylie's.

I took a draw then pulled it from my mouth and coughed my guts up. After a couple more draws my head began to spin.

'I feel dizzy,' I said. 'Is that normal?'

'It is the first time.'

Kylie struck up a pose with one arm bent across her torso, the elbow of the other resting on it while she waved her cig in the air.

'I could get used to this,' she said, exhaling a column of smoke skywards. She was a natural at it and she looked magnificent. It made me proud to be her friend. I did my best to finish my cigarette without too much coughing and spluttering. By the time I'd finished it I felt quite sick. Kylie seemed to enjoy hers.

'Fancy joining us tomorrow?' Seth asked. 'We're having a garage party. It's at my uncle's house. We'll have fun.'

I looked at Kylie and she looked at me. An unseen message passed between us.

'Yes,' we both said.

'Okay, give me your mobile numbers and I'll text you the details.'

I didn't have a mobile so Kylie gave him her number.

'Best be going,' he said, glancing at his watch. 'See you tomorrow.'

He stopped slouching against the wall, and managed somehow to slouch without anything to lean against. This talent lent him an insolent air which always enraged the teachers at St Benedict's. As he turned to walk back to the school, his followers did the same.

'Yes, see you,' I said, half-raising my hand to wave goodbye. Then I thought the better of it. Cool people didn't wave goodbye.

'What do you think "fun" means, Kylie?' I asked.

She shrugged.

'I don't know, but I'm game.'

I told my parents I was having a sleepover at Kylie's house. They would've had fits if they'd known I was going to a party organised by the most notorious boy at St Benedict's. My cover story wasn't a complete lie – I was staying over at Kylie's. I was, however, going to the garage party with her beforehand.

We got ready together in her bedroom with a Destiny's Child album providing background music. She had a new outfit from Miss Selfridge which showed off her trim figure, while I was wearing an old pair of tatty jeans and a T-shirt. She sat in front of her dressing table and used her make-up to transform herself into a precociously knowing and sexy teenage doll, very different to the studious mouse I'd met only weeks before. I felt rather inadequate next to her, having little more than the naked skin of my face on display.

'Amazing,' I said, observing her transformation.

She smiled with unnaturally full red lips and pointed to a pile of back-issues of fashion magazines.

'There's loads of how-tos in those. Why don't you wear any?'

'My mum won't let me.'

'You can use mine: just make sure you wash your face before you go to bed and she'll never know. I'll help you.'

She vacated the chair in front of her dressing table and, with a wave of her hand, invited me to sit on it. When I did she put a pillow-case over my shoulders to protect my clothes, then busied herself transmuting me for what seemed like ages, her fingers working make-up over my eyelids, my entire face, and lips. When she was finished, I turned my head to look in the mirror but she stood in front of it blocking my view.

'Not yet,' she said. 'Put one of my dresses on before checking what you look like.'

She ferreted around in her wardrobe and took out a red number.

I shook my head.

'Go on,' she insisted, 'give it a whirl.'

It was close fitting, rather too revealing for my liking, and made from a silky fabric. Against my better judgement I put it on and she zipped up the back. Finally, I looked at myself in her mirror.

The person looking back at me was a stranger to me. Just as Kylie was no longer Kylie, I'd become someone else – someone made-up and tarty. I wasn't sure I cared for the new me – but I didn't want to offend Kylie, so I said, 'Thank you, Kylie' and made a mental note never to allow this to happen again.

Her mum's eyes widened when she saw us. 'You do look different, both of you,' she said. 'You've become young women ready for a night out on the town.'

I wondered why she wasn't disapproving and why she didn't insist we at least tone down the make-up.

'Time to go, Mum,' said Kylie, and any opportunity I might've had to reverse things and look more like me was lost. Kylie gave her mum an address Seth had texted to her and her mum dropped us off.

'Call me when you're ready to come home,' she said.

'Don't worry, I will,' said Kylie.

I wondered why there was no curfew as there was in my own house. Had it been my mum dropping us off (which was impossible as she didn't have a car) her parting shot would've been: 'I'll be picking you up at midnight.' She would have added: 'And woe betide you, if you keep me waiting.' She would've meant it, too. That was the Sasquatch for you. I sometimes wondered whether her spitefulness was what made me mean. Beth wasn't the first person to have had an accident after crossing me.

We climbed from the car and Kylie's mum watched us make our way up the drive to a double garage, which, in size and appearance, resembled a small house with a pitched roof. It had eight small windows set high up in the big double doors at the front. A young man with dark hair and a round face was watching from one of them. He disappeared for a moment, then reappeared at the side of the garage. I recognised him – he was one of the group who'd been hanging round with Seth when he'd given us cigarettes.

'Hi,' he said. 'I'm Charlie. Follow me.'

When Kylie's mum saw Charlie and was satisfied we seemed to know him, and he didn't pose a threat, she drove off. It occurred to me the Sasquatch had her virtues. She did her best to make sure I was safe, even if, in other ways, she got right on my tits.

Charlie led us around the side of the garage to a door and opened it. A Limp Bizkit album boomed from within. We went inside where we encountered a crowd of teenagers. In a corner there was a table groaning under the weight of countless bottles of Two Dogs, Castaway, Hooch and Bud. Seth stood nearby, surrounded by admirers. With his confidence and good looks, not to mention his Superdry T-shirt and faded Levis, Seth was probably what a lot of young women would have considered attractive. I wasn't immune, but I had my doubts about him.

He saw us and pointed at the booze, so we got a bottle of beer each and began drinking. Kylie approached Seth, and I followed. He glanced at Kylie then turned to me, his eyeballs wandering slowly up and down my body from head to foot. I felt horribly exposed in my tight red dress, and was all too aware how provocative that, and my mask of tarty make-up, were.

'Wow, you look different,' he said, raising his voice so we could hear him above the din of the music. Then he leaned over and touched his face to Kylie's cheek, and kissed my cheek with his lips. I pulled away and he raised his eyebrows.

'Don't worry,' he said. 'I don't bite.' It seemed to be his stock saying. I wish I'd known it was a lie.

'I know, it's just that we've only just met,' I said.

There was more to it than that. There was the secret which was eating me up and throwing me off balance.

'Grab yourselves some beer and have a good time,' he said. 'We'll get to know each other later.'

Me and Kylie walked around sizing up the other partygoers, finished our beers, and went back to the booze table to get some more.

'Who paid for this stash?' Kylie asked no-one in particular as she opened hers.

Charlie was standing nearby talking to a girl, but even so he heard her. 'Seth did,' he said. 'Seth always has money. He's loaded.'

'Where does he get it from?' she asked.

Charlie tapped his nose and got back to his other conversation.

'Weird,' said Kylie, putting her bottle to her bright red lips.

I did the same – I didn't like the taste, but forced it down. We mingled for a while, and fended off the attentions of the teenage boys who kept hitting on us. Just as my head started to spin, Seth appeared. By now people were dancing. He took my hand and pulled me into the moving throng. I didn't object, being drunk and relaxed. He danced in front of me, and I could see he moved well. I caught the rhythm of the music and danced myself, basking in the attention as his eyes again moved appreciatively up and down my body. In spite of my feelings about him, it sent a thrill of excitement through my guts. I don't know how long we danced together but after a while he said, 'We could go out and enjoy a cigarette.'

I brushed back my hair with my hand. It was hot in the garage, and I felt I needed some fresh air, so I said, 'Yes, all right. Good idea.'

He led me outside to the back of the garage. A garden lay beyond it, bathed in a pale light from the outdoor lighting. Above us the moon gleamed in the night sky. He looked into my eyes and put his arms around my waist.

'You do know I like you a lot, don't you?' he said, bringing his face close to mine until he was kissing me on the lips.

For a moment I responded then I pulled away. There was something about the situation I found uncomfortable. I had reservations about Seth, but that wasn't what stopped me responding to his advances. In spite of my reservations I was attracted to him. He had a charismatic something I liked. Most girls liked it. But I wasn't ready for this sort of thing yet, not after what'd happened to me. Maybe at some time in the future he'd do something like this again and I'd be able to respond the way I should. Or when I'd got my head right, I'd come on to him in a situation like this. But not now, not here.

'Sorry,' I said. 'It's not you, this just doesn't feel right to me.'

I feared he'd be disappointed with me but he wasn't. 'No worries, it'll feel right to someone,' he said, lighting up a cigarette. 'I'll soon find her, whoever she is.' He proffered the open cigarette packet to me. 'Want one?'

'No, thanks.'

I went back inside, leaving him to smoke alone. Minutes later he came in. Kylie was dancing with someone else. When she saw Seth go to the drinks table she went to get a drink herself, and when he looked at her, she seemed to melt beneath his gaze. It wasn't long before they both disappeared outside for rather a long time.

When they returned she was adjusting her dress, and her make-up didn't look quite right.

Monday evening after school I called at the local supermarket and asked to see the manager, a short fat man with greasy hair. He wore a plum-coloured nylon jacket with the supermarket's logo on the breast pocket.

'I'd like a part-time job, please, anything you've got,' I said.

He looked me up and down. I wondered whether the interest he was showing was altogether savoury. Then he said, 'We've got a shelf-filling job going but it's hard physical work. Are you sure you're up to it?'

'I'm a hard worker,' I said. 'I'm definitely up to it.'

'Tuesday and Thursday evening, five till half-nine?'

'Okay, you're on.'

'Can you start tomorrow?'

'That's ideal for me.'

The following week when I got my first pay packet I put some of the cash in a Tupperware container in the bottom of my wardrobe. It was money I referred to as my escape fund. Sooner rather than later I planned to leave home, and this would help me on my way.

On Wednesday I took my usual short cut through the park. It was a chilly but bright September day, with the sun low in a clear blue sky. As I passed the children's play area I noticed a boy, about my age, sitting on a swing while texting someone. Apart from him, the place was deserted. He looked up and saw me walking by.

'Hi,' he said.

I quickened my pace, heading along a tarmac path which would take me past rolling lawns and through a copse of trees to the nearest exit.

'What's the hurry?' he shouted.

I ignored him.

'Fancy a smoke?' he shouted. I stopped. I wasn't sure I fancied a smoke after my previous experience but decided to give it a try.

'All right then,' I said, retracing my steps. I sat on the swing next to him.

He broke out a packet of cigarettes and gave me one, which I stuck awkwardly in my mouth. He put one in his own mouth, where it seemed to belong, and lit them both with a single match. He put the spent match back in the packet, which impressed me as I didn't like the way some people throw rubbish all over the place.

For a while we didn't talk. We just looked at each other, him smoking and me doing my best to smoke. After a while, he said, 'What were you doing, walking through the park?'

I took my cigarette from my mouth in what I hoped was a sophisticated smoking gesture. 'Going home. How about you?'

'Yeah, the same.' His eyeballs moved up and down as he scrutinised me. 'Is that a St Benedict's uniform?'

'Yeah, what's yours?'

'Mount Briar.' He chuckled. 'We shouldn't be talking really.'

I laughed too, but wondered what my friends would think if they knew about the conversation I was having with an enemy.

He took his mobile from his pocket. 'What's your number?' he said.

'I don't have a phone.'

'Home number?'

I shook my head. 'My parents are a bit weird. They'd go apeshit if you called me at home.'

'Okay. I've got to go now. Meet you here tomorrow for another chat?'

I looked him up and down. He was tall and slim, had a face I found attractive, and a disarming smile.

'All right,' I said.

'See you tomorrow, then,' he said, 'same time, same place. By the way, I'm called Tony.'

He headed off on a tarmac path which took a winding route between the trees to one of the many exits. I used a different one.

The next day we met as agreed, and the first thing he did after saying hello was to light up a cigarette. He took a draw from it and handed it to me.

'I only have the one left, otherwise I'd offer you your own one,' he explained. 'Do you have any friends your mum and dad approve of?'

I nodded. 'There's a girl called Kylie in my class. I'm allowed sleep-overs at her house.'

'Why don't you tell them you're seeing Kylie so you can spend the evening with me?'

I took a good pull on the cigarette while considering his sugges-tion. Then I blew smoke in the air the way I'd seen Kylie do. I had grave misgivings about meeting Tony, but liked him, so after a moment's hesitation I replied, 'That's a great idea. When?'

'Saturday?'

'Okay, Saturday.'

He turned on the swing, the metal chains which secured it to the frame twisting as he did so, and kissed me, no more than a peck really.

I glanced down at my ill-fitting school uniform, grateful someone fancied me in spite of the way I was dressed. Then I stood up. 'I have to go now.'

On the way home I felt like I was walking on air, but at the same time I was anxious about whether I could get Kylie to cover for me, and, if I could, whether I'd get away with lying to my parents, and, if that went well, whether I'd recovered enough from what'd happened to enjoy my assignation.

The next day during the first school break I had a word with Kylie. 'I need a favour.'

'What's that?'

'I need you to cover for me so I can go out on Saturday night.'

'With a boy?'

'Yes, with a boy.'

Her eyes widened. 'Who is it? Do I know him?'

'He's called Tony and he goes to Mount Briar High.'

She made her index fingers into a cross as if warding off a vampire.

'I know,' I said. 'But we like each other.'

'He's a Montague and you're a Capulet – it's a risky business.'

'We'll take our chances.'

'Too bloody right – I would if I were you. And of course I'll cover for you. I'm going to Seth's house on Saturday night. I'll tell Mum you're coming too, and you can stay over at ours. My mum'll confirm it, if your mum checks up.'

I began to see the virtues of having a slack mum who didn't carefully police everything you did.

'Thanks, Kylie.'

On Saturday afternoon I dipped into my savings and bought the cheapest pay-as-you-go mobile phone I could. It was getting obvious I needed one to negotiate my blossoming social life.

That night I got ready to go out at Kylie's house. I didn't wear any of her clothes this time, though. Just my own faded jeans with the tears in them – the fade and tears were genuine, not artificially put there by the manufacturer – and a T-shirt. I borrowed some make-up but insisted on playing it down.

'I don't want to look like I'm trying too hard, Kylie,' I explained.

'Good idea,' she said. 'I'm making an effort, but it's not for Seth, it's for me. I like to look my best.'

When we'd got our outfits and make-up sorted we went downstairs.

'We're ready to go now, Mum,' said Kylie.

Her mum was watching something on the TV. She stood up and looked at us, eyes widening in surprise when she scrutinised my face. 'Not wearing much make-up tonight are you?' she said.

'I don't usually wear a lot except for special occasions,' I told her.

'I can't go on a night out without it,' she said. 'Kylie's the same. Anyway, let's be going.'

She dropped us off at Seth's house then Kylie called a taxi for me on her mobile. We said goodbye to each other, and she went to the door, while I waited by the gate for my taxi. It wasn't long in coming. I got dropped off and went to the pub where I'd said I'd meet Tony. I was ten minutes early. I didn't try to get served. I just found a seat and tried not to look too conspicuous, all the while wishing I'd arranged to meet him outside. After five minutes I felt so uncomfortable being on my own that I got up and went out, and stood near the door waiting for him. He came round the corner and grinned at me, kissing me on the cheek as soon as he got close enough.

'Follow me,' he said.

'Where are we going?'

'Another pub. I've discovered one that's better than this. By the way, I've got fake id so I'll get the drinks. You stay out of sight while I get them.'

He led me to a small pub up a back alley called The Grosvenor. 'Beer's cheap here,' he explained as he opened the door. 'Remember, stay out of sight. What do you want?'

'A bottle of lager, please. Anything will do.'

We went inside and I found a booth to sit in. The place was

crowded, so I was concealed by the customers standing around drinking, and in any event the bar staff were too busy to look in my direction. Hopefully, if any of them did see me, my make-up would make me look eighteen. After a while Tony appeared with our drinks.

'Kronenbourg 1664,' he said, pushing a bottle across the table. 'Hope you like it.'

I took a slurp. I wasn't used to drinking but I forced it down. Our conversation was awkward and slow at first, but once I'd had a couple of beers and got a bit tipsy I relaxed, and things improved. We went to another pub and by the time we came out of it I felt well and truly drunk, even though I'd only had three bottles and had taken them slowly.

'I have to go meet my friend now. I'm going home with her,' I told Tony.

'Fair enough,' he said. 'I'll walk with you.'

By this time it was dark. We took a short cut through an archway, then along a back alley to another street. In the middle of the alley he stopped. The only light came from a streetlight on the road at far end of the alley.

'Wait a minute,' he said.

'What?' I asked.

He put his arms around me, pressed his lips against mine. I responded eagerly for half-a-minute or so, then pushed him away.

'What's wrong?' he asked.

'Sorry,' I said. 'It's nothing to do with you. I need time, that's all.' I wondered if time was really all I needed.

'Are you sure it's nothing to do with me?'

'Yes.'

'What is it then?'

'Sorry, I can't explain,' I said, and I couldn't.

Because Tony couldn't know what it was.

No-one could.

Ever.

3

HERE AND NOW

I propped myself up against the bar and ordered another drink. Even after all I'd had, which included a double brandy Seth had bought me, I didn't feel drunk. Not drunk enough, anyway. Charlie's death had had a sobering effect on me. My mind felt like a hamster on a wheel as I tried to make sense of it.

Poor Charlie had endured a sad life haunted by regrets – much like my own in fact – and had met his death without coming to terms with the events which had caused his woes. It occurred to me that what I'd been watching when Charlie had passed away was my own sad future. It was inevitable that on the day of my own death, I'd be in the same state as Charlie – a nervous wreck, haunted by the past, unable to move on. With my drink habit, I might die the same way he had done, and in similar circumstances, just keel over while drunk and breathe my last on a sticky, beer-sodden carpet. It was enough to drive anybody to drink.

I took a ten-pound note from my purse and waved it in the air. 'Another glass of red wine, please, and make it a large one,' I said to no-one in particular.

A passing barman heard me. 'Coming right up,' he said, grabbing a bottle and uncorking it.

He filled the glass up to the 250 ml line and pushed it across the bar to me. I took a sip and wiped my lips with the back of my hand, still dwelling on the subject of Charlie's death.

'Penny for them.' It was Seth.

'What?' I asked.

'A penny for your thoughts,' he said.

I felt as if he'd seen right through me and worked out I was a liability.

'I'm just sad about Charlie,' I told him. 'Gutted in fact.'

'Sad business,' he replied, looking around to check what the policemen were doing. When he saw they were having an earnest conversation with Raymond Wells, he grabbed my arm and pulled me close. 'Just remember,' he hissed, 'we have a pact. Charlie's death makes no difference to it. Understand?'

I tried to pull my arm free, but couldn't even move it, his grip was so fierce.

'Of course I understand,' I said, as calmly as circumstances allowed. 'When have I ever let you down?'

That seemed to convince him, and he let me go. 'You haven't – and it better stay that way.'

My heart should've been pounding my ribs, but it wasn't. The booze I'd drunk had taken the edge off pretty much everything life could throw at me. I'd reached the stage where my existence had become a somnambulistic dream, and I didn't care too much what happened.

Then I became aware of a presence at my shoulder and turned around. It was one of the policemen. He asked me to follow him. We went together into another room in the conference complex – a small office – and he invited me to take a seat on one side of the desk it contained. I did so, glass in hand, and he sat at the other side.

He fished into his pocket, removed a notebook and pen, and placed the notebook on the desk. 'Could I have your name and address, please?'

I told him my full name, house number, street name and postcode.

'I believe you knew Mr Duggan,' he said, giving me the sort of piercing look which coppers are well-schooled in. I noticed he had grey eyes which matched the greying hair at his temples.

'Mr Duggan?'

'Charles Duggan, the deceased.'

Those words – 'the deceased' upset me again, in spite of the amount of drink I'd had, and I emerged from my dreamlike stupor into a cold reality.

'Yes, I knew Charlie.'

'And you were with him when he died?'

'Yes.'

'Can you describe what happened in the period leading up to his death?'

I took a thoughtful sip of my latest glass of red wine. 'We had a couple of drinks together, then he keeled over, and that was about it.'

He scribbled in his notebook then looked up at me. 'Keeled over?'

'Yes. He got up from the table we were both sitting at, staggered a little, regained his balance, took a couple of steps and fell on his face.'

'Does he have any illness you know of?'

I shook my head.

'All right, that's all for now. I'll be in touch if I need to speak to you again.'

'You mean I can go?'

'Yes, you can go.'

I left him with his head down, engrossed in completing his notes.

As soon as I was back in the event room I booked an Uber. There was one close by. Less than a minute later I was on my way home. I got there in such an alcohol-fuelled daze I barely had the wherewithal to stagger from the back of the car and open my front door. I hurried upstairs, undressed, got into bed, and tried hard to forget I'd seen another death, the second in under two weeks.

The words of 'Born under a bad sign' came to mind. Bad luck was all the luck I seemed to have.

On the morning of Sunday 4 March I woke up with a raging thirst and a pounding hangover. It was an all-too-familiar feeling. As soon as I climbed out of bed, I felt my stomach heave, so I ran to the bathroom to throw up. In a way, those moments throwing up were the best I'd had in a long while. Bad as it felt, I was incapable of thinking of anything else but how ill I was, as I jettisoned the contents of my stomach into the toilet bowl.

When I was done, it all came back to me: the guilt over mowing down the young man, the worry that I'd get caught for doing it, my past sins which I felt were fast catching up with me, courtesy of the baseball bat I'd received in the mail (who sent it, and why?) And the mystery of Charlie's death, coupled with the possibility that it augured disaster for me.

I put my fears and negative predictions to the back of my mind, and, like all drunks the day after a bender, I said 'Never again.' How many times had I said that? *But you mean it for once, Jaz. You really do mean it this time.*

When I'd had a shower and a coffee I was able to pull myself together enough to lie on the sofa with the television on. The one thing I felt I had going for me was that it was Sunday, which, being a quiet day, would give me respite from the world at large. There would be no post – no chance of getting any unwanted presents delivered to my door, no shitty driving to work, no awkward conversations with work colleagues, no demoralising court cases, and probably no callers. Not that I ever got callers.

Tomorrow it would be Monday, and I'd have to face another week of hell. It didn't bear thinking about.

By mid-afternoon I was able to take a walk to get some fresh air. There's a saying that the criminal always returns to the scene of her crime. It turns out there's some truth in it. I followed a route which took me up Fosby Street and found myself staring at the lamp post I'd driven my car into. Then I thought it might make me look like I was guilty of something – even though no-one seemed to know there'd been a hit-and run incident at the very spot I was standing on – so I tore myself away.

A young man came towards me from the other end of the street. From a distance he looked like my – I didn't want to use the word, but I had to – my victim. I wanted to turn and run, but that would've been incriminating, so I didn't break my stride. When he got nearer, he looked like someone else – maybe the brother of my victim? He seemed to be staring at me. Did he know something? My pulse quickened as he got nearer still.

He walked right past me.

I should've calmed down but I couldn't, because I felt as if an unseen pair of eyes was watching me from every window of every house on the street. I made myself walk more quickly, so much so I almost ran to the end of the street. It was a relief to turn the corner at the end of it and get away.

The eight-till-late beckoned. I found myself heading towards it. Would it lure me in, or would I be able to resist its temptations? I knew I ought to, knew I was ruining my life and digging an early grave for myself with my drinking habits, so much so that I'd joined Alcoholics Anonymous in an attempt to break out of my self-destructive drinking cycle. But then again, all I wanted was a bottle of red wine to calm my nerves. Maybe two bottles, then I'd go back on the wagon, and tell them all at the AA meeting on Thursday how I'd fallen from the wagon and made a supreme effort to climb back on and get into a state of alcohol-free grace again. They'd applaud me and think me a hero for managing to do that.

The matter was settled.

I was going in.

I picked up two bottles of cheap merlot and took them to the counter. There was a woman ahead of me, middle-aged, overweight, and tattooed, putting her shopping into a bag. 'Terrible thing it was,' she was saying to the proprietor. 'He was in a right state. His mum'll never get over it.'

I guiltily wondered if she might be talking about my victim.

'All right, thank you, goodbye,' she said.

'Goodbye, Mrs Sandford,' said the proprietor. He hailed from somewhere in London but had an Indian background and spoke with a slight Asian twang. It was one of those places where the shopkeeper knows most of his customers and addresses them by name. He didn't know mine, because I avoided conversation with him. All I ever bought there was booze, and I didn't want him telling anyone who I was, and how much booze I bought.

I put the bottles on the counter and he scanned them into his till.

'Anything else?' he asked.

'No, thank you,' I said, avoiding his eyes in the vain hope it might make it harder for him to recognise me.

'Fifteen pounds, please. Do you need a bag?'

'If you don't mind.'

I handed over the cash, snatched up the bottles – noticing he raised his eyebrows as I did – and rammed them into the bag he gave me, after which I shot out, quick as I could.

When I got home there was a scruffy old woman outside my house rooting through my bins. Next to her was a battered-looking child's buggy with a pile of random stuff in it which I surmised was all her worldly possessions.

I wondered if I should tell her to move on – it didn't feel right having a complete stranger on my property going through my stuff, even if it was stuff I didn't need or want. She turned to look at me when she heard me walking up the path, and our eyes met. Hers were rheumy, grey, and disturbingly yellow where they should've been white. Mine were brown and, I hoped, clear.

In the instant we looked at each other, I saw my own future: I was going to become a bag lady like her, probably by the time I turned fifty, and I'd be helpless and alone, spending my days rooting through other people's discarded waste in order to survive. My liver would be so decayed by cirrhosis that my eyes would be yellow like hers, and it wouldn't be long before my skin followed suit. My death would be a painful one in a back alley, surrounded by overflowing bins, with no-one to hold my hand during my final, desperate moments.

I decided to let her carry on with what she was doing, hoping my generosity would be paid forward in some mystical way, and that someone would be as understanding with me, when I caught up with my dismal future.

I went indoors shaking my head at the thought of what I had coming, uncorked a bottle of wine, and wondered why I hadn't thought to check if the bottles were equipped with screw tops. I prefer screw tops. You can open the bottles quicker.

When I'd gotten the cork out, I poured a good big glass and took a sip of it. Then I thought about the baseball bat, and got it out of the cupboard I'd put it in to examine it.

It was black, sleek, and deadly, just like the ones which had done the damage all those years ago. It occurred to me I ought to put it under my bed. Then, if an intruder entered the house while I was in my bedroom, I'd have a weapon to hand to fend him off with.

I guessed the chances of an intruder had gone up, because, having given the matter much thought, I couldn't believe I'd ordered the baseball bat myself. I was convinced someone else must have ordered it. This could mean I had an enemy who was out to get me.

I put the bat down and took myself and the bottle to the front room, finding comfort in watching TV while slowly getting slaughtered. I knew that comfort couldn't last, and I was right.

The next day, Monday 5 March, I woke up with no recollection of having gone to bed the night before, and had what was becoming the usual raging hangover. When I raised my head from the pillow it hurt. When I put it back down on the pillow it hurt more. But as it was Monday, I had to motivate myself – I had a job to hold down. Somehow I got myself up, noting a pile of abandoned clothes in the middle of the bedroom floor. It told me what a state I'd gotten myself into the previous night.

After showering and putting on my work clothes, I grabbed my car key off the hook in the kitchen I have for it, then put it back – it was obvious even to me that I was still over the limit, and in no fit state to drive. I booked an Uber, and before long it disgorged me outside the unsightly red-brick offices of Womack and Brewer LLP, my place of work.

I got there late, which caused a number of people, including the receptionist, to raise their eyebrows at me as I swanned in, and made my way to my office. Their disapproval didn't bother me. I'd reached the stage where my concerns outside of work were so pressing that work-related issues didn't seem important anymore.

When I got to my desk and checked my diary, I found my secretary had booked me an appointment at 10.30am. with a woman called Mrs Duggan, who must have called first thing, before I'd arrived.

Mrs Duggan.

The same surname as Charlie.

It couldn't be a coincidence. I had a horrible feeling about it, and wanted to cancel the appointment, but felt I had to go through with it. There was just time to get a coffee to clear my head, which I did, then I got a call telling me she was in reception.

'Thank you, I'll come and get her,' I said, hoping the worry in my voice wasn't too obvious.

The firm of Womack and Brewer LLP was what I privately referred to as a semi-backstreet outfit. It operated from an ancient brick building far from the fashionable shops and offices of Crystal Palace. The windows were grubby, and, thanks to our specialism – criminal defence – the clients were grubbier still. The inside was unsuited to a modern business concern, being a rabbit warren of narrow corridors and stuffy ill-lit box-like rooms.

I went to reception – a considerable walk away from my office – and opened the door. A row of obvious reprobates was already taking up the chairs, all of them fiddling with mobile phones. Among them was a gentle middle-aged woman, who looked as if she didn't belong in the same building as them, let alone the same room. I guessed she was my client – if, indeed, she had any intention of using my services. She might have other motives for paying me a visit.

'Mrs Duggan?' I said.

She got to her feet and I let her through the door, taking in her appearance. She looked to be in her late fifties, was overweight with plump pink cheeks, and had hair which was dyed a vivid shade of red. The colour accentuated a railway junction of worry lines on her face.

I stuck out my arm and we shook hands in a business-like way.

'I'm Jasmine Black. Follow me.'

I led her along darkling corridors, past judgemental secretaries in the one open-plan area, and, at length, to my office. By the time we got there she was out of breath, which led me to suspect she was a heavy smoker. I caught a whiff of her clothes which confirmed it.

'Take a seat, please,' I said, gesturing towards one of the two chairs permanently stationed in front of my desk for the use of clients. She gratefully sat down and I sat behind the desk in my revolving leather chair, a position which normally gives me the feeling of being in control, but today it didn't. 'How can I help you, Mrs Duggan?' I asked, hoping to God she needed advice on some aspect of criminal law.

'Please call me Clara,' she replied. 'My son was Charlie. He told me – he told me –' she paused and let out a huge sob. 'He told me you knew him.' Then her body heaved, and tears cascaded in rivers down her plump cheeks.

I kept a box of tissues on my desk for these awkward moments. When you work in criminal law, you often get the parents of the young crims you have to defend coming to see you. Some of them are honest, hardworking people, who can't understand why their progeny ignore the values they were brought up with, and who struggle to believe any child of theirs could stoop so low, as to, say, mug an old lady who isn't much different to them. This sort of crime, by their own kids, often reduces parents to tears.

I pushed the box towards her. She took a couple of tissues from it and wiped her eyes. Afterwards, she carefully mopped up the snot which had started running from her rather large nostrils. Her cheeks had turned from pink to a vivid shade of red which almost matched the colour of her hair.

'He mentioned you quite a few times,' she said, when she'd regained her composure. 'You were part of the crowd he used to run around with at school. He talked about you a lot. He rather liked you.' She found the strength to look me straight in the eye and asked: 'Were you with him when he died?' The directness of the question shocked me. It must have shown in my expression, because she immediately added: 'I'm sorry, but I need to know.'

I took a deep breath.

'Yes, I was with him, Mrs Duggan, that is, er, Clara.'

It was her turn to take a deep breath. 'I'm so glad he was with someone he cared for. It might have been a comfort for him.'

I felt myself welling up. Charlie had been a nice person from what little I knew of him, and although we only met once a year, I felt something for him. Forcing myself to be strong, I held back my tears and did my best to say something to make things better for Clara. 'If it helps, he didn't appear to be in pain. He passed away peacefully as far as I could tell.'

She shook her head. 'He must have fooled you,' she said. 'But he couldn't fool me.'

I desperately wanted to end the conversation and get her, and the memories she was dredging up, out of sight and out of mind. At the same time, I was curious to know more about Charlie. He'd told me the game was up. *Why had he said that?*

'What do you mean?'

'He was hiding something.'

My insides turned cold. I knew of at least one thing Charlie had been hiding, and I didn't want it to get out. That said, I wanted to know how much Clara had found out. 'Do you have any idea what?'

She repositioned herself in the chair and I hoped she wasn't making herself too comfortable. 'No, only that it was something serious. My son was a troubled man. He'd been such a happy boy, but it all went wrong in his teens.' She gave me a stare which made me feel like I was looking directly at the business end of a drill-bit. 'Something happened to him, I don't know what. You were part of the gang he used to knock around with. Do you have any idea what happened to my Charlie?'

Sometimes when I took statements from clients they'd tell me about shocking crimes they'd committed. There was, for instance, the gangster who nailed a rival's hand to the floor. At times like that, I'd assume an air of icy professional composure no matter what I was feeling inside. It had become second nature with me in those situations. I used the skill to blank Mrs Duggan.

'I'm sorry, I don't,' I lied. 'It's as much a mystery to me as it must be to you.' My hastily constructed stonewall wasn't enough to stop her relentless line of questioning.

'Did you notice the change in him?'

I assumed a pensive expression as if reaching into the depths of my memory. 'It was a long time ago. I can't be sure.'

'I did, and whatever changed Charlie stayed with him. What's more, the day he died he was worse than ever, very agitated.'

I could guess why – he probably got the screaming abdabs every year, same as me, at about the time the school reunion came up. I couldn't let on to Clara, of course, so nodded blandly.

'Then he died,' she continued. 'So I'll never get to know what was troubling him. That's what hurts me more than anything. I wish someone could tell me why my son was such a troubled soul.'

Someone can, I thought, *but I'm not going to, which is awful of me, but I have to protect myself.* She needed to know her son's secret to set her mind at ease. Or did she? Would the knowledge help her, or make matters worse? 'I can't, and I'm not sure anybody can. I'm sorry, I can't help you, Clara.'

Her shoulders slumped. 'I wanted to know what happened to my son, now I never will,' she said, resignedly. 'He'll always be a mystery to me.'

I stifled the relief I felt as I got to my feet. 'I'll show you out.'

'Thank you. If you hear anything, or remember anything that could help me, please get in touch. Here's my number.' She handed me a piece of paper with her name and a mobile number scribbled on it.

'I will. Leave it with me, Clara.'

When I'd taken her to the exit I closed the door behind her, and stood with my back to it, breathing deeply, while wondering whether she'd continue with her enquiries, whether she'd get anywhere, and whether she'd find a way to bring the whole dirty wall of silence which protected me crashing down around my ears.

Somehow I managed to convince myself there was no point in worrying about something I couldn't do anything about, and returned to my desk with its overflowing in-tray. But my fears about Clara hadn't left me permanently. They soon came flooding back, along with all my other worries. The things that'd happened in the recent past, and the distant past, including my drink problem, my relationship problems, the fact I felt my job was slipping away from me because I couldn't handle it any longer, and even little things like the pile of dirty washing in my laundry basket began to get to me. Soon I was such a nervous wreck that I couldn't do so much as a stroke of work. It took all my inner strength and then some just to sit at my desk and pretend to be working until lunchtime.

At 1pm I left my office, went for a walk, and didn't go back. Instead I called in sick.

'I've had to book an emergency appointment with the doctor,' I told my secretary.

'I hope it's nothing serious,' she replied.

'It probably isn't,' I said bravely.

'I'll hold the fort for you till you can get back in.'

'Thank you, Camilla. You're a star.'

I headed home thinking I'd call in the eight-till-late on the way for three bottles of red wine. I reckoned I'd need that many, because I had a lot of hours to get through – most of the afternoon, as well as the evening. But when I got to the eight-till-late I managed to get a grip and walk right by it.

You have to stay on the wagon till your AA meeting on Thursday, Jaz, I told myself. At the end of the street I muttered: 'Easier said than done,' turned around, and headed back to the eight-till-late.

I spent the next three weeks avoiding work and AA meetings. Bernie, my AA counsellor, called a few times but I refused to pick up when he did and deleted his voicemail messages without listening to them, and his texts without reading them. Those twenty-one days passed by in an alcoholic blur. I recall very little of them beyond the fact I didn't venture out except to get food and drink – most of it wine – and I ate a lot of takeaways.

I rolled downstairs in my dressing gown one day and made a coffee, noticing while I was in the kitchen that it was Monday 26 March. It would soon be time to turn the calendar on the wall to a new page. When I looked at the worktop I saw that some considerate person had gathered up three weeks' worth of mail and deposited it, unopened, in a neat pile, next to the cooker.

The considerate person must've been you, Jaz, you dope, I said as I poured myself a generous mug of coffee, my usual prelude to a day of oblivion. I looked at the clock. It was 10am, too early to start drinking, even for me. I liked to try to postpone it as late in the day as possible, which in practice meant the back-end of the afternoon at the latest. The rest of the day could be filled in with walks, television, reading, and fretting, not necessarily in that order.

Two of the letters caught my eye. They were from Womack and Brewer LLP. I opened the envelopes and picked up the first, dated the 12 March 2018. It was from the senior partner, and he was enquiring whether I was okay, and asking me to ring in and let him know the reason for my absence. That was nice of him.

The later one was dated the 20 March 2018. This one was also from the senior partner, and it informed me that when he'd had no response to his earlier letter dated the 12 March, he'd called me and we'd had an interesting conversation during which I'd insulted him, sworn at him, and told him where to stick his bloody job. All-in-all he was none too impressed with my attitude and the top-and-bottom of it was I'd been sacked for gross misconduct.

In my drunken state I must've been unable to stop myself from telling him how I truly felt about representing guilty criminal types and getting them off. Too bad I hadn't been able to be more diplomatic.

I must've been completely off my head when he rang, because I couldn't remember talking to him.

Anyhow, I'd handed in my notice, in a manner of speaking, before I was ready to go. I had no other job to go to, and I'd blown it as far as getting a good reference went. So if I did interview well for a new job, there was a chance I wouldn't get it because my references from Womack and Brewer LLP would stink the place out.

Naturally I panicked, wondering how I was going to pay my bills. Then I reasoned I didn't have to worry, not yet, anyway, because I had a credit card I wasn't yet maxed out on and a generous overdraft limit, and could probably hold out for six months without a salary. Then the crunch would come. But being as the crunch was still over the horizon, I could put it to the back of my mind and focus on my more immediate woes.

I sipped my coffee and watched some-or-other mind-numbing breakfast show, padded upstairs, had a leisurely bath, and got dressed. Somewhat illogically, not having a job began to feel better than having one, and lifted my spirits.

This could be a fresh start for you, Jaz, I told myself. *You could retrain and be a nurse or something, work in a capacity where you help people who deserve it.*

As I reflected on those happy possibilities I heard the doorbell ring and went downstairs, wondering who my visitor was. I never had visitors, so it was a mystery. It occurred to me it might be Bernie chasing me up about bloody AA. If it was, I'd tell him politely I liked drinking more than not drinking, and didn't want to go anymore. Then I speculated it could be the postman dropping off an item I didn't want – another baseball bat, perhaps, or some other deeply unpleasant reminder of my past. The thought made my heart shoot up to the roof of my mouth and cling to it tightly.

When I got to the small hall at the front of my house I saw, through the frosted glass in the middle of the front door, that whoever was there was wearing a uniform. It was a policeman. What was happening now? Was he here to arrest me for my hit-and-run crime? Fear gripped me so ferociously I nearly keeled over. I wanted to pretend I wasn't in, but that would only be delaying the inevitable. In any case, it was too late to give him the slip. If I'd seen him, he'd seen me.

I opened the door a crack, as if that would help, because he wouldn't be able to fit through the gap I'd left. Sticking my head in the narrow gap, I said, 'Can I help?'

He was a huge man, maybe six foot four, with broad shoulders and the beginnings of a paunch. 'Good morning, madam,' he replied, his face giving nothing away. 'Are you Ms Jasmine Black?'

This sounded very much like the preliminary to an arrest. My skin prickled with anxiety. 'Yes, I am.' My eyes probed his for indications of whether he might be in any way hostile, but he remained impassive.

'Can I come in please, Ms Black? I'd like to talk.'

I brushed a few stray strands of hair from my eyes. I'd not been to the hairdresser for weeks, and it was beginning to show. I was getting to look like the bag lady I'd seen rooting through my bins. 'What about?'

'It's about your friend – the late Mr Charles Duggan.'

My body relaxed, making me aware of the tension I must've felt, worrying he was here to arrest me for killing a young man. I was relieved this was just going to be about Charlie. Then I had an unpleasant thought. What if he was going to probe into Charlie's past? What if he had done already? What if he intended to get to the bottom of the crime we were all involved in eighteen years ago? I wasn't out of the rough yet. I'd have to be on my guard. I opened the door fully.

'Come in,' I said, leading him into the front room. 'Would you like a coffee?' I thought I might as well try to ingratiate myself with him.

'Don't mind if I do.' He had a layer of flab under his chin which wobbled disconcertingly when he spoke.

'I won't be a minute.' I went to the kitchen and made us both one, using the time to breathe deeply and get into a calm frame of mind to deal with whatever pointed questions might come my way. When I returned to the front room he was holding his notebook and pen, his huge bulk completely filling one of my armchairs.

'Thank you,' he said. 'I need to ask you about Mr Duggan.'

I twisted my features as best I could into the very picture of unsullied innocence. 'Fire away.'

'How much did he drink the night of your school reunion?'

I shrugged. 'I don't know. A lot I guess, but I couldn't tell you exactly how much.'

'Did he take anything?'

My face became a question mark. *Take anything? I have no idea what you might mean. I'm not that kind of girl.* 'Sorry?'

'I mean, did he take any drugs of any kind. You're a solicitor – you work in the criminal courts defending perps. You must know what I'm talking about.'

Oh dear, slipped up there. I should've known a local copper would know how I made my living. 'I didn't see him taking any drugs.'

'Was he a drug user?'

'No, they never interested him. His recreational drug of choice was scotch on the rocks.'

'Did you have reason to believe someone might have tampered with anything he ate or drank on the night he died?'

'No. What's this about, constable?'

He closed his notebook and returned it to his pocket. 'I'm just pursuing lines of enquiry, Ms Black. I'll show myself out.'

He finished his coffee and left, and I cupped my mug in both hands, wondering what on earth was going on. When I finished my coffee I did some tidying, watched some TV, had a walk in the park and a mooch around the shops, and by the time I got back to my house I was able to crack open my first bottle of wine of the day with a clear conscience.

The next week or so passed by in a blur. Each morning began the same way with me getting up hungover, checking the calendar, and making a coffee while still in my dressing gown, then showering and getting dressed, and eating a late breakfast before the drinking began.

One thing stood out from my drunken haze: a body was found in a wood way out of town. It belonged to a young man who lived locally: Sean Price. I was drunk when I heard the news, having consumed one-and-a-half bottles of wine. I sobered up right away. It was the most sober I got during my month-long binge. Actually, it was more than a month.

Sean Price. How had my hit-and-run victim ended up dumped in a wood miles away from the place I'd run him down? Had I somehow imagined the entire episode? Surely not. Had I identified him wrongly? Definitely not.

Either I'd moved his body myself during my blackout, or someone, for some bizarre reason, had decided to help me by covering up my crime.

Neither possibility seemed likely, but one of them had to be true.

It made my head hurt just thinking about it.

Eventually I put the matter to the back of my mind, along with all the other stuff that was bothering me, and polished off the remaining half-bottle, and I probably opened a third and got stuck into that, too. I was well and truly back to my old bingeing ways.

April 3, 2018: I'd just rolled downstairs after showering and getting dressed when the doorbell rang.

'Fucking hell, Jasmine,' I said. 'What is it this time, a delivery man with another reminder of the past, the postman with more bad news, or the copper again come to arrest me?'

When I got to the hall I saw through the door that my visitor, whoever it was, wasn't in uniform, which ruled out a policeman or postman, and moreover he wasn't wearing the sort of high-viz jacket favoured by delivery men. With feelings of relief I opened the door.

My relief lasted precisely the amount of time it took me to get it open enough to see who my visitor was. It was Clara Duggan, Charlie's bereaved mother.

'Jasmine, can I come in, please?' she asked. I wanted to say no, and slam the door in her face, but hadn't the heart to do that, so instead, against my better judgement, I said, 'Yes, of course, Clara. Follow me,' and led her to the kitchen.

'Take a seat,' I said. 'Coffee?'

'Yes, please.'

I made a mug for her and one for myself before joining her at the table. Her puffy cheeks were pale instead of pink, making her face seem a chalky white when viewed against her unnaturally red hair.

'Are you all right?' I asked.

She nodded, then changed her mind and shook her head. 'No,' she said. 'That's why I'm here. The police have had a toxicology report done on Charlie. He didn't die of natural causes.'

I'd assumed Charlie had suffered a heart attack or stroke, or possibly overdosed on Valium, or something. I suppose we all did. Now she'd teed up the question I had to ask it. 'What did he die of, Clara?'

'He was poisoned. Some sort of date-rape drug.'

Charlie was one of the few people I'd known at school who hadn't, to the best of my knowledge, ever taken recreational drugs. He stuck to booze and fags. If he'd been depressed, he might've taken a prescription drug if his doctor had written him a scrip. He'd never have self-administered any kind of date-rape drug. It wasn't in his nature to do that kind of thing.

'Could he have taken it himself to get a high?' I asked, wondering if Charlie might've started taking substances without letting on.

'Definitely not. My Charlie never took drugs. The police have searched his flat and haven't found any trace of what killed him among his things, so they think someone might have given it to him on the night of the reunion. But, like you, they also said it's possible he took it for recreational purposes. He didn't.'

She stared me in the eye with an unwavering gaze which felt like an accusation.

'You don't think I gave it to him do you?' I asked.

'No, but you must've seen something, even if you didn't know at the time it was significant.'

I shook my head. 'The police have asked me what I saw, Clara. I couldn't help them because I didn't see anything amiss. Maybe someone gave it to him before he went to the reunion.'

'Whenever he took it, I'm sure he didn't know he was taking it. It was slipped into his food or drink by someone who knew what they were doing and wanted him dead. My Charlie was murdered.'

Hearing Clara tell me her son had been murdered left me struggling to come up with a reply. Anything of a sympathetic nature was likely to be inadequate, and as for saying something positive, there was nothing positive to say – other than to express the hope the police would catch Charlie's killer. That would've sounded lame. In the end I settled on, 'I'm so sorry to hear it, Clara. I can't imagine how you must feel.'

Her puffy cheeks seemed to droop. 'I still haven't come to terms with his death,' she said. 'Knowing he was murdered is almost more than I can bear.'

It was another conversation I wished I wasn't involved in and wanted to end quickly but couldn't. Good manners and humanity demanded that I listened to Clara for as long as she wanted to talk to me. I could only hope it wouldn't be for long.

'I can imagine.' Was there a more trite cliché than that to offer someone who had recently been bereaved? Probably not, but it was the best I could think of other than 'sorry for your loss' – a formulaic response I was desperate to avoid.

'There's something else,' she said.

My heart sank. She wanted to talk some more and I wanted to be alone to watch the television, drink coffee, and generally while away the time until wine o'clock. I decided to get the 'something else' issue out of the way as quickly as possible, in the hope I'd then be able to usher my unwanted guest out of the door.

'What is it, Clara?'

'Something arrived through the post for him a few days after he died. I didn't think anything of it at the time, but I keep wondering if it's important.'

'Perhaps you should let the police decide,' I said, with a horrible suspicion I knew what sort of thing she was referring to. 'What was it, anyway?' I added, trying my best to sound like I was making a casual enquiry.

'It was a baseball bat. I gave it to the police and they said they'd look into it, but I got the impression they weren't much interested.'

'A baseball bat?' I asked, forcing my eyebrows into twin arches of surprise, though in truth the emotion I felt was closer to horror than surprise.

'Yes. Charlie has never shown the slightest interest in baseball. There's no reason he should have got one. It seems so odd.'

My spine tingled. 'It is odd, but it's nothing I can help you with unfortunately,' I said.

'I suppose I knew it'd be a waste of time coming here. No, that's ungrateful of me. It hasn't been a waste of time at all. It's been good to unburden myself, and you've been really generous with your time, Jasmine. Thank you so much, I really do appreciate it.'

I lowered my eyes as her praise made me feel uncomfortable, particularly since I hadn't earned it. Far from helping her, I'd concealed what I knew.

'You're welcome, Clara,' I said, like the liar and hypocrite I'd become.

She glanced at her watch. 'I ought to leave you in peace,' she said, and relief flooded my body but I didn't show it.

Instead, I assumed an air of concerned gravitas. 'Anything I can do to help,' I said.

We both stood up and I led her to the door. 'Well, goodbye, Clara, sorry we've had to meet in such awful circumstances,' I said.

'Goodbye. Thank you again, Jasmine. You've been a great comfort to me at a very difficult time.' She walked slowly away, turning once to glance over her shoulder and give me a forced smile, before disappearing down the street. I closed the door, thanking God I was on my own once again. Then my mind began working overtime on the issue of Charlie's death.

'Charlie keeled over after being drugged,' I muttered to myself. 'Then he got a baseball bat delivered to his home. I got a baseball bat delivered to my home. What happened to me before that? Did someone drug me, or try to kill me?

'I don't remember being drugged, but I got myself into a state and ran a young man down. Or did I? Maybe I just assumed I did, because I get myself into a state so often.

'But what if I hadn't gotten myself trolleyed when I'd run him down. What if I was in a state because I'd been drugged at some time before I ran him down? That'd explain a lot. For instance, how it all felt so unreal and nightmarish, and how I only remembered having one drink at O'Shaughnessy's.'

It'd also lead to a troubling possibility – namely, that someone was trying to kill me.

4

TUESDAY, JANUARY 23, 2018

Patience and stealth – these are the qualities required for the job I've set myself. Namely, keeping watch over Jasmine and following her around, getting to know her routines.

Last night I waited in my car for three hours before she emerged from her house. It would've taxed the resources of a lesser person, but I stuck to the job without faltering. That's because I'm highly motivated. There's a lot hanging on this.

She drove to the Crystal Palace Police Station with me following at a discreet distance. She didn't notice she was being tailed – she never does. Jasmine isn't very observant, probably because she's a lush, and drink is all she thinks about. It's one of the things I've learnt about her recently. During the week I've been monitoring her movements, she's bought enough wine to hold a party every day, but as she doesn't see anyone, she must be drinking it all herself. Strange habit, if you ask me. Still, I'm not interested in judging her habits. There's only one agenda I want to pursue: her death.

She turned into the police station car park and I tucked my car discreetly among the other cars on the street, facing the direction I knew she'd take to go home when she was done. She was in there an hour, no doubt doing her best to prise a criminal from the tight embrace of the law. I eventually saw her pull out of the car park in her blue Audi.

On her way home she took a detour into the car park outside O'Shaughnessy's pub, and I realised I might have been presented with the perfect opportunity to erase her from the planet. It'd be somewhat opportunistic, but sometimes life is like that. You plan things when you can, but that shouldn't rule out taking your chances when they come.

I drove past O'Shaughnessy's and parked on the street nearby, just in case they kept a CCTV record of their parking area. I got out, taking my stash of GHB with me. The way I saw it was that if I was able to administer it, there'd be a better than evens chance she'd die of the stuff, or leave O'Shaughnessy's and plough fatally into the nearest brick wall, or similar obstruction, on her way home.

I'd taken the precaution of disguising my appearance, as I always do when I'm stalking someone. Moreover my car can't be traced back to me. It was a second-hand Ford Fiesta – just about the most common car on the road – and the registered keeper didn't exist.

I was wearing a black baseball hat pulled down low over my eyes, a black bomber-jacket, and grey cargo pants with black trainers. My wraparound sunglasses were a somewhat incongruous touch, given that it was 10.55pm, but who cared? What mattered was they hid my features rather well, and the lenses weren't too dark to see through at night.

I entered O'Shaughnessy's looking like a chav from the local housing estate and walked with an uncharacteristic lolloping gait to the bar, where I ordered a half of weak lager weakened still further with a good deal of lemonade. When it arrived I picked it up, and found a seat at a table. I'd clocked Jasmine sitting on her own in a booth, and positioned myself so I could keep an eye on her from under the brim of my baseball hat. I was pretty sure that if anyone had to help the police with a photofit of me at a later date, the result wouldn't look anything like me. No-one who knew me would be likely to recognise me if they gave me a casual glance – and casual glances are, for the most part, what people give strangers in bars, so as not to cause offence. But even a penetrating stare might not have uncovered my disguise, it was so good.

Jasmine sipped her drink, which was undoubtedly stronger fare than mine, then took a gulp of it. She left her glass two-thirds full and headed for the toilet. That was when I seized my chance, draining my own glass, wiping my mouth, and heading for the exit. To get there, I had to walk past the booth Jasmine had been sitting in. As I did so, I theatrically lost my footing and fell off balance, then recovered my poise with a wave of my arm. The wave took my hand over the top of Jasmine's glass, and deposited a squirt of GHB into it from a small plastic container.

I left the premises and returned to my car to await developments.

Ten minutes later Jaz's car pulled out of the car park. I followed at a discreet distance behind her. She lost control of her car on Fosby Street and ploughed into a lamp post. She ran over a young man in the process, causing unplanned collateral damage.

I pulled into a space at the side of the road. Ahead of me, where Jasmine had crashed, the road took a lazy curve to the right, so I was able to see her vehicle, even though I was parked on the left-hand side of the road. I should've turned my lights off, but I was so excited by what I'd seen, I forgot. I sat in my car with the lights on and watched, wondering whether her car would burst into flame, or whether the man would get to his feet.

I was about to drive off when she climbed from her car. This was unexpected. Not only was she not dead, she didn't even appear to be badly hurt. The way she wobbled about suggested she was groggy, but that was all. I'd obviously miscalculated the dose. I made a mental note to double it in future.

She tottered to the side of her car and crouched low, disappearing from view behind its bulk. I guessed she was looking closely at the boy. She stood up, got back in her car, reversed it, climbed out, and looked at the boy a second time. Then she stood up and stared in my direction. I crouched low to avoid her gaze.

This was potentially a problem. If she had seen me, and thought I was calling the police, she'd turn herself in, because she'd have nothing to lose. She could end up in prison. Killing her in prison could prove difficult.

So the best scenario for me would be if she left the scene of the crime without telling anyone.

I didn't know if she was the sort of person who'd do that, but I knew she definitely wouldn't do it if she thought I was a witness who was contacting the cops.

Was there some way to reassure her I wasn't?

I decided to take a calculated risk.

I pulled out of my parking space and drove towards her, then took a right turn up a back street and drove off. It began to drizzle so I turned on my wipers. I made three more right turns, which took me back to Fosby Street. By the time I got there, Jasmine was gone, having left her victim lying on the pavement.

Now I was faced with another problem. There was a chance the crime could be traced back to her. If the boy she'd run down was alive he might be able to identify her car. Even if he was dead he might be a liability because there could be forensic evidence linking his body to Jasmine's Audi.

I pulled up at the side of the road so that my car masked his body from the houses across the way. Directly opposite there was only a derelict warehouse to worry about. The street was deserted. The only sound to be heard was the swish-swish my wipers made on my windscreen, and the hum of my engine as it idled. I pulled on a pair of the surgical gloves I kept in my car for situations which required discretion, made sure the coast was clear, and climbed out.

By this time the pavement was glistening with rain and a pool of blood by the boy's head was fading as the rainwater washed it away. I crouched over him and quickly established he was dead. Then, after ensuring the coast was clear, I got my hands beneath his armpits and dragged him onto the back seat. He was short with a slim build, but was strangely heavy, as if the dead might weigh more than the living.

After my first attempt to get him in the car, his legs were left sticking out the door. I grabbed his feet and stuffed them in the back, then drove off to dispose of the body. I got rid of the car while I was at it – leaving it a burnt-out wreck, far away from the woodland in which I'd left his corpse.

5

WAY BACK WHEN

After I told Tony I couldn't explain what was wrong, he stared at me and my face got hot. I looked up to avoid his eyes, and caught a glimpse of the crescent moon against a dark sky. Then I told myself the heavens don't have any answers, and forced myself to look at Tony.

'Does this mean you'll finish with me?' I asked.

He put his arms around me.

'No,' he said. 'I'll give it time, like you said.'

My tears flowed freely – I couldn't have stopped them if I'd tried – while he held me tight, little knowing that part of me wanted more than ever to push him away. Lurking in the recesses of my mind were unnatural impulses urging me to keep away from Tony. Drunk though I was, I hadn't been able to push them aside and let myself go when he'd tried to kiss me.

'It's all right,' he said. 'Everything's all right.'

Against all the evidence of my experience I believed him, at least for the few minutes I was in his arms, and stopped crying.

'You don't think I'm a freak for not letting you kiss me?' I asked.

'No,' he said, letting me go. 'You're no freak.'

I wiped my eyes and, as he so often did, he pulled a pack of cigarettes from his jacket, put one between my lips and one between his own, then struck a match and lit them both. I took a draw on mine, and wondered how long he'd give it before deciding he didn't want to date a puzzle like me.

'What are you thinking?' he asked.

'What do you mean?'

He reached over, smoothing my hair away from my forehead. 'Your eyebrows arched as if you were worried. You must have had something on your mind.'

I shook my head. 'That's just a habit, it doesn't mean anything,' I lied, wondering whether everyone could read my thoughts as easily as Tony seemed able to.

When we'd smoked our cigarettes, we headed for a taxi rank.

'We could share a cab,' Tony said. 'My place is on the way to yours. You could drop me off. I'd pay for the cab.'

We got in a taxi and gave the driver Tony's address and mine, telling him to head for Tony's first. When we pulled up in front of his house he pressed some cash into my hand and kissed me on the cheek before getting out of the taxi. When it set off again, I asked the driver to head over to Seth's house then I dialled Kylie's number.

'Hi,' I said when she answered. 'I'm on my way. I'll be there in five.'

Her voice came back at me through the ether, slow and drawling. 'Whad? Whad're you talking about?'

'I'm in a taxi like we arranged. I'll be there to pick you up in five.'

Silence. Then, 'Oh yeah. Five. Did you say five?'

I realised she was seriously drunk and I was wasting my time. 'Let me talk to Seth.'

Moments later I heard Seth's voice. 'Kylie's a bit tipsy, but no worries – she'll be waiting for you when you get here.'

As the taxi pulled up, the door to Seth's house opened and he emerged with one arm around Kylie, supporting her, and propelled her to the rear door. I opened it and he eased her in next to me.

'Bye, babe,' he said, kissing her on the cheek.

She blew him a kiss as I fastened the seatbelt around her. Seth shut the door and the taxi moved off.

'Did you have a good time?' I asked.

'Dunno, think so,' she slurred, her head lolling around on an oddly limp neck.

Kylie's mum was waiting for us when we got to her place. 'What sort of state have you got yourself in?' she demanded as soon as she saw her daughter. I thought she was going to bollock Kylie for once, but instead she said: 'You're just like me when I was your age. You'll learn.'

I more-or-less pulled Kylie upstairs, put her to bed, got my jammies on and climbed into the spare bed next to her, and switched the lights out. I should've given some thought as to how Kylie had got herself wrecked, but I didn't. I was too preoccupied with my own concerns to worry about her. Maybe if I had done, I would've been able to prevent the disaster that overtook me later and blighted my life forever.

HERE AND NOW

The thought that someone might want me dead was too much to bear. I went to the cupboard where I keep my wine but was disappointed to find I was fresh out. After a minute or two of trying to do without, I left the house, and headed, inevitably, in the direction of the nearest eight-till-late.

Three questions exercised my mind as I walked:

1. What measures could I take to ensure my survival?
2. What kind of wine was I going to get?
3. How many bottles did I need?

By the time I'd reached the eight-till-late, I'd revised my priorities. I'd relegated the life-threatening circumstances I faced to number three in order of priority. As I scanned the liquor shelves, it fell from my priority list entirely, because I was too busy thinking about merlot and shiraz to give it any consideration. I bought two bottles of each, which was approximately twice as much as I needed for a day's drinking, and headed home with a plastic carrier bag in my hand, the bottles clinking noisily together as I walked.

I told myself for at least the fiftieth time that I ought not to keep getting plastic bags from the eight-till-late, and I should, in future, use one of the half-dozen bags for life I'd bought from the super-market for situations like this.

Minutes after getting back home I gripped the top of one of my purchases intending to open it, when I noticed the time – it was only 11am – and began to feel guilty about having a drink so early. I resolved – like I'd already done a thousand times before – to give up. Then I told myself: *that's not possible, Jaz, get real.* So instead of trying to give up, I decided to try something which might be doable: getting through one lousy day without having a drink.

To divert my thoughts from alcohol, I took a book into the front room and tried to read, but found I couldn't because I was too fidgety, so I switched on the television. I put it on just in time to catch the local news show.

The first story which aired got me sitting straight up in my seat, because it was about one of my old muckers from school – Stuart Foss. He'd been present at the incident we'd all been covering up for eighteen years, and he was dead, just like Charlie, and seemingly he'd died in a similar way to Charlie. He'd been found by a neighbour in his own home, where he lived alone. He hadn't been seen for a while, and someone had noticed a bad smell coming from his house. The neighbour who discovered him broke in and found Stuart slumped in an armchair. It was too early to tell what'd killed him – but I was willing to guess it was the same drug which had killed Charlie, and – I was becoming more certain of this – which had been used in the attempt on my life.

It made me wonder whether something I'd feared for a long time was at last happening: namely, that Seth was eliminating all the witnesses to the incident we'd both been involved in, to ensure his own safety. If so, I could be next in line for the chop. I'd been lucky once. I was unlikely to have the same good luck the second time around.

What was prompting him to do it now, after all these years? Presumably something had spooked him, made him think that one or more of us couldn't be trusted to keep his – or her – mouth shut anymore. The baseball bats Charlie and I had received would be a typical Seth touch. He'd always been one for pranks of various kinds. I wondered if he'd sent one to Stuart.

The rest of the day passed in a frenzy of cleaning, tidying, dusting, clothes-washing, and ironing to keep my mind off things. By 5.30pm I'd cleaned everywhere, including the kitchen cupboards, skirting boards, and even behind the books on my bookshelves.

When I was done with housework I felt hungry and opened the fridge, intending to get something to eat. Then I had a thought: my provisions had the potential to kill me if there was, as I suspected, a poisoner out to get me. I resolved that while I was at home in future, I'd eat nothing I kept in the house unless it came out of a virgin packet, and drink nothing unless it came from a bottle which hadn't been opened. If I half-finished a bottle and left it, I wouldn't drink it.

As most of my meals were ready meals, and I generally finished a bottle of wine once I'd opened it, this resolution didn't necessitate any drastic lifestyle changes on my part.

I also decided that if I ate or drank anything while I was out and about, I'd keep an eye on it to make sure it wasn't tampered with.

For added protection I'd start using the lock the previous owner of my house had installed on the bedroom door. I'd always thought of her as a paranoid bitch, but now I felt more in tune with her way of seeing things.

I fished a shepherd's pie ready meal from the fridge and checked the packaging. It looked sound, so I microwaved it and got it eaten.

While I was washing up, an all-too-familiar panic gripped my insides. It was something I'd had many times before, a sort of floating anxiety which would catch me unawares and put me totally on edge. I needed a drink to sort myself out. I reminded myself about my pledge to stay dry, if only for a day, put on my coat, and wandered out into the dusk, in the hope a walk would help me calm down.

The walk didn't do the trick, and by the time I was passing a bar known as The Alma – the window of which showed how pleasingly illuminated the interior was – I was gagging for a drink. It was impossible for me to walk past the door, so I pushed it open and went inside. It was buzzing with the after-work crowd. The hubbub of excited conversation in the air gave me an instant lift, but it didn't lift me enough, so I sidled up to the bar and bought a half-pint of a rather warming stout, perfect for this cool spring night. *Just one*, I told myself, *that's all I need to keep sane.* One became two, two became three, and after that I was on the red wine.

I tried to keep my pledge to myself to make sure my drinks weren't tampered with, but I doubt I watched them too closely because the rest of the night passed by in a crazy whirlpool of events, none of which I remembered when I woke up. Which was why I was surprised to find myself sharing a bed with someone else. I found out when he moved and woke me up. At least I was in my own bed – I knew, because the freshly-laundered sheets smelled of the fabric softener I used.

As for the person in my bed, I had no idea who he was. I was curled up on my side and he was in a spoon position behind me, one arm over my body. His hand began moving, stroking first my arm, then my belly. I rolled over to face him as it didn't feel right being groped by a stranger.

The man looking at me had a smooth, firm face devoid of the ravages that only experience can inflict, and I realised with a shock he was at least a decade younger than me. He was good-looking, too, with chiselled features and clear blue eyes, which made me wonder if I wasn't so much of a dog as I was accustomed to thinking I was.

His name came to me from somewhere in the drink-clouded recesses of my mind. 'Listen, Jake, I don't think we should be doing this,' I said.

He smiled and I had to admit to myself he had a winning smile.

'Doing what?' he asked.

'You know,' I said, trying to strike a balance between dignified and easy-going, 'sex.'

His smile broadened into a filthy grin. 'That's not what you said last night.'

I felt myself reddening like a naïve virgin. 'Last night I was drunk,' I snapped. 'Today I'm sober and my head's throbbing.'

'Okay,' he said, 'no worries.' He got out of bed and as I watched him put on his black boxer shorts, I couldn't help but notice how lean and muscular he was, not to say desirable, and wondered if I'd had a good time with him. I wished I could remember.

'I'd like to see you again when you're in a better mood,' he said, pulling on his jeans.

'Not so fast,' I replied then I fed him the classic line: 'I'm old enough to be your mum.'

He shook his head, laughing. 'No you're not, I'm older than I look.'

He pulled his T-shirt over his crew-cut head and put a check shirt over it, unbuttoned, with a navy jacket over the shirt.

'How old are you then?'

'Nineteen,' he replied, as he put on a pair of Vans, completing his ensemble. It was a good look, particularly the trainers. I've always had a weakness for Vans.

But what was I doing with a man – I worked it out – fifteen years my junior? – I'd become a cradle-snatcher, and flattering though it was in some ways, it was embarrassing in too many others to contemplate.

I rolled my eyes.

'You insisted on locking the bedroom door last night,' he said, turning the key. 'Why did you do that?'

'No reason. It's just a silly habit of mine. When you're a woman living alone, you can't be too careful.'

'I'll call you,' he said as he left the bedroom.

'What?' I shouted after him.

'I'll call you!' He shouted, descending the steps. 'Last night you gave me your number!'

I lay there for a while wondering who, or what, I'd gotten myself involved with, and what I was going to say if he carried out his threat to call me. Probably thanks, but no thanks, or something of the sort.

Then it hit me that I was a jobless alcoholic who'd run down her victim and left him lying in the road, and was being hunted by someone who – it seemed – was intent on killing her. I spent the next ten minutes sobbing uncontrollably before I somehow pulled myself together.

Jake had woken me up earlier than I would've wanted, but I couldn't sleep so there was no point staying in bed. I got up and stood under the shower. I could only hope I'd find the courage to face the rest of the day, and survive whatever evil it might bring.

7

WAY BACK WHEN

I lay awake in the spare bed next to Kylie's, worrying that I'd never be able to properly kiss Tony or any other man, and even if I crossed that hurdle, I wouldn't be able to have sex with him. Then what? He'd tell my friends and they'd laugh at me. Or some of them would, anyway. Others would pity me. I could never let that happen. But how could I avoid it? Finish with Tony now before it all gets out of hand? I liked him too much.

There's nothing for it, I told myself. *I'll have to carry on seeing him. But I have to minimise the fall-out if it goes horribly wrong, lead a separate life with Tony. I won't ever introduce him to my friends.* I knew he'd understand, because people from his school and mine never mixed, being sworn enemies.

It'll ensure he won't be able to tell my friends anything about me if we split up. The worst that could happen is rumours might reach them which I'll deny.

Hopefully Tony isn't the sort who'd kiss and tell, or not kiss and tell in my case. He doesn't seem to be. But you can't be too careful.

The following morning I woke up before Kylie, in spite of the fact I'd taken ages to get to sleep. I lay in bed fretting about things until she opened her eyes, put her hands over them, and said, 'My head, oh my God, my poor head. What have I done to it?'

'Headache?'

'I've got the mother of all headaches. Can you go ask my mum to give you some paracetamol for me, please?'

I went downstairs and found her mum in the kitchen, cleaning. Everywhere was spotless.

'Er, can I have a couple of paracetamol and a glass of water please?' I asked.

She looked at me and frowned. 'For you or for Kylie?' she asked.

I opened my mouth to say 'for me', to keep Kylie in her mum's good books as far as possible, but before I could get the words out of my mouth she shook her head and said, 'Don't tell me, I already know.'

She gave me two paracetamol and a glass of water which I took upstairs. Kylie sat up in bed, put the paracetamol in her mouth, and eagerly rinsed them down with the contents of the glass. 'I have this feeling,' she said, putting the glass on her bedside table.

'What sort of feeling?'

Her eyebrows knitted together forming furrows on her forehead. 'About Seth. I like him, but I wonder if he's cheating on me, and if I should finish with him.'

I sat on the edge of the bed. 'Where's this come from?'

Her eyes glistened with tears which weren't quite ready to run down her face. 'Sometimes he says he can't see me, and when I ask why, he clams up. It's as if he's hiding something.'

I'd often wondered if Seth was a player. He was always so self-assured, as if he thought he could have any girl he wanted just when he wanted her. But I didn't want to tell Kylie how I felt – she might tell Seth and he'd think I was trying to put her off him, and then he'd freeze me out of his gang.

'You've never mentioned it before.'

'I wanted to pretend everything was good, but I can't anymore, not after last night.'

'Why? What happened last night?'

'He was so evasive. There's something else.'

'What's that?'

'I didn't want to have sex with him but then I got drunk and we ended up in bed together.'

This revelation saddened me and I decided to risk sharing with Kylie some of my misgivings about him. 'Kylie, you like Seth but he has his faults. He might not be right for you. If he's not making you happy, you shouldn't have sex with him. You should end it.'

She nodded. 'You're right,' she said. 'I should. I tried to last night, but couldn't get the words out. I love him too much. I'm in too deep.'

I knew how she felt. I'd fallen into a deep well of my own I couldn't get out of. My secret had hold of my legs and was dragging me down deeper. There was no escaping it. I wondered if Tony might be able to stop me from drowning but it seemed a forlorn hope, especially when I saw him next, and he asked me a tricky question. 'So who do you hang out with at school?'

It should have been an innocent enquiry, but to me it was the stuff of nightmares. I was desperate to keep my two worlds separate – school life, and life with Tony. If ever they should become known to each other, me and Tony would have to split up because of the risk management issues associated with Tony getting to know my friends.

So I concocted a lie, based at least partly on the truth to make it plausible. 'Hardly anyone, as I have an evening job at a supermarket, and I spend a lot of my time on my homework because I want to do well in my exams. So I don't have much time left over to see people – apart from you, of course.'

In fact, I met with my friends on those evenings I wasn't seeing Tony or working, and rushed through my homework before going out. I never once broke a sweat over it. My marks weren't too good, but I didn't give a monkey's. Scraping a pass would be good enough for me. I was pretty sure that further down the line, I'd be able to make a supreme effort and get some half-decent A level results. They were what counted.

'Who are the people you don't often get to see?'

Christ, he was persistent.

'You know, Kylie. I see her as often as I can.'

This seemed to satisfy his curiosity about my social life, thank God. He turned to another subject, 'Do you fancy coming back to my place? My dad's away for the weekend, and my sister's gone out for the night.'

I desperately wanted to say yes, but instead what I said was, 'I do, but you have to understand–'

He cut me short. 'We'll just listen to music. I've got the latest Stereophonics album.'

I managed to look him in the eye. 'Thank you, Tony.'

He arched his eyebrows. 'You don't have to thank me.'

We left the pub we were in, and I linked his arm during the short journey to his house. My mind was in a turmoil. What would we do when we got there? He'd said we'd just listen to Stereophonics, and I was okay with that. But what if he wanted more? And what if I said no? What then?

We turned off the street onto his garden path, and as we traversed the few yards leading to the front door, I felt as if I was walking the plank. He turned and grinned at me before unlocking the door, and I responded by forcing my lips into an uncertain U-shape.

'You don't have to look so worried,' he said. 'We're just two people enjoying each other's company.' He pushed open the door and stood back to let me in. I stepped into the entrance hall. It was an actual hall, albeit a modest one, rather than a cramped lobby like the one in the house my parents owned.

I looked into the front room. It smelled of vanilla. My eyes roved the walls until I detected the source of the smell – a plug-in air freshener.

'Would you like a coffee?'

'Yes, please.'

'Follow me.' He led me to the kitchen at the back of the house. 'Take a seat. Make yourself at home.'

I sat at the table trying my best to enjoy the situation. At least the pressure was off for now. He was busy making coffee, and I didn't have to worry about physical contact for the time being. I prayed that if it was on the agenda, my flesh wouldn't crawl. I tried for a moment to imagine Tony touching me in an intimate way, and squeezed my legs together, but couldn't get excited. At least I didn't feel altogether repelled by the image. Maybe that was progress.

'Let's go to the other room,' he said. 'It's more comfortable there.'

We went to the front room. It was furnished with a large two-seater sofa and an even larger three-seater. I wanted to sit in an armchair I could occupy on my own, but no such item was available. Then I conjured up an image in my mind of Tony in an armchair, me sitting on his lap, and shuddered, wondering what'd made me think of it.

After a moment's hesitation I chose the three-seater, imagining I could put more space between me and Tony if I sat there. He placed an occasional table near me and put our coffees on it, then switched on the sound system and put on some music, which I hardly noticed, being in a tizz.

He sat next to me, so close we were touching, reached behind me, and put his arm around my waist.

'Relax,' he said, and I realised I'd stiffened up.

We sat there for a while, and I allowed myself to rest my head on his shoulder, all the while telling myself, *This is what normal teenagers do.* The music stopped and I realised we must've been sitting in that position at least half an hour. Tony stood up.

'I'm going upstairs to get a book I want to show you,' he said. 'Back in a mo.'

His feet pounded on the steps as he ran up, and when he got to the top there was silence for a few seconds, after which I heard knocking on a door. Then I heard him say, 'Sarah, are you in there?'

He sounded concerned, knocked harder, and shouted, 'Sarah! Are you okay? Sarah? Sarah!'

Another silence.

'Sarah, answer me! Please answer!'

Another brief silence.

'Sarah, I'm going to kick the door open if you don't answer right now!'

I wondered what could possibly be going on. The thunderous crash of a door being kicked open interrupted my thoughts and made me jump.

'Oh my God, oh my God, oh my God! Sarah!'

The tone of Tony's voice alarmed me and I felt frightened for him. It was my cue to run upstairs. I found Tony in the bathroom, crouching over the bath, which was half-full. He had both hands in the armpits of a naked woman – presumably his sister, Sarah – and was holding her up, out of the water. Her head was lolling forward on a limp neck; her black hair was plastered to her scalp. I caught a glimpse of her pretty face. It had an unearthly pallor and was soaking wet. Her expression was peaceful, and her eyes were as dull as the grey tiles covering the bathroom floor.

'Help me get her out,' he said. 'We're going to have to stand in the bath to do it.'

I stepped over the side of the bath into the water which entered my trainers and lapped up my legs almost to my knees. I was surprised how cold it felt. I plunged my hands in near her feet and when I grabbed her ankles, they were cold too. She must have been in the bath quite a while for the water to have gotten so cold.

'Okay,' Tony said. 'One, two, three, lift.'

We straightened up, and stepped sideways onto the bathroom floor, then lowered Sarah onto the tiles. Illogically I wanted to make her comfortable, and tried to slip the bathmat under her.

'Don't bother with that, call an ambulance,' Tony said, kneeling astride her, and pressing his hands repeatedly on her ribcage.

I dialled emergency services on my mobile phone, noticing a growing puddle beneath Sarah's body.

'Hello, what service do you require?' A female voice asked.

I gasped my reply in something of a panic.

'Ambulance, please, right away. A woman has drowned in a bath. We're trying to revive her.' Then I gave her Tony's address.

Tears were running down his face – she'd failed to respond to his CPR. He tried the kiss of life, which similarly achieved nothing, so he resumed CPR. The puddle around her prone form grew bigger. I picked up her arm. It was limp as overdone spaghetti. I felt vainly for a pulse. When I couldn't detect one, I tried her neck, with the same lack of success.

'It's too late, Tony,' I said. 'I'm sorry.'

He ignored me and carried on with the CPR, performing the action more energetically, almost brutally, in his efforts to get it to work. Finally, he accepted it wasn't going to, got to his feet, then sat on the side of the bath with his head in his hands, sobbing. I sat next to him and put my arms round him, felt his body heaving with each loud sob. We remained in that position until a knock on the front door disturbed us. I took the stairs three and four at a time, almost falling down them. When I opened the door two paramedics were on the doorstep.

'Come in,' I said. 'She's upstairs.'

I followed them up. They knelt next to Sarah's body, checking her pulse and temperature. 'I'm sorry, there's nothing we can do,' one of them said.

'What do you mean?' Tony asked.

The paramedic looked almost as sad and uncomfortable as Tony. 'I'm so sorry, she's dead, and judging by her body temperature she seems to have been dead for a while. We need a doctor to certify the death. Can you give me the name of her general practitioner, please?'

'Yes – yes of course.'

Tony reeled off the details and the paramedic called the surgery. Then he called the police.

'What are you doing?' I asked.

'Standard procedure,' said the paramedic. 'Where the circumstances of a death are unusual, we have a duty to alert the police.'

A policeman arrived within minutes. The paramedics had a brief discussion with him before leaving. He turned his attention to us. 'I realise this is difficult,' he said. 'But could you give me your names, please?'

By this time Tony had stopped crying but was unable to talk, so I answered the question, 'He's my boyfriend Tony Fulgoni, and the... the dead girl is his sister, Sarah.'

The policeman recorded my reply in a small notebook. 'Could you tell me what happened here today?'

My head was all over the place and for a moment I couldn't think what'd gone on, then I made a massive effort and pulled myself together. 'I was in the front room with Tony. He went upstairs to get a book, and I heard him knocking on the bathroom door. When there was no answer, he broke in, and must've found his sister in the bath. I could tell he was upset and went upstairs to see what was going on. We got her out of the bath, and he tried to revive her, but it was too late.'

He made a note. 'Were you and Tony here when Sarah got in the bath?'

I shook my head. 'I don't think so. I didn't hear any noises from upstairs after we arrived, so she was probably in the bath already.'

'How long were you in the house before you found her?'

'About an hour.'

'Did she have any health issues you know of?'

I couldn't answer so I looked at Tony. He was still sitting on the side of the bath with his head down. I put my hand on his shoulder and shook him gently. 'Tony,' I said.

He looked up and replied. 'Sorry, no she didn't.'

The policeman turned to face him. 'I'm sorry to ask, but did she have any mental health issues?'

Tony's eyes narrowed. 'What are you trying to say?'

'I'm not trying to say anything, sir. I just have to rule out certain possibilities.'

'She definitely had no mental health issues.'

'Any history of drug use?'

Again, Tony's eyes narrowed. 'No.'

'Was she on any prescription drugs?'

'No.'

The policeman shut his notebook. 'I'll wait here with you until the doctor arrives,' he said.

Doctor McGee, the family practitioner, arrived shortly afterwards. After conferring with him, the policeman left us with the words, 'I'll be in touch if I need any more information. If you need to contact me for any reason I'm based at the Crystal Palace Police Station. When you call, ask for Police Constable Fanshaw, number 1098.'

Doctor McGee examined Sarah and said, 'It'll be impossible to establish the cause of death without an autopsy, I'm afraid. I'll get one organised. Sorry it has to be this way.'

Tony just nodded.

'Had you better call your dad?' I asked him.

'Oh my God, yes.' I thought he'd cried himself out, but he began to cry again. 'How can I possibly break this news to him?'

Some weeks later I received a text message from Tony.

Dad's out can u come round asap? xx

I typed my reply.

No probs be there v soon xx

When I got to his place he let me in before I had the chance to press the doorbell and I was scarcely through the door before he was saying, 'We've got the results of the autopsy.'

He showed me into the front room.

'What – what do they say?'

129

His voice choked with emotion, 'She'd been dosed up with GHB. They think she took it or more likely was given it before she got into the bath. Then she fell unconscious and drowned. I know for a fact she didn't take it voluntarily. Someone must have spiked her drink, and I'm going to find out who.'

At some point after that I met Tony in the park. The sky was overcast and he was waiting for me on a swing, looking – to my young eyes – as glamorous as Marlon Brando in the famous scene with Eve Marie Saint. I sauntered over, he stood up, and we briefly kissed, and I wondered how long he'd stick with me, a girlfriend he couldn't have sex with, or even kiss properly. Surely our days were numbered. I could only hope that the end, when it came, wouldn't hurt me too much and the fall-out wouldn't tarnish my reputation. When our lips parted he said, 'I've got a secret to tell you.'

I wondered what he could possibly tell me which would rival the secrets I was keeping. 'What is it?'

He put his arms round my waist and looked into my eyes. 'Promise you'll keep it to yourself.'

'I promise.'

'I found out who gave the GHB to my sister.'

I don't know why, but those words filled me with dread. 'Who was it?'

'It was a piece of low-life called Seth Delaney. He goes to your school. Do you know him?'

Tendrils of panic took root in my intestines. 'Only by reputation,' I said, feeling something like Peter must have done when denying Christ. I didn't feel able to admit I regarded him as a friend. Something told me I ought to be up front about my relationship with Seth, but a darker voice told me to keep it quiet, and it was the darker voice I listened to.

'I gave his name to the police but they're useless. They reckon there's not enough evidence to take it to court. That means he'll get off scot-free.'

This was developing into an intolerable situation even though

Tony knew nothing about who I associated with. It wouldn't require much for him to find out. Even if he didn't do any digging, my name could easily come up, depending on who he talked to about Seth. I decided to act as an advocate and steer him away from what seemed unreasonable suspicion.

'Are you sure it was him? If the police can't get enough evidence to charge him, it probably means he didn't do it.'

'He did it all right.'

Tony's eyes glowed with hate, and I knew he wouldn't listen to me. Even so, I had to try. 'How do you know?'

'Call it gut instinct. That and the fact he was with my sister the day she died.'

I considered marshalling some more arguments in defence of Seth but it was obvious from the look on Tony's face I'd be wasting my time.

All I could do was cling to the hope he wouldn't do anything stupid.

The following Saturday Joshua was lying in his carry-cot, eyes wide open, looking up at me longingly, or so I liked to think.

My mother had warned me not to pick him up, but she was in the kitchen and we were in the front room. I scooped him up and held him. He felt like pure love and smelled of heaven. Then I heard my mother's footsteps approaching, so I put him down again. She glared at me as soon as she came in.

'What have you been up to?' she said.

I nudged the toes of one foot with those of the other. 'Nothing.'

Her glare got harder. 'You're lying. You've been up to something.'

She examined Joshua's covers and I wondered whether she'd notice anything amiss. I'd done my best to tuck them in the way she always did, but I couldn't be sure I'd done enough to deceive her. My stomach churned. I could do without a bollocking from the

Sasquatch. After a few seconds she turned her attentions to me. 'Just remember, I've got my eye on you,' she said, heading back to her steamy kitchen.

I remembered all right. It was something I was unlikely ever to forget.

When she was gone I whispered in Joshua's ear, 'One day when you're grown up enough to understand, I'm going to tell you all the secrets this family has kept from you, Joshua. I'm going to explode all the lies you've been told.'

Then I watched him for a while and held his tiny hand. He was briefly interested before he nodded off. I looked at the time. It was 11am. and I was due to meet Kylie, Seth and the others. As I was still in my jammies and dressing gown, I went upstairs to get ready. I showered and was putting on my jeans when my mobile rang. It was Kylie. Oddly, she couldn't talk to me. She'd rung me, but she didn't say anything. She just blubbered on the other end of the line. Even though she didn't say anything, I could tell it was her by the tone of the blubbering. I'd heard it before. I was pretty sure it was to do with Seth and he'd finished with her.

'Kylie, what's wrong?' I asked, but she was so distraught she couldn't tell me, so she hung up and texted:

Meet me in half an hour at the entrance to St George's Hospital xx

This was all very mysterious. I wondered what could be going on. Was her mum ill or something? The hospital was about a half-hour's walk away, so I said goodbye to my mum and Joshua, and left. Kylie was waiting for me as promised. Her face was puffy, pink, and blotchy and her voice croaky – but at least she was no longer sobbing her heart out.

'Kylie, what's happened?' I asked, feeling scared for her, and scared for what her future might hold.

'It's Seth,' she said.

Hearing his name made me shiver with apprehension.

'What about Seth?'

She shook her head as if trying to deny the horrible news she had for me.

'He's been attacked.'

My shivers of apprehension became more pronounced.

'How – how badly?'

Her face distorted with sorrow.

'Really badly. He's in a mess.'

'Is he well enough to receive visitors?'

She nodded. 'Yes, and I'm sure he'd like to see you, but we won't be able stay for long. His mum and dad have been with him all morning. They'll be back for another visit later.'

She led me into the hospital, took me down long white corridors smelling of antiseptic, then into a lift which transported us to a ward on the fourth floor.

Seth was in bed, head propped up on a couple of pillows, a drip of a clear liquid connected to his arm. The drip impressed on me the feeling that his condition was serious, even grave. But what really did it was his head, which seemed to be twice the size I remembered it, and a variety of colours – red, purple, even blue in places, but nowhere was it a normal, healthy skin colour. The one eye he could open rolled to the side, he looked at me, and smiled, or did the closest thing to a smile he could manage.

'Oh my God, Seth, what's happened to you?' I asked, and saw a hint of fear in his eye. Maybe he hadn't realised how bad he looked. I cursed myself for my lack of tact.

'Got beat up,' he said in a low murmur. It cost him so much effort I decided not to ask him anything else.

'Just lie still, Seth,' I said. 'We'll sit with you for a while.'

We both pulled chairs up close to his bed, and Kylie held his hand. The visit soon became boring because we couldn't talk, but I felt I had to hang in there for Kylie. After half an hour Kylie said, 'We should go now,' so we said our goodbyes and left.

'Do you know who did that to him?' I asked, as we made our way back to reception. I had a horrible idea I knew the answer to my question, but didn't want to admit it to myself.

'No, he wasn't able to say, he doesn't remember much of what happened because he got concussed. Maybe when he gets better.'

I wondered whether he would get better, but didn't want to express my doubts to Kylie. He looked so bad it seemed inconceivable he could ever make a full recovery.

'Yes, when he gets better he'll tell us.'

'I love him and it breaks my heart to see him in such a state.'

So, Kylie was still in love with Seth, it seemed.

It made me question how I felt about Tony.

I'd been so concerned with keeping my relationship with him in a hermetically sealed container that I hadn't allowed myself to dwell on my feelings for him. But if I really thought about it, I liked him a lot. The patience he'd shown with me made him into something akin to a saint in my view. Maybe I did love him, although I had little idea what love was. My feelings for Joshua were probably my only touchstone. What did they tell me? It was impossible to say.

I realised I'd been silent for too long, lost in my own thoughts. 'I'm sure. What kind of an animal does that to a person?' I said.

Deep down I had an idea what kind of animal did it – a vengeful one who's lost his sister. I just hoped my suspicions about Tony weren't true.

'I keep asking the same question. Who would do a thing like that? They deserve locking up, whoever they are. They deserve worse than locking up. Someone should do to them what they did to Seth.'

Those words made me wince, but nevertheless I made a show of agreeing with her. 'Yes, it'd serve them right.'

We headed in the direction of Kylie's house, both of us with heavy hearts. This was a bad day, but not my worst – I'd already had my worst, or so I thought.

Little did I know, my worst was yet to come.

One day as I was kicking my shoes off in the hall, having just got back from school, my mother shouted, 'Come here!'

I braced myself and pushed open the door to the front room. She was sitting on our sofa, her vast bulk taking up more than half of it, her crimplene dress straining at the seams. In her lap there was a translucent rectangular object. It was a moment or two before I recognised it for what it was: the Tupperware container I kept in my wardrobe with my savings in it. Over the months I'd saved up as much as I could, and had amassed, what to me, was a small fortune. My mother held it in a hand the colour of corned beef and stood up.

'What d'you think this is?' she asked.

'It's a Tupperware container,' I replied as calmly as I could.

'I don't mean the bloody well container,' She replied, taking off the lid and ostentatiously presenting the inside of the open container to me so as to show me my own money.

'My savings,' I told her.

'And what were you planning on doing with those savings?'

'I was planning to keep saving them and maybe open a post office account,' I said.

Her lip curled and her face wrinkled into one of her mean expressions. 'Is that so? Well, now you're earning, you should be paying me and your father some board to stay here, so I'll tell you what I'm going to do.'

She reached into the container and took from it most of the money I'd worked so hard to accumulate. 'I'm taking this to pay for your board for all those months when you've been working and you haven't paid any. It'll go towards the fund I'm going to use to send Joshua to university.'

I tried to snatch the money and container from her hands, but my mother was too big and strong for me.

'Right, you defiant little sod,' she said. 'As a punishment, I'm going to take all the rest of your bloody money.'

I'd kept my secret because I'd been too ashamed of what'd gone on to discuss it, and perhaps also because I'd known it'd destroy my mother if she got to know about it. But in that moment of anger I couldn't keep it in. It leapt from my mouth of its own accord.

'Your brother – my uncle – is Joshua's father,' I said, in a surprisingly calm tone of voice I barely recognised as my own.

Her mouth opened into a speechless O-shape. She stood holding the Tupperware container in both hands, perfectly motionless. It was as if she'd become part of a freeze frame in a movie. It was only a moment, but it was one of those moments which seem to last forever. Then she let go of the container. It fell, seemingly in slow motion, to the floor, and the noise it made on impact broke the spell.

My mother's face reddened. 'You bloody what?' she asked, advancing on me with her hand raised. I prepared myself for a crack which would send me flying, the mother of all cracks.

'Nothing,' I said, although I knew it was too late. The cat was well and truly out of the bag – and it wasn't any tame domestic kitty, it was a snarling, man-eating brute.

'You accused my brother of fathering your child. That wasn't nothing.'

'He raped me,' I said.

Then I watched as she deflated like a balloon, and wished I'd let her just take my money without saying anything. Her face was no longer red. With hunched shoulders she silently sloped off downstairs, leaving me to ponder on what would happen next. Probably she would speak to my dad, there'd be ructions – to put it mildly – with her brother, she'd have a nervous breakdown, and life would never be the same again.

I sat on my bed with my head in my hands. My stomach was churning so much I felt as if my entire body might rotate with it.

Later when I went downstairs, my mother was in the kitchen cooking one of her ghastly stews, and there was steam everywhere. Joshua was in his carry-cot next to the kitchen table, gurgling happily. I picked him up right in front of her, something I wouldn't have dared to do an hour before.

She looked at me and I stared her right in the eye, daring her to say something. After a few seconds she turned her attentions to a bubbling pan on the hob, stirring the contents with a wooden spoon. I carried Joshua to the front room.

'You're my son, not my brother, Josh,' I told him. 'It's all out in the open now.'

But it wasn't. The pretence had to continue to the outside world, and even to Josh. We couldn't expect a young boy to keep our dark secret. I made a promise to myself that one day, when he was old enough, I'd tell him everything.

When I went to my bedroom to read, I heard my mum on the telephone so I sneaked downstairs to eavesdrop.

'How could you?' she was asking. 'How could you?'

My uncle was obviously on the other end of the line, and I got the impression he was denying everything but my mother accepted my version of events. I peeped round the door just in time to see her hang up. Tears were coursing down her flabby cheeks. She wiped them with her hands and retreated to the kitchen, while I returned to my bedroom.

My dad came home an hour later and I heard raised voices which I found unsettling. My parents were in the kitchen out of earshot so I sneaked downstairs to eavesdrop, but by the time I got close enough to hear them, they'd stopped talking. Likely they were whispering to prevent me from overhearing. With a fast-beating heart I went back upstairs.

In the evening we ate together as normal, even though our world had suffered a massive perturbation. The only difference to usual was that me and my mother were both in poor appetite. When my dad finished eating he said, 'I'm going out.'

My mum turned down the corners of her mouth and began clearing away the dishes. I helped her. My dad returned much later. We never saw or heard from my uncle again.

Later I went into the bathroom, bolted the door, and took off all my clothes. Then I looked at myself in the mirror, studying every tiny detail of what made me uniquely me.

My hair was dark brown, unstylish, and a bit lank, if truth be told. I took a bobble from my pocket and tied it up into a rough bun, with straggly bits sticking out. It made the bony nature of my face more apparent. I had cheekbones – just – and was pretty, apart from having a nose which was too big and pointy. My lips just about passed muster, although they could've been fuller and more luscious. My chin was small and childlike.

My breasts were pert, but not as big as I'd have liked them to have been. Waist and stomach: still suffering the effects of having carried a baby, but almost back to normal. Hips: probably too boyish and narrow. Legs: definitely good. Feet: a size too big, but okay in the right shoes.

Why was I conducting this audit? It was because something had changed, and I wanted to know if it was obvious to all, or if only I would know about it.

I faced the mirror, then turned three-quarters-on, and finally side-on, examining my profile via the corner of my eye.

I fully expected to see something leap out at me which said: *this is a changed woman.* But nothing did. I sighed and put my clothes back on, then went outside with my mobile, so there would be no chance of anyone overhearing me, and rang Tony.

'Have you got a minute?' I said.

'For you, always.'

'I want to tell you something. I think I can do it now.'

There was a tangible silence which must've lasted five seconds, or even ten. Then he said, 'What? What do you mean?'

'Don't you get it? Do I have to spell it out for you?' I asked, unable to supress the surprise in my voice. I'd assumed that even though my change wasn't visible, it would somehow be manifest in my tone of voice and demeanour.

'Sorry, I don't get it. What're you on about?'

'I think I'm ready to have sex with you.'

There was another tangible silence. Then he said, 'Sorry about the silence. I don't know what to say.'

'Then don't say anything.'

'Okay, great, I'm just surprised, that's all.'

'Meet you tomorrow in the park after school?'

'Sure.'

The next day Tony was sitting on a swing waiting for me.

'Hi,' I said.

'Hi,' he said. 'I've got the house to myself again.'

'And?'

'And I could show you a good time.'

'You'll have to do better than that,' I said, laughing.

He got off the swing and we took one of the tarmac paths which led through the trees to the exit nearest his home.

'Cigarette?' he asked.

'It would be rude not to.'

He took a pack of Embassy Regal from his pocket and handed me one, putting a second between his lips. We stopped and he took a pack of Swan Vestas matches from his other pocket and lit them both. Then we casually smoked as we sauntered along the path.

When our cigarettes were finished we made sure to put them out properly, and threw them in a bin at the side of the path. After that, it was as if we both had ESP, and both of us knew what the other was thinking. He lowered his face to mine and we kissed, and for a few moments we were all that mattered to each other. We were caught in a spell in which the world beyond us had ceased to exist.

The spell was broken by the sound of a hostile voice.

'There he is, and look who he's with.'

Then I felt myself being manhandled and my head exploded with a million painful stars, and I was on the ground, on my hands and knees, staring down at the surface of the tarmac path. None of it made any sense. I raised my head and saw five young men with two young women.

Lying at their feet was Tony, who wasn't moving. My instincts told me he was well and truly dead. I realised then I was on my hands and knees because I'd been hit on the head.

I looked closely at the ones who'd done it, the people responsible.

They were: Seth Delaney, Charlie Duggan, Mike Stone, Stuart Foss, Danny Scott, Kylie Wood, and Jasmine Black.

8

HERE AND NOW

W hen I finished showering I selected a clean outfit for the day. I was able to choose from virtually every item I owned, thanks to my cleaning frenzy. I selected a maroon sweater and mid-blue stonewashed jeans with a tear at both knees which the manufacturer had inserted in the interests of fashion.

Once dressed, I headed for the kitchen, grabbed a couple of paracetamol, and rinsed them down with a glass of water. Afterwards I glanced at the calendar: it was Wednesday, April 4, 2018.

I made a coffee, strong and black, no sugar, went to the front room, and switched on the TV. My stomach was churning with the panic all alcoholics feel when they're not liquored up to the eyeballs, and on top of that was the panic which comes of being a hit-and-run driver, and on top of that was the additional panic which comes of being part of a cover-up of a murder that took place a long time ago, and knowing someone is out to get you because of it.

That's a pretty stiff cocktail of panic, and it took everything I had to not head straight back to the kitchen, grab a bottle of wine, open it, and demolish it in record time. Maybe the fact I could resist it – if only for a while – was a sign I wasn't an alcoholic after all. I hoped so.

My thoughts were interrupted by my mobile phone. As I picked up, the thought occurred to me that I ought to change the noise it made, possibly to something more funereal. I glanced at the screen before answering. It was Kylie – not the most welcome person in my life. It was only 9am Why would she be calling me so early?

'Hi, Kylie,' I said with what little enthusiasm I could muster.

'Jaz, have you heard the news?' She sounded concerned, scared even.

'What news?'

'Stuart's dead.'

I already knew this. Hearing it again wasn't as painful as receiving the information the first time around – but it still made me shudder.

'That's awful, Kylie.'

'I need to see you.'

This was odd. We never saw each other, except occasionally during the run up to a school reunion. As I didn't feel any need to see her, I prevaricated. 'Can't you tell me what you want to say over the telephone?'

'I'd rather do it in person.'

My heart sank. While my relations with Kylie weren't anything like as bad as those with Seth, they hadn't been good in a long while. She wasn't someone I relished spending time with.

'When?'

'Twelve noon at TNQ.'

I was still groggy from my night's drinking. There was no telling how long it'd take my system to get shot of the alcohol I'd poured into it. I must've had a lot – waking up with Jake next to me was proof enough of that. I couldn't risk driving. I'd have to take a train to TNQ.

'Okay,' I said reluctantly, 'I'll see you there.'

When I got to TNQ Kylie was already ensconced at a table for two in a dark corner. She looked sad, almost tearful.

It suddenly occurred to me that Seth might be using Kylie to wipe out the rest of us. They'd always been close, and she'd done some of his dirty work for him, like organising the reunions and making sure the rest of us showed up. I made a mental note to keep my eyes on my food and drink, and on Kylie herself. Whatever else she was going to do today, she wasn't going to poison me.

'Very intimate,' I said as I sat opposite her. She gave me a rueful grin, more of an exposure of her pristine teeth than anything else.

'Isn't it? Let's get ordered.'

She looked as if she was bursting to tell me something. I was tempted to ask her what, but decided instead to let her get to it in her own good time.

She waved her arm to attract the attention of a waitress who came over with a notepad and pen and took our orders. Kylie scanned the menu for a minute, struggling to make up her mind. 'I'm not really hungry today,' she said, then added: 'I'll just have a small salad, please, the smallest you've got. And a coffee, an Americano.'

This meant for once I'd be eating a more expensive meal than her.

'Bad news about Stuart,' I said. I couldn't think of anything more original. Death is like that. It leaves you with little scope for originality and you end up falling back on tired clichés like the old 'I'm sorry for your loss' – which wasn't really appropriate in our situation, though we were both truly sorry. It's just that we were sorry for ourselves rather more than for Stuart.

'You don't know the half of it,' she said.

In an attempt to show concern, even though I'd never really liked Stuart, not since the business with Charlotte, anyway, I said, 'How did he die?'

She got this look on her face I'd never seen before, sort of like a rabbit trapped in the headlights. 'They're saying it's a drug overdose.'

That struck me as eminently possible. Stuart, I knew, had worked for Seth. Seth had been an entrepreneur since school – and his line of work wasn't one you'd want your son or daughter to enter. He dealt in drugs. Few people at St Benedict's had known this because he was discreet about it, and he had a policy he adhered to quite strictly.

'Never shit on your own doorstep,' he used to say.

After leaving school he continued in the same line of work but he wasn't your conventional gangster-style back-street drug overlord. He dressed like a stockbroker and dealt strictly with professionals and even a few low-end celebs. By going upmarket he avoided, for the most part, the turf wars gangster-types have to contend with. Mind you, if anyone trod on his toes, they didn't do it twice.

Because of his work for Seth, Stuart would've had access to every recreational drug going, at least those that bankers and the like use. It was possible he'd developed a habit which had killed him.

However, I was willing to bet someone had poisoned him. I wondered whether Kylie had come to the same conclusion. I didn't want to influence her views, so I avoided putting it to her directly. 'Well, he did deal in drugs,' I said, 'so it's none too surprising he died of them.'

She shook her head, her golden hair shimmering as it caught a beam of light shafting in from a distant window. 'He might've been a dealer, but he didn't take anything. He was clean. Stuart didn't even drink much.'

I couldn't argue with that. I hardly knew the guy. I only ever spoke to him at the reunions. It was fully eighteen years since I'd last had a meaningful conversation with him. Kylie knew him far better than I did.

'What are you saying, Kylie?'

I knew exactly what she was saying. It was what, deep down, I'd known, but hadn't wanted to believe.

'I'm saying he wouldn't have overdosed himself. He didn't do drugs, and even if he had done, he wasn't that stupid.' My stomach lurched. I knew what was coming. 'Someone killed him.'

'Probably one of Seth's business rivals,' I said.

It was the sort of remark which would normally have drawn denials from her. Before today, she would never have admitted Seth was anything other than a respectable businessman, and the people who worked for him were business associates. But now Stuart was dead, she didn't try to put a gloss on what he did.

'Sometimes I think so,' she replied. 'But other times I think: first Charlie, then Stuart. Two members of our old gang – it can't be coincidence. How long will it be before they come for you and me and the rest of us?'

The answer was all too obvious.

'It's already happening,' I said softly.

Her eyes widened just as our food arrived. The waitress probably assumed from her big eyes that Kylie was impressed by what she saw on her plate. At any rate she looked pleased, perhaps anticipating a generous tip, and went smiling to the next table.

'What do you mean?' Kylie asked, picking at her salad without much real appetite.

'I mean they've sent me a sign they're out to get me – whoever they are. A baseball bat. I take it you haven't had one yet.'

She opened her bag and took an e-cigarette from it, put it between her lips with shaking fingers, then, remembering e-smoking wasn't allowed in TNQ, returned it to her bag and picked at her food again.

'No, I haven't. A baseball bat. That's always been Seth's trademark.' She was being unusually frank with me.

'Why would his enemies target us? They can't think we're part of his operation, surely?' I asked.

I could practically see the blood draining from her face. 'I am,' she said. Then she corrected herself. 'I was part of Seth's business. I used my interior design work to get contacts for him.'

She was being honest for once about helping Seth – and she'd just let me know she wasn't helping him any longer. They'd always been so close. I wondered what had come between them, and whether she was ready to consider what to me seemed obvious – it could all be Seth's doing. He could be behind it, orchestrating the murder of everyone who'd been mixed up in things to make damn sure no-one would ever grass him up.

'But why Charlie and Stuart, and why me?' I asked, setting it up so she could work through the logic of it and arrive at the same conclusion I was fast coming to, namely, the love of her life was the culprit.

She didn't answer, she just looked pensive, so I tucked into my duck liver parfait. I wasn't hungry, but I knew my erratic habits had made me unhealthy, and I ought to try to eat better.

'There's something I have to – have to – tell you,' she said, and as the words left her mouth she burst into tears. I'd only ever seen her like that twice before, both times at school. The first time was when she thought Seth was messing her about, and the second time was when he got badly hurt and had a spell in hospital.

'What do you have to tell me, Kylie?' I asked gently.

By then she'd taken a pack of tissues from her handbag and was loudly blowing her nose and wiping her face, which was pink and blotchy, like the face of a small child that's just cried its heart out.

'I wanted to tell you this before but I couldn't. I couldn't talk about it, couldn't risk getting the words out because I knew it'd choke me up.' She sounded so upset that I felt uneasy about the unknown revelation she was going to spring on me.

She lowered the tissue. 'It's Seth,' she said. 'He's dead.'

With that she burst into a fresh bout of sobbing and there was no consoling her for at least the next ten minutes.

While she cried herself out I tried to come to terms with this latest news. It had shocked me to the core. If there was one person I would've said was un-killable, it would have been Seth. But now he was dead, which meant he couldn't be responsible for the murders. So who was, and what was the motive?

Was it, as I'd theorised, a business rival who was in the process of retiring Seth and his team from their enterprise? Had I got caught in the crossfire?

When Kylie had finally composed herself I said, 'How did Seth die? How do you know about it?'

She'd taken a pack of tissues from her bag while she'd been crying and used at least half of them to staunch the flow of her tears. She pulled another one out and dabbed at her face.

'I called him this morning right after I called you. He didn't answer so I drove round to his place. It was surrounded by police and reporters. The police wouldn't let me in the house. I asked one of the reporters what was going on and he told me Seth had been found dead in his front room. No sign of a struggle. We both know what that means.'

So he'd been wasted the same way Charlie and Stuart had been.

'Who did it, Kylie? We have to work it out. If one of Seth's business rivals is behind it, why did he kill Charlie? I understand why he'd kill Stuart but not Charlie.'

She took a sip of her coffee. It must've been stone-cold by then.

'Charlie was on Seth's payroll,' she said. 'Stuart always had been ever since school. Charlie tried to distance himself at first but he got drawn in when he needed money. Seth lent him what he needed and Charlie ended up doing delivery work for him to repay the loan.'

I knew Stuart had been working for Seth, but not Charlie. It seemed Seth was even better at manipulating people than I'd always given him credit for. 'What about me? Why should I be a target?'

'It could be enough that you knew me, Seth, and the rest of us.'

'I wondered if I'd been caught in the crossfire.'

She lowered her voice and looked apprehensive. 'I'm pretty sure someone's been following me.'

Was this paranoia? Or was she really being followed? Was I being followed? If I was, I'd probably been too drunk to notice most of the time.

'Kylie, what are we going to do?'

'I don't know. I can't go to the police for obvious reasons. Maybe you can. You could tell them about the baseball bat you got.'

'I could, but by the time they got round to doing anything about it, we'd all be dead if that's what's on the cards. And in any case, I doubt they'll be able to get anything from it which would help them catch whoever sent it. Even if they did, what would they charge them with? Abuse of the post?'

'I see what you mean.'

We finished our meals in silence, having tacitly concluded we were both doomed and there was nothing we could do about it – except hope we were somehow mistaken.

'Okay,' I said, as we left TNQ. 'Until next time, then.'

Kylie hugged me with genuine affection, something I hadn't had from her since our schooldays. Maybe the feeling she was being stalked with a view to being killed made her appreciate me all of a sudden.

'Yes, till next time,' she said. 'If there is a next time, that is.'

9

WAY BACK WHEN

Fear turned my insides into knots. It wasn't only fear I felt, though. There were other emotions, and anger was part of the mix.

I was on all fours, helpless, but I swore to myself that if I possibly could, then somehow, some way, they were all going to pay for this, in the same currency they'd demanded from me and Tony: blood.

Seth stepped over Tony's prone form and I noticed something in his hand: a black baseball bat. He wielded it clinically, bringing it down in a vicious arc onto my head. I tried to raise an arm to protect myself but couldn't. I was too dazed, presumably because I'd been hit once already. I was aware of the bat striking me, then it was lights out and I entered the void.

The void is the place where you cease to exist as a person. It's a dark place of silence and nothingness. How long I remained there, I don't know.

It was a voice which brought me out of it for the first time.

'When will Charlotte wake up, Mum?'

That's when I began to surface. I didn't know who I was, or where I was. Then I smelled disinfectant. I felt myself tilt slightly, and realised I was in a hospital bed, and someone was sitting near me on the edge of it.

In the same instant I knew something very bad had happened to me, and was gripped by panic. I screamed, but no noise came from my mouth – I couldn't even open my mouth. The scream was entirely in my mind, and it almost drowned out the voices I was hearing, 'When will she wake up, Mum?'

'I don't know, love. Soon, I hope. But it might be never.'

I felt sensations on my scalp. Someone was gently stroking my hair. It made me feel better, so I stopped screaming, and began to wonder who my visitors were.

I recognised their voices, but when I tried to bring their names and faces to mind, it proved impossible. Then I felt sleepy. Experiencing consciousness of sorts for only those few seconds had exhausted me, and I sank back into the void.

A hand held my own hand tightly. Was this the same visit or another, later visit? If it was another visit, was it hours or months later? I don't know. All I can say for sure is that the sensation of my hand being held roused me, and I was able to listen to two people conversing for what seemed like several minutes.

'Charlotte, can you hear me?'

It was my mum – the woman who'd made my life hell. But now I was delighted and grateful to hear her voice.

'Mum,' I said, but the word never left my lips. I heard it in my head but knew I hadn't been able to say it.

'Charlotte, me and your dad are both with you. I hope you know that, love.'

My heart leaped in the knowledge that my parents were both present and I realised I loved them both. I tried to tell them I knew they were there, but didn't succeed. My nervous system wasn't ready, so I just did my best to enjoy their company.

The knowledge my parents were visiting me gave me reason to get well and recover. I promised myself I was going to get out of the place I was in, for their sake. Once I'd made the promise, my recovery began. I felt a tingling in my nervous system which told me positive things were happening to my body. I couldn't yet make any conscious movements, but I convinced myself I'd be able to, sooner rather than later.

That was when I remembered another promise I'd made to myself a long time before – that I was going to make a select group of people very miserable indeed. Who were they? Surely it'd come back to me. It had to. Something told me it was desperately important.

It took time, but gradually the lost knowledge I was seeking emerged from the mist. Namely, seven people had murdered my boyfriend and put me in hospital.

The seven people were: Seth Delaney, Charlie Duggan, Mike Stone, Stuart Foss, Danny Scott, Kylie Wood, and Jasmine Black.

HERE AND NOW

A s I left TNQ and Kylie headed back to her car, I couldn't help but notice I was only a few yards away from a pub called Psycho Jack's. It was an unusual name for a pub, and it caught my eye. I decided to explore the place to find out what it was like. You never know when such information is going to come in useful, after all. That was the lie I told myself at the time, anyway. But the real reason I went in there was to get a drink, because Kylie had set my nerves on edge.

I pushed open the door and went inside. The place had a pleasingly dark interior with plenty of good places to sit. Psycho Jack, or someone employed by him, a good-looking middle-aged man who looked like he could've gotten a bit-part in a movie, was busy polishing glasses behind the bar. He put his latest glass down as I approached. Naturally, there were craft ales on draft. Every pub in London has craft ales on draft these days. One of Psycho Jack's craft ales was fully nine point five per cent by volume. It looked like my kind of drink.

'A half of Crazy Jane, please,' I said.

'Coming right up,' he replied putting a glass under the nozzle. As the glass filled, I cast my eye over the place and saw a TV lounge through a doorway at the back. It was a touch I liked. I'm not a fan of TVs in pubs unless I want to watch one. This pub gave me the option of a room with a TV and another room without one.

Jack handed me my glass and I paid him using my contactless credit card. Then, as there was no-one around I wanted to talk to, I went through to the TV lounge so as not to have to endure my own thoughts.

The news was on, and the headlines were, as usual, relentlessly grim, which made me feel better about myself. There's nothing like somebody else's misery to make you realise you're not in as bad a place as you thought you were.

As I watched a procession of depressing news stories about war and death, refugees and famine – the all-too-usual fare – I wondered if I wasn't behaving too much like a sheep under a carving knife, the way I was just sitting around waiting to be bumped off. Maybe, I thought, instead of fretting about who had sent the baseball bat and what it might mean, and which of Seth's many enemies was out to get me, I should start thinking about how to save myself.

But what could I do?

No sooner had I had that thought then another struck me.

What if I'd been barking up the wrong tree entirely?

It wasn't Seth who was behind the killings. What if it wasn't one of his business rivals either? What if it was someone from the mutual past I shared with Seth who had reason to hate me?

Think, Jaz, who could hate you enough to kill you?

Then I began to think the unthinkable, the impossible, for only one such person came to mind: Charlotte Hawkins.

And it couldn't possibly be Charlotte.

She was the nearest thing to dead there could possibly be.

And the very nearly dead don't kill.

They can't.

Can they?

Charlotte was a member of the gang I used to hang around with at St Benedict's. There were eight of us: Charlotte, Seth Delaney, Charlie Duggan, Mike Stone, Stuart Foss, Danny Scott, Kylie Wood, and myself, Jasmine Black. I'm ashamed to say it wasn't a very nice gang, which is putting it mildly.

It hadn't been nice back in my schooldays, and it wasn't nice now, during my adulthood, insofar as it still existed. Four of the gang members were no longer around: Charlie was dead, killed at the school reunion. And so was Stuart, having been killed around the same time. And more recently Seth had shuffled off the mortal coil. As for Charlotte, she might as well have been dead, owing to what happened to her in the park near our school one night.

Seth was the leader of our gang. My relationship with him had been unusual, and probably unhealthy. He was my protector throughout my school years, the person who'd step in to save me if I was in jeopardy. Mind you, Charlotte helped me too, sometimes. She had a reputation for being 'hard', and I, for one, would never have crossed her.

Seth roped me into activities I'd sooner have missed. That was the price I paid for his protection. Because of my devil's bargain, I was never able to turn him down. An unholy mix of fear, respect, obligation, and perhaps even sublimated love made me do more-or-less everything he wanted. He had a kind of hold over me because I went to a rough school, and would've lived my life in fear, if not for him. Yes, we had sex together, but he asked me to keep it secret, and I did – he was going out with Kylie at the time. It was weak-willed of me to have sex with Seth behind Kylie's back, I know, but I've come on a lot since then.

I was sixteen, and a seasoned member of Seth's gang, albeit one who was unproven. I knew I'd be expected to prove myself at some time or other, and was dreading that time coming. The others had all proven themselves in the way Seth expected them to: by helping him inflict violence on an unlucky individual when required.

But he got his comeuppance: another gang beat the tar out of him and he had to spend time in hospital recovering. When I visited him, he said it'd been a surprise attack and he hadn't stood a chance. When he was discharged, he said he'd get even. Nothing seemed to come of it, and, as time passed by, I forgot about the incident.

Then one evening Seth called me on my mobile after school. 'Where are you?' he asked.

'On my way home.'

'Meet me at the park entrance. There's something we have to do.'

'What?'

'Remember the gang that attacked me? I know who one of them was.'

My stomach turned over. I knew what was coming.

'We're going to sort him out tonight,' he continued. 'It'll be your chance to show us what you're made of.'

The last thing I wanted was for Seth and the rest of them ever to find out what I was made of. I tried desperately to think of an excuse to go home, but none came to mind, so instead I decided to pretend to go along with things, but to definitely not hurt anyone – or get hurt myself, if I could help it. That said, I reckoned I'd sooner get hurt myself than hurt whatever victim Seth had singled out for vengeance.

When I got to the park entrance, Seth was there with Charlie, Mike, Stuart, Danny, and Kylie.

'Right, let's go, follow me,' he said.

'Where's Charlotte?' I asked.

'Never mind her,' said Seth. Kylie just shrugged.

We made our way along the tarmac paths running through the trees towards the middle of the park, where the children's playground was. As we neared it, we rounded a corner and practically bumped into two people, a teenage boy and girl, embracing each other and kissing.

'There he is, and look who he's with,' said Seth. 'What are you waiting for? Get stuck in!'

The others moved forward with Seth while I hung back, partly because I wasn't the violent type, and partly because I was shocked to see the teenage girl was Charlotte.

Charlie and Mike grabbed the boy while Stuart and Danny grabbed Charlotte, pulling them roughly apart.

I think everyone, except possibly Seth and Kylie, were shocked to see Charlotte in a clinch with one of the boys who'd beaten Seth up. They understood they were expected to pummel the boy, but were unsure about what to do with Charlotte. In the end it was all academic.

Seth had a baseball bat hidden under his jacket and so did Kylie. They pulled them out at the same time.

Seth smashed his on the boy's head. Kylie did the same to Charlotte, but caught her only a glancing blow. Even so, it was enough to knock her off her feet. As she lay on all fours on the tarmac path, eyes open and with a dazed expression on her face, Seth turned his attentions to her, belting the back of her head.

After Seth struck Charlotte she looked dead, or as close to death as it's possible to be without actually dying.

'Let's get out of here,' he said, running back along the path. We followed him like sheep back to his uncle's house. He took us there by way of a winding route and assembled us in the garage for a debriefing when we got there.

'No-one can ever talk about this,' he said. 'If any of us says anything, we'll all go down. Have you heard of joint enterprise?'

I shook my head.

'It means that if you're with a friend when he commits a crime, you'll get sentenced for it just the same as if you'd committed the crime yourself, so keep schtum. Anyone who doesn't will have me to answer to.'

None of us were likely to grass after what we'd just seen, irrespective of the law on joint enterprise. The thought of Seth wielding a baseball bat was enough to keep us all quiet.

For at least the next six months I was sick with worry.

I expected a knock on the door from a policeman at any minute, every hour I was at home. I don't know what I would've done if it had come. I couldn't grass up my best mate to the police, of course, but I'm far from certain I would have had the bottle not to crack under pressure. Anyway, the policeman's knock never came.

Apparently the police visited Seth's house, but he was so cool he was able to lie convincingly to them, and the coppers who came to question him went to other homes to pursue their enquiries, which never came to anything.

Seth's parents would have been horrified if they'd known about the incident, but of course, he never let on. To this day they probably think he can do no wrong, and that he's a respectable businessman.

'What the mind don't know, the heart don't grieve over,' was the way he explained it to me. It worked for him. At any rate, his parents were probably one of the reasons he got away with it. Softly spoken and deeply religious, who could have failed to believe them when they said their son would never do a thing like that, and he'd come home far too early to have been involved? (He managed to pull the wool over his parents' eyes about how long he'd been out exactly.)

The next day at the school assembly, the head teacher made an announcement about the crime, asked if anyone knew anything about it, and if so, would they please come forward with details? No-one did, although seven of us did know about it. Fear of, or admiration for Seth, or the Code of Silence, kept us from spilling our guts about who'd done what.

The boy who was with Charlotte – his name was Tony – died.

Charlotte herself, it later emerged, was terribly disabled due to brain damage. She ended up lying in a hospital bed, and she might as well have been dead to the world, given the prognosis which filtered out: she would never fully recover, and it was unlikely she'd ever think clearly, speak again, or communicate in any meaningful way.

Seth was cock-a-hoop when he heard the news.

'That's it,' he said. 'We're in the clear, as long as everyone sticks to the script. And everyone had better – if they don't want to end up like Charlotte or her dead boyfriend.'

Of course, he showed a different face to the world – a compassionate face, full of concern that one of his erstwhile best friends was in such a bad state. He was very accomplished when it came to that sort of thing. Looking back on it, the way he used to manipulate us with a combination of charm, charisma and menace, and the way he could so easily turn off one emotion (glee at Charlotte's injuries) and replace it with another (grief that Charlotte had been so badly hurt) he must have been psychopathic. I just didn't see it at the time, and when I eventually saw him for what he was, it was too late.

Anyway, the prognosis appeared to have been correct. If the medics had gotten it wrong, Charlotte would by now have told the police how she'd come to be injured so badly, and we'd all have had our collars felt.

Unless, that is, she'd recovered but chosen not to go to the police, and decided instead on a personal vendetta.

Could such a thing be possible?

It occurred to me that I ought to check on how she was doing. There might have been developments none of us had ever reckoned on – developments which were having life-shortening consequences.

I'd thought about Charlotte every day of my life since the incident, as I euphemistically referred to what had happened. I'd been racked with guilt and desperate to tell someone about it, and make a clean breast of things to the police. But the thought of Seth with his baseball bat put me off, as did the threat of being charged under the law of joint enterprise.

After leaving school I went to the University of Kent to study law, and eventually I qualified as a solicitor. What I saw, heard, and learnt, both on my legal courses and while practising law, convinced me the police were better kept in the dark about my part in Charlotte's fate, no matter what demands my conscience might make. There was a distinct possibility – not to say certainty – that everyone present when Tony was killed and Charlotte disabled, would be charged. The charge sheet would include at the very least: murder, attempted murder, and grievous bodily harm. It added up to a lot of sentence. In the worst-case scenario which featured in my paranoid imagination, it'd emerge at some stage during the trial I'd committed another serious crime – I was a hit-and-run driver who'd killed a young man, and I'd be convicted for that, too.

I made a determined effort to put my fears to the back of my mind, and to investigate the possibility, however far-fetched, that Charlotte had somehow made a miraculous recovery and was out to get me and the rest of the gang.

'Right, Jaz,' I said to myself, 'where do you start?'

The answer was obvious: at the hospital where she'd ended up. I had to find out if she was still hospitalised or if she'd been discharged.

11

WAY BACK WHEN

When I remembered the seven, I remembered something else, too: I needed to take their lives to make them pay.

The loathing I felt towards them gave me a new energy. It made me desperate to get better and get my revenge. I looked forward to the day that I'd be able to gloat over their dead bodies.

12

HERE AND NOW

I finished my half-pint of Crazy Jane and ordered another and another.

I should've been finding out what, if anything, Charlotte was up to, but I needed enough drink inside me to steady my nerves first. By the time they'd been steadied, I was thinking none too clearly, and it was tempting to carry on drinking all afternoon. Somehow I made myself stop and focus on my next move.

If memory served me correctly, Charlotte had ended up in St Thomas' Hospital. A quick search on my mobile gave me the details and I clicked on the number. Seconds later, I was speaking to a man who handled calls.

'Hello,' I said, and realised I hadn't taken the trouble to make up a convincing lie to get the information I needed. I had to think on my feet – luckily I'm a lawyer.

'Erm – my name's erm – Jackie Clarke. I think a cousin of mine is a patient here and I'd like to pay her a visit. Could you tell me what ward she's on, please?'

There was an ominous silence. Then, 'What's your cousin's name, Ms Clarke?'

'Charlotte Hawkins.'

Another silence but when I listened carefully I could hear keys being punched on a keyboard.

'Yes, we have a Charlotte Hawkins here. Ward thirty-five.'

My heart bounced in my chest. Why the news made me so excited I didn't know. It could've been apprehension as much as anything else.

'Thank you so much. Goodbye.'

I hung up. The thought struck me that if the Charlotte Hawkins in the hospital was the same Charlotte I knew at school, she couldn't have drugged me and posted the baseball bat to me, far less have killed three men. Anyway, I had to find out. It might be a different Charlotte they had in there. Maybe – if I was to entertain every possibility – Charlotte had found a way to replace herself with a fake Charlotte and she was walking around causing mayhem.

Or maybe she was faking disability and sneaking out of the hospital to kill people.

It was unlikely, but it'd been done. I'd seen a news story in 2015 about a man who'd faked a coma to avoid going to court. He'd convinced doctors he had a mystery illness, and it was two years before he was found out. Even then, it hadn't been medics who'd seen through his con – he'd been caught out by video footage which showed him shopping in a supermarket. It wasn't beyond the bounds of possibility that Charlotte was doing the same.

I stood up on legs which were only a little bit unsteady and headed for the railway station. It was about 2pm, the sky was a muddy sort of grey colour, and as I made my way through the crowded streets I felt as if I was being followed. Then I told myself I was being stupid – what Kylie had said had got to me, and I oughtn't let it. *God knows, Jaz, you have enough real worries to concern you without taking on any fake ones.*

The train got me to Westminster in half an hour including changes. I arrived there seven pounds and fifty pence the poorer because of the fare, and headed in the direction of the hospital. Soon enough I saw it: a huge concrete-and-glass box rearing up into the grey sky. I made my way to the entrance and looked around. The place was vast, and I didn't understand the signage, probably because my mind was in too much of a turmoil to interpret it. I sought help and saw a glass-walled reception area. Joining the long queue leading up to it, I noted an unmistakable smell in the air – an odour of disinfectant, mingled with, I fancied, serious illness.

Eventually I reached the head of the queue. A middle-aged male receptionist with grey hair, grey stubble, and green-framed spectacles stood before me, behind a glass screen. It had a rectangular hole in it. I spoke into the hole, beads of perspiration breaking out on my forehead. Was the unnatural level of heat in the place responsible? Or was it the stress I was feeling?

'Can you tell me the way to ward thirty-five please?' I asked.

He gave me a grin which was meant to be reassuring but did nothing to make me feel serene – not his fault. Then he pointed to his right.

'That way, straight along the corridor, lift at the end to floor three. You should find it easily enough from there.'

'Thank you.'

I turned and walked along the corridor, feeling deeply apprehensive about what I might find. I felt almost as guilty about Charlotte's injuries as if I'd inflicted them on her myself. I didn't want to have to face the results of what I thought of, in some ways, as my own handiwork, even though it wasn't. There was nothing I could've done to stop it, but I shouldn't have been there. What's more, having gotten myself into that situation, I shouldn't have run away with the others, and left Charlotte for dead. I should've called an ambulance and the police, to make sure she got prompt medical attention. For all I knew, it could have made all the difference. If I'd called an ambulance, maybe she would have been in a better state now.

And of course, Seth and Kylie, her attackers, had gotten clean away with it, and it was all down to me.

I entered the lift, pressed the button, and got out at the third floor, narrowly avoiding a bed being pushed by a porter, because I was too preoccupied to watch where I was going.

'Watch your step, madam,' he said. 'You'll cause an accident if you're not careful.'

'Sorry,' I said, avoiding the eye of the elderly patient on the bed who was giving me a filthy look.

Before me was a large rectangular landing with corridors leading off it. One of them was sign-posted 'Wards 30–35'. I made my way down the corridor under the glare of the artificial lighting – it had no windows to speak of – and pushed on the door of Charlotte's ward, number thirty-five. It wouldn't open. That was when I saw two further signs: 'Press buzzer for admission to ward' and 'Please make sure you use antiseptic handwash before entering and leaving the ward'.

I pressed the buzzer then doused my hands liberally in handwash, and rubbed them together until it dried, feeling distinctly like Lady Macbeth as I did so. And, just like Lady Macbeth, I found I couldn't wash off the stain of my guilt.

A click told me the door had been unlocked, so I opened it and proceeded through the corridor beyond, stopping at the nurses' station to ask for further directions.

'Charlotte Hawkins?'

The nurse on duty, a young woman with earnest blue eyes, glanced up from her papers and said, with a sideways nod of her head, 'Room eight, over there.'

'Thank you.'

When I got to room eight I saw Charlotte's name clearly written in felt tip pen on a whiteboard next to the door. All I had to do was push the door open and see, for the very first time since the incident, what my victim looked like – if indeed she was my victim. If she wasn't, then it was just possible Charlotte Hawkins had somehow made a miraculous recovery, and was going after everyone who'd taken part in turning her into a comatose wreck.

I grabbed the steel handle and slowly pushed the door open, hesitating before stepping through. When I did, and let go of the door, it closed on an automatic catch with a loud click which made me jump.

Classical music was emanating from a radio. It sounded like Mozart's *Piano Concerto Number Twenty-one*. The window was open at the far side of the room. A gentle wind briefly rattled the blind. Ahead of me was a bed, and in it a prone form. Could it be? I moved closer, hardly daring to look. Above the head of the bed, slightly to one side, a small handwritten placard informed me for the second time that the patient was Charlotte Hawkins. I approached until I was standing over her, my heart beating wildly. When I looked down at her face, I felt so weak I could've keeled over.

The patient's eyes were closed and she was wearing a peaceful expression. But who was she? Did I recognise her? She looked different, but she would, wouldn't she? The last time I'd seen her, I'd been in my mid-teens, nearly two decades ago. I'd changed since then, and didn't doubt she had, too.

'Charlotte,' I whispered. Then I said her name out loud: 'Charlotte.'

Her eyes opened, she looked up at me, and I swear to God there was recognition in those eyes. I stepped back in horror, as, beneath the covers, her body started moving.

I half turned to flee before realising she was moving because her bed was equipped with a special mattress to prevent her from getting bedsores.

When I turned back to Charlotte, the peaceful expression she'd had before was gone. In its place was something else. It looked like – and I didn't want to admit this – fear and loathing.

I should've left then, so as not to cause her any more distress, but didn't. Instead, I put my own needs first. I pulled up a chair, the legs squeaking on the tiled floor as I did so, sat next to her, and held her hand.

'Charlotte,' I said, 'it's me, Jasmine. I'm sorry I haven't visited before. You'll never know how much I've wanted to, and how sorry I am you're... you're – how sorry I am about what's happened.'

The expression on her face softened, or so I thought, and I felt her hand grip mine.

'My God,' I said. 'You know who I am, don't you, Charlotte?'

She didn't reply, not in any way anyone could have understood. She opened her mouth and a sound came out of it, a hoarse whisper, nothing more than a collection of meaningless vowels, 'Aaaahuuuooo.'

Was she trying to talk to me? If so, was she being friendly, or expressing her hatred of me? It was impossible to tell.

'I want you to know I had no idea you'd be in the park that day, and I never wanted you to get hurt. I didn't do anything to you. I just watched. I know I should've done something to stop it, but it all happened so quickly, and in any case, I was too scared to stop it, even if I'd thought to. I should have been a better friend to you, Charlotte.'

'Aaaahuuuooo.'

There it was again. What did she mean?

'I'm so sorry. I ought to go now, Charlotte. Goodbye.'

As I got to my feet the mattress made a creaking, breathing noise, and first raised, then lowered her legs with a wave-like motion. I retreated to the door. When I'd opened it I gave her a final backward glance and a pathetic wave, noticing when I did that her eyes seemed to be fixed on me. The knowledge chilled me to the soul, and I hastily made my way to the ground floor. As soon as I got outside I realised I'd been damn near holding my breath all the way to the exit. I stopped and breathed deeply, bending at the hips as if I'd just run a quick 400-metre race.

So that's it, Jaz. Charlotte couldn't be involved in the killings. Whoever's after you, it's not her. It must be some nutter Seth was involved with, just like Kylie said.

I headed back to the railway station, and, via two changes, ended up at Crystal Palace where I walked home. I couldn't remember if I'd stocked up with booze, so on the way I made further inroads into my credit limit by visiting the eight-till-late and buying a couple of bottles of red wine. Then, just in case two wasn't enough, I bought a third for good measure.

If you're going to die, I reckoned, you might as well look death fearlessly in the eye with a drunken smile on your face, and a glass of something in your hand strong enough to toast him with.

Back at my house I glanced at the clock on the kitchen wall. It was 5.09pm Where had the day gone? I put two wine bottles in my cupboard, noting it already had two in it, and placed the third on the table. 5.09pm was as good as any time to have a drink in my view. I unscrewed the top and poured about two-fifty mil into one of my best wine glasses. If Seth's enemies came round to get me tonight, they'd have it easy. I'd be too busy getting drunk to run away. But at least I'd die happy, sort of.

Thursday 5 April began with a hangover. When I got out of bed I felt sick, and had to rush to the en suite bathroom to throw up. It told me I'd had my money's worth the night before. Being hungover and throwing up my guts wasn't altogether a bad thing. It stopped me from feeling anxious, at least for a while, because I was preoccupied with feeling ill.

I donned my dressing gown and unlocked the bedroom door, cursing the lock for being a minor inconvenience I'd rather not have to deal with while suffering from the mother of all hangovers, and descended the stairs.

I started feeling anxious again almost as soon as I got to the bottom of them. There's a door from my kitchen, leading, via a small utility room, to my tiny back garden. The handle on the door was a bit stiff. I'd been meaning to get it fixed for ages, but never gotten round to it. I noticed the handle was down. I knew that whenever I used the utility room, I was always careful to force the handle up, because it wouldn't spring up of its own accord. As the handle was down, it could only mean someone else had been in my utility room. I pushed open the door, and saw the small window set in the outside door leading from the utility room to the garden had been broken. Glass was everywhere, all over the floor and worktop. The door itself was shut. When I tried it, it was obvious a very unprofessional burglar had smashed his way in. It must've been a noisy operation carried out late at night, but I'd been too trolleyed to hear it.

I went back indoors to check what had been taken. My iPad was missing, that was all, so far as I could see.

I'd left an unfinished bottle of wine on the worktop. It pained me to pour it down the sink, but I did, just in case the burglar hadn't really wanted my iPad, and had only taken it to make an assassination attempt look like a burglary.

My iPad had an app which meant that the person who'd stolen it could look at my E-mails without knowing the password. I went online and closed down the account. There weren't any other security leaks I could think of. The E-mail address wasn't linked to my bank account.

I called an emergency service and organised a UPVC glazing specialist to come out right away to secure the door and fix the glazing. While waiting for him to arrive, I cleared up the mess of broken glass my visitor had left.

The repairman came and went, and by late morning the damage had been fixed, and I'd taken a shower and had a couple of mugs of strong coffee. That was when the full horrible reality of my situation came back to me yet again and I had a panic attack. I remembered something about breathing through a paper bag, and I happened to have one in a kitchen drawer, so I clamped it over my nose and mouth and used it like an oxygen mask for a minute or two. It eased my panic just enough that I was able to function. I still felt lousy though.

What are you doing, Jaz? You're sleepwalking to death, that's what. You ought to be figuring out a way to survive. Put on your thinking cap for God's sake and do some figuring!

I made a third mug of strong coffee and sat at the kitchen table with it, then grabbed a notepad and pen and put them on the table in front of me.

Jaz, I told myself, *you have to become a private eye. You have to use all your skills – everything you've got – to figure this thing out and turn it round, and protect yourself, and maybe even – think the unthinkable – stay off the booze.*

I wrote some names on the first page of my notepad then crossed out the first three of them and put a question mark next to the fourth:

~~Charlie Duggan~~
~~Stuart Foss~~
~~Seth Delaney~~
Jasmine Black?
Danny Scott
Mike Stone
Kylie Wood

I'd thought this might shine some light on why people had been killed in a particular order, but was unable to make either rhyme or reason of it. It was probably just a matter of being in the wrong place at the wrong time. If things had worked out differently, I'd be one of the crossed-out names by now, the first one on the list. It was pure good luck which had spared my miserable life, the only good luck, it seemed, I'd ever had.

Given that four of us were left, it occurred to me we ought to get together and compare notes, maybe try to fight whatever we were up against as a team. I didn't really want to work with Mike and Kylie, as I didn't much care for them, but I decided if that's what it took to prolong my life, I could get on board with the idea.

I called Kylie. Her mobile went straight to the answering service so I left a message, 'Kylie, these people who are after us, the nutters that Seth got on the wrong side of. Can we talk about it? Maybe there's something we can do to stop them. It's worth discussing, anyway.'

As I hung up, I wondered if she was dead already and that's why she hadn't answered. I picked up my pen and put a question mark next to Kylie's name.

I tried Danny with the same result, so I put a question mark next to his name, too.

When I called Mike Stone he picked up immediately.

'Jaz,' he said, 'I haven't heard from you in quite a while. We didn't get to talk at the reunion. How are you?'

'I'm a barrel of laughs, Mike.'

He laughed uneasily. 'Anyway,' he said, 'let's cut to the chase. There must be a reason you're calling me.' Mike wasn't one for wasting time on small talk.

'You're right. I think you know what it is.'

There was a pause so pregnant it could have been an elephant about to give birth. 'Yes,' he said after a while. 'I think I do.'

'I'd like us to meet up. Maybe we could come up with a way to protect ourselves,' I said.

'I can't see how, but I'm willing to listen to what you have to say. You could come round to my place tomorrow morning to discuss it.'

'Yes, okay, I will, thank you.'

'About 11am?'

'That works for me.'

'Good, I'll see you tomorrow morning, then.'

He hung up, and I felt marginally better for having talked to him. I had the feeling I was taking, or trying to take, control of events, rather than just letting things happen to me. Maybe I should treat myself to some wine? Maybe not. I fought the urge with all I had. It was probably a losing battle but I didn't get to find out – my mobile rang, putting an end to my thoughts about wine. There was no name on the screen – it was a number I didn't know.

'Hello,' I said.

'Hi!' It was a youthful male voice, and whoever was speaking, he sounded in good cheer, unlike me.

'Who is it?' I snapped, wondering, for a moment, if it might be someone out to kill me.

'It's Jake, don't you remember?'

Of course, Jake. How stupid and paranoid of me to think my murderer was calling me on my mobile.

'Jake,' I said, 'it's good to hear from you.'

The truth was, it wasn't good to hear from him but I was so mightily relieved it was him who was calling me, and not someone sinister, that, to some small extent, his call was a welcome one.

'Hey, I'm glad you feel that way. Listen, I'm at a loose end tonight. How about we get together?'

I didn't know whether to feel flattered or acutely embarrassed. While I wasn't quite old enough to be Jake's mother, I certainly wasn't in his age bracket, not by a long shot. I was reminded of television documentaries I'd seen about May-to-December relationships. They were toe-curling, as they featured deranged old men clinging to absurdly young women, and deranged old women clinging to absurdly young men. I could be lining myself up to be one of them. There were other things to consider: If I met him, what would we have in common? What could we discuss? Would people look at us, and think I was a cradle-snatcher? And what future could we possibly have, given the age difference?

Then I thought: *bollocks to that, I'm on a downer and I need cheering up.* 'Yeah, sure, why not?'

'Don't sound so enthusiastic!'

'Sorry, I've been going through a bad patch lately.'

'You can tell me all about it tonight.'

No I can't, I thought. 'It's a long story. Where do you want to meet, and when?'

'How about 7.30pm at The Grape and Grain?'

'Okay, see you there.'

I had a couple of hours in which to get ready. I showered and changed, and took extra care over my make-up in an attempt to make myself look younger, or at the very least more presentable.

Perhaps inevitably, I drank too much while I was out with Jake and woke up remembering little or nothing of the evening. At least I woke up in my own bed. The bad news was, Jake was in it with me. I'd have preferred him not to be. He was spark out, so maybe he'd overdone it as well.

I got up and took a shower, then put on some clothes and shook him until he woke up.

'I have to go somewhere this morning,' I said. 'I'll make you a coffee then we'll have to part company.'

He rubbed his eyes. 'Okay, got you.'

I went to the kitchen thinking about what I was going to say to Mike later in the morning. Jake soon joined me. 'What's this list all about?' he asked.

I had my back to him and didn't know what he was referring to. 'What list?'

'Charlie Duggan,' he said, 'Stuart Foss, Seth Delaney, Jasmine Black, Mike Stone, Danny Scott, Kylie Wood. Why are some of these names crossed out? And why is there a question mark next to your name, and next to Danny Scott and Kylie Wood, whoever they are?'

I turned and saw he had my notepad in his hands. This wasn't a discussion I felt I could have with him, or with anyone not connected with what remained of our group.

'I was planning a party.'

'Aren't I invited?'

'Wait and see. I've only just started making the list.'

I put a mug of coffee in front of him, praying to God he'd drink it quick and go. I was beginning to think I'd made a terrible mistake. A relationship with a nineteen-year-old – what had I been thinking? Plus, I had to get over to Mike's place for 11am.

'What kind of party is it?'

I couldn't help myself. The words just slipped out. 'The killing kind.'

He looked at me as if I'd become unhinged. 'What?'

I had to pull the fat out of the fire somehow. 'I'm sorry, what I meant is, it's a murder mystery. One of those dinner parties where you have to work out whodunit, a bit like a game of Cluedo.'

'Oh yeah, I know the type,' he said, slurping the last of his coffee. He stood up to go, and I walked him to the door, where he insisted on kissing me. Then he glanced at his watch. 'If I hurry I'll just be in time for the first lecture,' he said.

'What?'

'You haven't already forgotten I'm a student, have you?'

I had. I must've been dead drunk when he told me. 'No, of course not. Have a good day. Enjoy the lecture.'

Halfway down the path he gave me a backward glance. 'I'll call you,' he said. Then he was on his way, and I went back indoors wondering what fresh terrors the day would spring on me.

Mike Stone lived far enough away from me to justify using my car to visit him, but I was worried I was still over the limit, so I caught the train to Honor Oak Park then walked up the hill to his place, a rambling Victorian property which was far too big for one person. Still, he lived there alone for whatever reason.

I pressed the doorbell and he let me in, a skeletal smile on his face. He was wearing a red silk dressing gown over navy cotton pyjamas.

'Isn't it time you were dressed, Mike?' I asked.

'I've been too busy to get dressed.'

Mike's jowls wobbled when he talked. He looked just the way I remembered him from school, but more so: he was thickset and would've been good-looking if not for the fact he'd got too much weight around his middle, and lately he'd piled it on around his neck too, with the result that his neck flab made odd movements every time he spoke or turned his head. He was sweating like onions in a hot pan of oil, and not just because he was overweight. He was over-wrought, like me.

As he led me down the expansive hall of his grand house, I noticed a couple of suitcases on the floor at the bottom of the staircase.

'Come into the front room,' he said, ushering me through a door. 'Can I get you a drink?'

'Coffee, please, black, no sugar.'

As he turned to go to the kitchen, I noticed a bald patch on the back of his head. He was only in his early thirties. I wondered if his hair loss was stress-related.

He brought the coffee in and placed mine on a long low table in front of the sofa I'd chosen to sit on. He put his own on a similar table, went to a glass-fronted drinks cabinet, and took out a bottle of whiskey. He poured a generous amount into his coffee then offered the bottle to me.

'No, thanks,' I said. It took everything I had to refuse his offer. 'I'm recovering from last night's binge,' I explained.

'Best thing for a hangover, this,' he said, taking a sip of his fortified coffee.

I thought we ought to get down to the business at hand.

'Three of us are dead, Mike,' I said. 'Charlie, Seth, and Stuart. There's been an attempt on my life, and what's more, I haven't been able to get in touch with Danny or Kylie. What do you make of it all?'

He pursed his fleshy lips. 'What really scares me is they got Seth. I always thought he was untouchable.'

The smell of coffee wafted up from the mug on the low table in front of me. I picked up the mug, held it under my nose and breathed in deeply, enjoying the dark fragrance. Then I replied, 'So did I. The big question is what are we going to do? I suppose we all thought that if something like this ever happened, Seth would come out on top and save us. It seems we have to save ourselves. But how?'

'I've been giving it a lot of thought since you called me yesterday. We don't know who's out to get us, so frankly, there's nothing we can do, other than run away and go to ground. Danny's already done that. He advised me to do the same and I'm taking his advice. I've been packing my bags.'

I took a sip of the coffee. It was strong enough to stand up a spoon in, which was what I needed.

'Yeah, I noticed.'

He poured another slug of whiskey into his coffee. 'I suggest you go to ground too.'

I gave it some thought. Maybe he was right, but I didn't want run away. It seemed like such a complicated solution. What would I do about my house, how would I earn money to live, and how would I fix myself up with a new identity?

'Is that the best we can do? Just run away?'

He nodded, sending fleshy ripples up and down his neck. 'Yep, I'm afraid so.'

His solution was drastic, but I had to admit it made sense. If they'd got Seth, the rest of us wouldn't have a chance.

'But where, Mike, and for how long?'

He shook his head, creating more ripples on the second chin beneath his jaw. 'I'm not telling you. With the best will in the world, I daren't. You might tell.'

'I'd never do a thing like that, Mike. You know I can keep secrets. I've kept ours all these years. I haven't told a soul.'

'I know, Jaz. But some people would do anything to get the information out of you.'

My stomach churned when he said that. Until then, I hadn't really considered what sort of people we might be up against. Now it was clear to me: the sort who were willing to torture me before taking my life. They were probably like Seth, but even more vicious, if it was possible to be more vicious than Seth.

'I ought to go pack my own bags,' I said, finishing the dregs of my coffee.

'Yes,' he said softly. 'Sorry I couldn't be more help. Oh, one more thing. Watch your back. You never know who could be waiting for the right moment to see you off.'

'Have you been watching your back, Mike?'

'Yes, ever since Charlie died. I couldn't be sure at the time, but I took it as a sign that business in these parts might be getting danger-ous. I'm not sticking around to find out for myself how dangerous it could get.'

I stood up. 'I'll let myself out. You get on with your packing or whatever.'

'Okay, I'll see you around, Jaz.'

'Sure, see you around, Mike.'

I closed the door knowing I was closing it for good, as far as our relationship was concerned. I knew I'd never see him again, because before long, I'd be dead, or he'd be dead, or both of us would be.

If Mike was the one who carked it, it'd be no great loss as far as I was concerned – he reminded me of bad things in my past, so I was unable to enjoy his company. Even so, it saddened me to think I'd seen him for the last time.

As I headed quickly back down the hill to Honor Oak Park Station, dark clouds gathered overhead – a neat metaphor for the way my life was going.

When I got home I took my luggage from the cupboard beneath the stairs – a large and small wheelie case – and carried both cases up to my bedroom. I was about to start packing when the thought occurred to me: I'd have to tell my parents and brother I was leaving town. Then what? They'd want an explanation, obviously. What would I tell them?

Then I wondered, *If someone came looking for me, what would they do?* Would they try to find out where I was by torturing my mum and dad, or my brother? Or all three of them together? Those scenarios didn't bear thinking about.

I realised I couldn't follow Mike's example and leave. I had to hang around, and take whatever lay in store for me, to spare my family.

I put my bags away and wondered if I could arm myself and fight off my future assassin. Then I remembered his or her weapon of choice seemed to be poison and I couldn't fight that off. But I could continue to be a bit canny – and make sure nothing I ate or drank could be tampered with. Sooner or later, I reflected, that'd force my assassin to use another method – and in doing so, he'd have to show his hand. When he did, I'd be ready and waiting for him.

Such was the plan, anyway.

I only hoped I'd have the willpower to stay sober enough to execute it.

My mobile rang, interrupting my thoughts. Kylie's name appeared on the screen.

'Hi, Kylie,' I said, swiping it and putting it to my ear. 'Thank God you've called. I was beginning to think something had happened to you.'

'Sorry for worrying you,' she said. 'I've only just picked up your message. I'd love to get together, but I can't imagine what we can do to fight this thing.'

My free hand was resting on the back of a chair. It trembled slightly. I wondered whether that was due to withdrawal symptoms, or stress, or both.

'I have a few ideas. Let's meet up.'

'TNQ ASAP?'

I was feeling too strung-out to leave the house again. 'No, thanks, it'd be better if you came to my place.'

'Why?'

'I'll explain when you get here.'

'Okay, see you in half an hour.'

When Kylie arrived I made us both drinks and took them through to the front room.

'This is all very mysterious,' she said. 'You must explain why you didn't want to meet at TNQ.'

I looked at her over the top of my mug of coffee and took a sip before answering. 'I'm sorry, I was having a bit of a panic attack, that's all.'

She nodded. 'I suppose I shouldn't be surprised. I've had one or two myself lately. What are these ideas of yours?'

I put down my mug. 'I don't have a lot of great ideas, just one small one. The murderer, whoever he or she is, uses poison, so watch your food and drink. Make sure it isn't tampered with. That includes the food in your own house. I've been broken into, and it might have been more than a simple burglary.'

She nearly dropped her coffee but recovered without spilling any. 'What?'

'I had a visitor the other night. He came in through the back door and he didn't use the key. He left a pile of broken glass in the utility room and took my iPad. But what if he didn't break in to steal things from me? What if his real motive was poisoning me?'

'That's scary,' she said.

'I can't be certain, but someone might have been trying to poison my food. I'm making sure everything I eat and drink is tamper-proof. I suggest you do the same.'

She eased off her shoes and curled her legs under her body. 'It sounds like a lot of work, but I suppose it has to be done.'

'It's not a lot of work, it's dead easy. If you find it hard, motivate yourself by considering this: if we take away his best weapon – poison – he'll be forced to do something else. He might start making mistakes. With luck, we'll be able to get him.'

She frowned. 'Assuming there's only one of him,' she said. 'There could be a few people behind this.'

'Whatever. At least this way we might have a chance. Another thing you need to do is arm yourself. If he can't use poison, he'll try to find another way.'

'That's a cheerful thought. Do you have any more good news?'

'It was never going to be good news, Kylie.'

'I know.'

We sat in silence for a while, me mulling over my chances of survival, Kylie perhaps doing something similar. She finished her drink and stood up. 'I'm going now. I'll think about what you've said. Maybe I'll do it – or more likely I'll just leave town and hide out somewhere.'

I wondered if she'd got the idea off Mike. 'Following Mike's advice, eh?'

'Mike?'

'I saw him this morning. He's leaving town, like you. Haven't you heard?'

Her eyebrows shot up. 'I haven't been in touch with him since the reunion. Anyway, I can't say I blame him.'

I walked her to the door wondering if I should tell her she'd be putting her family at risk by leaving, then decided not to – she'd soon figure it out for herself, if she hadn't done already.

'All right,' I said. 'Good luck with that. Keep in touch.'

'I will. See you.'

As she climbed into her car, I got the feeling Kylie was another person I'd never see again. We weren't close, we weren't even on good terms, in fact we were barely on terms at all, but even so, I hoped my feeling was wrong. Death was getting to be a close companion and I'd already had more than enough of his company.

13

: WAY BACK WHEN

Once I'd recovered my ability to think, I devoted every hour of every day to directing my consciousness into every part of my body, starting with my toes.

I'd think about them individually, trying to feel them and get them to move. From there I'd work upwards, through my shins, knees, thighs and torso, trying to detect something – pressure on my skin, responsiveness – anything other than deadness. It was a fruitless task for a very long time.

Then at last I had a breakthrough: I opened my eyes. This caused great excitement among the medical staff who were caring for me. They immediately summoned a doctor. He murmured something about 'Glasgow Scale four' and said it was a very positive development. He leaned over my bed and spoke to me. 'Keep it going, Charlotte,' he said. 'We're all delighted with what you've achieved so far.'

Perhaps he said it to all his coma patients, but his words motivated me, whether or not they were his standard spiel. It was as if he knew that opening my eyes hadn't happened by accident, and he was praising me for working as hard as I had done. So I followed his advice and kept it up, teaching myself to move my fingers and make speech-like sounds. Eventually I learnt to take food through my mouth, as long as I was spoon-fed.

More than anything, I looked forward to the day I'd walk again. I was convinced I'd make a full recovery. The possibility I wouldn't fully recover never occurred to me. It was too horrible a fate to contemplate – a life in a hospital bed, devoid of activity, utterly devoid of meaning, and consumed by emotions I could barely cope with – hate, and the lust for vengeance being chief among them.

I lay there day after day, stewing in my own vengeful juices, aware of my stomach churning, bile often enough rising in my throat because I was so angry. Much as my anger gave impetus to my efforts to recover, I became aware I'd have to do something to quell it, because it was taking a toll on me. It made me throw up from time to time, gave me indigestion, and put me into a deep, dark downward emotional spiral.

My hate would've killed me in the end, but I saw the danger and turned it around. I listened and learned, hoovered up any information I could that would be useful to me, and discovered meditation. Then, by a sheer effort of will, I found a new way of thinking. It took time, but over the course of many years of meditation I reached a sort of inner peace and developed the strength to forgive my enemies. I became able to recite their names without feeling any negative emotions about them: Seth Delaney, Charlie Duggan, Mike Stone, Stuart Foss, Danny Scott, Kylie Wood, and Jasmine Black. I was able to wish them well, hope they'd found the same sort of enlightenment I had. I even hoped they weren't all living in fear because of what they'd done to me.

My days became tolerable, and at times good, once I'd jettisoned my hate and anger. I focussed on the positive things in my life – visits from my family and friends, radio shows, television – there was always some form of broadcast going on in my room, intended to provide me with stimulation – and I lost myself in my thoughts.

By the time I realised I'd never fully recover, and this was as good as it was going to get, I was mentally equipped to deal with the situation, courtesy of my new approach to life in a hospital bed.

My peace was only broken when one day I received a visit from someone I never expected to hear from.

She pushed open the door slowly, and hesitated before coming into my room, unlike my other visitors, so I knew it was someone who hadn't been before. I had my eyes shut. I was tempted to open them, but decided to wait to find out who it was. After all, this was a big event, probably the high point of my day – a new visitor – and I wanted to milk it for all it was worth.

Footsteps on the tiled floor told me my new acquaintance was advancing slowly, cautiously towards me. I heard my name, 'Charlotte.' It was a woman's voice, speaking in a whisper. 'Charlotte,' she repeated, speaking my name out loud this time.

The voice was all too familiar to me: it was Jasmine Black. Being helpless and alone, I felt threatened. *What is she doing here?* I wondered. My mind went into wild speculations about the purpose of her visit. *She is here to kill me,* I decided, *to make sure the truth about what she and the others had done never gets out. Seth has sent her.*

I opened my eyes to make sure I was right. I was: there, looking down at me I saw her, Jasmine Black. She stepped back, the expression on her face mirroring the fear I felt deep in my soul, and I realised our meeting was as scary for her as it was for me, possibly even more so. Lines of concern were etched in her face. I knew then that she wasn't visiting in order to kill me, and I relaxed. She pulled up a chair rather noisily, sat next to me, held my hand and squeezed it gently, affectionately. My senses have in some ways become more acute during my incarceration in hospital. I was vividly aware of the feeling of her skin against mine. It felt smooth, dry, warm, and reassuring. I sniffed the air, and smelled the remains of a recent binge drinking session oozing from her pores. Then I noticed she wasn't wearing any perfume, and, taking another sniff like a dog, I detected the pleasing fragrance of the shower gel she'd used, the shampoo on her hair, and the deodorant she'd applied to her armpits.

'Charlotte,' she said, gently squeezing my hand again, 'it's me, Jasmine. I'm sorry I haven't visited before. You'll never know how much I've wanted to, and how sorry I am you're... you're – how sorry I am about what's happened.'

What purpose she had I didn't know, but at least it didn't seem sinister.

'My God,' she added. 'You know who I am, don't you, Charlotte?'

I was surprised she seemed able to read my emotions from the expressions on my face. Then I thought, *The nursing staff can do that, so why not Jasmine?* I answered her as best I could. I wanted to tell her I knew her, and I'd long since let go of my bad feelings about her. I knew any attempt on my part to communicate with her was doomed to failure, but I had to try. 'Aaaahuuuooo.'

She didn't understand, of course.

'I want you to know I had no idea you'd be in the park that day, and I never wanted you to get hurt. I didn't do anything to you. I just watched. I know I should've done something to stop it, but it all happened so quickly, and in any case, I was too scared to stop it even if I'd thought to. I should've been a better friend to you, Charlotte.'

I attempted to reassure her, tell her all was forgiven. 'Aaaahuuuooo.'

The puzzlement on her face told me she hadn't understood. 'I'm so sorry. I ought to go now, Charlotte. Goodbye.'

I would've liked her to have stayed longer but she let go of my hand and left after that.

For the remainder of the day, my thoughts were in a state of turmoil, and it was several days before I managed to rein in my feelings and restore the peaceful frame of mind I'd been so carefully cultivating for many years.

14

HERE AND NOW

With Kylie gone, I was alone with my thoughts. The situation wasn't entirely welcome. I retreated to the kitchen to make another coffee and glanced at the calendar. It was still 5 April, and I was still feeling out of sorts, partly from the drink I'd imbibed the day before, partly from the general shitness of my existence. I considered having a hair of the dog to make me feel better, or at least well enough to make it through to five o'clock, when I could allow myself to drink without a getting a guilty conscience about it.

I reached into my wine cupboard but managed to summon up the willpower to stop myself from taking a bottle out of it. As I stood in the middle of the kitchen wondering what to do to kill time until I could drink with a clear conscience, my stomach spoke up. It told me I should eat, so I looked in my fridge, selected a spaghetti bolognaise meal for one, and gave it a dose of full-on radiation in the microwave oven on my worktop. That got it so hot I nearly burnt my tongue on the first morsel I spooned into my mouth. As for the taste, the flavour had something of a chemical edge to it, making me suspect it might contain poison, but of a kind put there by the manufacturer rather than by an assassin. When I'd finished I washed up and went to the front room to chill out with a cup of tea.

Chilling proved impossible because I was about as strung-out as it's possible for a body to be. But I was dealing with it, at least for now. I picked up the remote and switched the TV on to a news channel, being the news junkie I am. There was lots of stuff going on in the world, all of it bad. It occurred to me that sometime soon, my own death was probably going to get a mention. It wouldn't be a big item, and it probably wouldn't make the national news, but it'd definitely be reported locally. I could see the *London Evening Standard* giving me a couple of column inches, and there'd be something on one of the radio stations covering my area – maybe KISS if I was lucky – and a brief item on local TV.

'Defence lawyer poisoned – foul play suspected'. That'd be the headline, or something like it. A couple of weeks later there'd be a tiny two-line obit paid for by my parents, something about a loving daughter who'd be sorely missed. It made me sad to think about my parents and brother missing me. It was almost worse than the thought of death itself. I wished there was something I could do to spare them the misery of having to find me dead, or be informed by a grim-faced copper that I'd died.

The thought of my parents having to answer questions like 'did your daughter have any enemies you know of?' was too much to bear. I finished my tea and opened a bottle of merlot. The first glass hit the spot so well I promptly poured another, and another. By late afternoon my nerves were well-settled and I was multi-tasking. I had a cheap tablet on my lap (the one my iPad had superseded before being stolen), a paperback novel on the sofa next to me, and the TV spewing out as much news as anyone was capable of taking in on any given day. I turned my attention from one to the other to the other, lost in my own little world.

Mid-evening when I got hungry I ordered a takeaway pizza – I reckoned the chances of the poisoner working in the self-same fast food outlet I was ordering from were too remote to bother about. It was a margherita which proved disappointing, and I made a mental note never to use the place again. Nevertheless I ate it all, even including the burnt bit of crust around the edge. It filled my belly and made me drowsy.

At some point I must've fallen asleep on the sofa. When I woke up the TV was on, an open bottle of red was in front of me on a low occasional table with an empty glass next to it, telltale red stains in the bottom, and there was an empty pizza carton next to me. *Christ, I'm not a slut,* I thought. *Why didn't I get myself a plate and eat properly? I must've been pretty drunk to eat straight out of the carton and leave the mess by my side.*

I was about to clear it away when a news item caught my attention. Something about a man overdosing and dying in his own garden. There was a shot of the street where the death had occurred. It looked like the Honor Oak Park area where Mike lived, but it couldn't be Mike who'd died. He'd left town. Anyway, whoever it was, he was probably just a junkie who'd taken too much of the wrong stuff, so there was nothing for me to worry about.

I poured a final glass of wine and dragged myself off to bed, wondering at the coincidence of the death on Mike's road.

When I woke up, somewhat the worse for wear, I'd forgotten about the body that'd been found in Honor Oak Park. After I'd showered and dressed, I brewed a coffee and sat in front of the TV to watch the morning headlines, first nationally, then locally. Christ knows why I enjoy such stuff. Maybe 'enjoy' is the wrong word. It's more that it has always had an eerie hold on me.

When the local news was broadcast the main subject covered was the death I'd heard about during the night. It was no longer being attributed to an overdose. Foul play was suspected. As a result, a lot of airtime was given over to it. Nothing excites the interest of the public at large – including me – as much as 'orrible murders do.

The name of the victim was a shock: Mike Stone. How could it be? Obviously, when I'd first heard about the death, I should've worked it out, but I'd been too pissed to think straight and in addition I'd given Mike's survival instincts more credit than they were due.

Poor Mike had been found behind his car with two suitcases next to him. It seemed someone had gotten to him before he'd had the chance to make his getaway. By the time he was ready to go, it was already too late. He'd been poisoned and was very nearly dead.

He'd picked up his cases and taken them to his car, then collapsed on his gravel drive without even having opened the car door to stow his cases in the luggage area. He'd remained on his drive for an hour or two before being discovered, as his car, a large four-by-four, had hidden him from the view of passers-by walking up and down the street.

It was devastating news. The more members of the gang who were killed, the more likely it became that I'd soon be a target on the killer's list. The list was now very short, consisting only of Danny Scott, me and Kylie, which gave me a one-in-three chance of being taken out next. I'm not the betting type, but even so I knew those weren't great odds. My hands shook with fear just thinking about it.

I wondered if there was any chance the killer would leave me alone. After all, he might think he'd done enough to me by slipping me a Mickey Finn and sending me a baseball bat through the mail. It was a notion which gave me succour for approximately five seconds. No, I soon decided, whatever the reason he hadn't killed me, he'd be coming to get me in the near future. If he was out to slay all the members of the old gang, and it seemed he was, there was no reason he'd spare me. I was probably meant to die in a car crash, but fate had stepped in and I'd survived. The killer would undoubtedly have a second bite of the cherry and he'd make damned sure he bit enough of it to finish me off next time round.

My mobile beeped interrupting my thoughts. It was Bernie, my AA counsellor. I couldn't bring myself to admit to him I'd fallen off the wagon and watched it drive so far up the street I didn't have any chance of climbing back on, so I ignored it.

The mobile stopped ringing then started again, about two seconds later. It was Bernie again. The pattern was repeated until I picked up, on the fifth time of being rung.

'Bernie,' I said, wondering how to explain myself, what excuse I could give. 'I've been... ah...' my voice tailed off. What had I been doing? More to the point, what could I claim to have been doing?

'You've been drinking,' he said.

He'd got me bang to rights. 'How did you know?'

'For a start you haven't been to any meetings lately, which is always a sign. Secondly, you felt obliged to explain yourself to me, but you couldn't come up with any sort of an explanation. You're not a good liar. Thirdly, you slurred your words when you answered.'

Christ, I'd slurred some words and I hadn't even noticed. I'd thought I'd delivered them with perfect diction. What was I coming to?

'I'm sorry, Bernie, things are tough for me right now.'

'I'm here to help. We could meet up if you want support, even if that just means complaining to me about all the shit things in your life.'

I wondered what he'd think if I did as he suggested. He'd probably fall down with shock if he knew I'd killed a young man and left the scene of the crime; and been a member of a gang which had killed a young man and left a young woman with such life-changing injuries she might as well have been dead; and was involved in a cover-up; and was doing my best to survive a mad killer who was out to poison me the first chance he got.

'That's very good of you, Bernie, but I can't. I've got a lot on at present.'

'Just remember I'm here for you. And no matter what, you can always come back to the meetings. Drop in tonight if you can.'

'I'll do my best. See you, Bernie.'

'I'll keep in touch. I'm not going to let you go. You're too young and too talented to fall by the wayside.'

'Thanks,' I said, hanging up.

Too young and too talented – it's not how I saw myself, but I'd gratefully take that praise from anyone.

I had the rest of Friday to kill but how would I do it? By hanging around pointlessly until someone murdered me? If they tried, would I manage to escape them? If I managed to escape, would it grant me anything more than a temporary reprieve?

My internal debate, I realised, amounted to a very good argument for staying on the sauce. But I wasn't going to spend every minute of the day drunk. I had to find other ways of diverting myself.

For lack of anything better to do I called Jake. I needed buoying up and he could provide some buoyancy. There's something about being a woman in your early-to-mid thirties. You feel as if the clock's ticking, your bloom is fading, and you've lost, or are on the verge of losing, your allure. So having a man – a younger man at that – who acts as if you've still got it in spades is quite the morale booster. Or at least it was for me.

'Hi, Jake,' I said when he answered. I almost added 'how's it hanging?' When you spend time in the company of younger people, it's tempting to talk young, but if you did you'd get it all wrong. It's one of those pitfalls you have to avoid, so instead I said, 'How are you?' Far more appropriate for an older woman.

'I'm good, Jaz.'

'Do you fancy getting together?'

'I thought you'd gone off me the way you couldn't wait to get me out of your house the other day.'

'Sorry if I was a bit brusque. I had a lot on.'

'No worries. When do you want to meet?'

That's what I liked about Jake. He was easy-going, he enjoyed seeing me, and was good-looking to boot. What was not to like? 'When are you available?'

He was silent for a moment, presumably considering his plans for the day. 'Let me see, I've got a couple of lectures and an assignment to finish but I could get out to meet you at seven.'

Seven. I didn't want to meet him after I'd been drinking and wondered if I could possibly stay dry until then. It was going to take a mighty effort.

'Okay, how about Westow House?'

'Yeah, I like the place. See you there at seven.'

I glanced at the clock. It was only 11am. There was a lot of day to get through before seven o'clock in the evening. I did a few chores, got some lunch, took a walk, read part of a novel, and somehow by sheer effort of will got myself to Westow House at 7pm stone-cold sober. Mind you, my heart was racing and I was in desperate need of alcoholic nourishment. As Jake wasn't around I got myself a pale ale. It was strong enough, at nine per cent, to do the job I needed it to, and I figured it'd last longer than a small glass of red wine. It didn't. But by the time I'd finished it my nerves were slightly less ragged. It was partly down to the alcohol but also something else. You can only spend so much time worrying. When you're up against it, your body occasionally turns off the worry switch to give you a break. You should never get complacent when that happens – it gets turned back on again soon enough.

Jake showed up just as I was about to go to the bar to get another. He looked at my empty glass. 'What are you drinking?' he asked – so considerate.

I managed to give him a big grin. With the worry switch at 'off' for a change, I was, for once in my miserable life, feeling something approximating to happy and I wanted to make the most of it while it lasted. 'I'll have a glass of merlot please – a large one.'

Then I felt tight asking for it, because he was a student and presumably on a limited income.

'I tell you what, Jake, I'll go Dutch with you on this round,' I said, getting my purse from my bag.

He shook his head. 'No need, you get the next one.'

We were buying rounds then, which suited me. I just hoped he could afford the number of rounds I'd need to get properly relaxed. If he couldn't, I'd sub him. I could think of no better use for my overdraft than applying it to getting dead drunk as I waited for death to catch up with me. Then as Jake headed for the bar I had a horrible thought: what if the poisoner knew I was here and was hanging around just waiting for an opportunity to slip something into my drink? I stood up and followed Jake so I could keep an eye on things.

'I can manage to carry two drinks on my own,' he said when he saw me standing next to him. 'You sit down.'

'I... er... just wanted to make sure there wasn't any other red wine I would've liked more,' I told him. Then, when the barman appeared, I was forced to ask: 'What red wines do you do by the glass, please?'

'We have a shiraz, a cabernet sauvignon and a merlot.'

I looked at Jake. 'I'll stick with my first choice,' I told him. 'Merlot.'

I linked Jake's arm as we stood at the bar so as not to arouse suspicion I might be watching over him. He must've thought I'd become more affectionate than usual but he didn't comment on it.

We returned to our table armed with drinks. Halfway through my red wine I had the urge to have a pee. I was about to go to the loo when I had another of my horrible thoughts: Jake doesn't know to keep watch over my drink. Then I had an even worse one. *Hang on a minute, Jaz. Maybe you're missing something. Maybe you've been missing it all along. Jake has a tattoo on his arm – the letter 'J'. It's in an ornate script and it's about four inches high. Charlotte has a brother called Joshua.*

Is it possible Charlotte's brother is the one doing the killings? And if so, is it possible that Jake is really Joshua? That he's had to use a pseudonym beginning with the letter 'J' because of his tattoo? And he's dating me in order to find an opportunity to kill me? He's the right age to be Joshua, when I think about it.

When I visited Charlotte in hospital I wasn't able to understand a word she said – but possibly the people who know her well can interpret those sounds she's making. I've heard of disabled people communicating by blinking out Morse code with their eyelids – so it's not too much of a stretch to suppose she's told Joshua what happened to her and Tony.

The more I thought about it, the more worried I got about going to the loo and leaving my drink unattended. And the more I worried about that, the more I became convinced Jake was really Joshua. I decided I better not act suspicious. If he was Joshua, it was best to keep him in the dark about what I knew, or thought I knew. That way I might be able to outwit him. Anyway, I needed the loo so I necked the remainder of my wine so as to prevent anything from being slipped into it while my back was turned, then I stood up.

But I couldn't go right away – Jake might be tempted to buy me a drink during my absence and I'd have to decline to drink it, which would tip him off I was on to him. A subtle change of plan was needed.

'Drink up,' I said. 'I'm going to the bar.'

His eyebrows shot up into his unlined forehead giving it enough creases to rival my own for once.

'You gulped that down,' he said.

I ignored the remark. 'What're you having?'

'A pint of pale ale, please.'

'I have to pay a visit,' I explained. 'Back in a mo. I'll get the drinks on my return.'

When I came out of the loo I went straight to the bar and bought another round.

'This is going some, even for you,' Jake said when I put them on our table. He'd noticed I drank a bit by the sounds of things.

'I suppose you're right. I ought to slow down. We have the whole night ahead of us.'

That wasn't the only reason I was planning to slow down. I had to be alert to what was going on. There was no telling what might happen if I wasn't – and if I was right about Jake being Josh, I'd have to really be on my toes. I kept my glass near me so he'd have to stretch to reach it if he wanted to put something in it.

'Something wrong?' he asked.

Damn – what was I doing to make it obvious? I shook my head but did so rather too quickly. 'No, why do you ask?'

'You just seemed to be looking at me in a funny way.'

I was in danger of giving away what I suspected – that Jake was really Joshua. Somehow I had to make a recovery. I gave him a semi-sideways and furtive sort of stare. 'Oh, that. It's been noticed before. It's just the way I look at people when I like them.'

'It's spooky.'

'Sorry, I'll stop doing it.'

'I need to go myself. It must be catching,' he said, standing up and heading for the loo.

He left his jacket – a black leather number – hanging on the back of his chair. As soon as he'd disappeared through the door I jumped up, dashed to his side of the table, had a furtive look around to make sure no-one was watching me, and went through his pockets. He'd left his wallet in his jacket. It contained a student id card. I looked at the picture: it was him. The name on the card was Jake Thurman. I shoved the card back in the wallet and the wallet back in his jacket and sat down just before he emerged from the loo.

'Are you okay?' he asked as he resumed his seat.

'Sure, why?'

'You seem to be out of breath.'

I must've gotten myself worked up worrying about whether Jake was really Joshua while I was going through his pockets. At least I now knew he was who he said he was, which meant I could relax. I did my best to slow down my breathing and get a grip on my fears.

Then I thought, *When I was younger people used to get fake student id cards so they could go drinking under-age – which means I haven't proved that Jake isn't Joshua. His ID could be fake.*

I started worrying again but managed to keep it within reasonable bounds, so I didn't end up hyperventilating.

After getting well-oiled we went back to my place. I reckoned I'd be safe as long as I didn't let him near any of my food before I ate it or my drink before I imbibed it. After all, violence wasn't Joshua's style. He was a poisoner.

We went upstairs, I locked the bedroom door much to Jake's – or Joshua's – puzzlement, then we undressed and got drunkenly into bed. As we did so, I belatedly remembered my intention had been to lock the door to keep the danger out of my room, not to secure it in there with me.

Having sex with someone you think might be out to kill you is an odd experience. I'll leave it at that.

When I woke up the next morning he was having a shower in my en suite. While he was occupied with his ablutions I jumped out of bed and went through his pockets, quickly finding his wallet and examining the contents. He had a full driving licence confirming he was Jake Thurman, which was a relief. I hadn't slept with my would-be killer after all.

My relief was short-lived. The bathroom door opened and he came out wrapped in a white towel, steam swirling all around him, and saw me with his wallet in my hands, his cash and a few other items from it on the bed.

'What the hell are you doing?' he asked.

At that moment I wanted the earth to open beneath my feet and swallow me whole. What could I say? 'I can explain,' I said, but I couldn't, not in a million years.

He strode over and snatched the wallet off me then started putting his money and everything else I'd taken out back into it. 'What is this?' he demanded. 'Some kind of a weird shakedown or something?'

'You know I wouldn't do that to you, Jake.'

He glared at me. 'So what are you doing?'

I couldn't tell him about my past, couldn't tell him I'd suspected he was a murderer out to kill me, so I had no explanation to offer.

'It was just a bad mistake, Jake, honest,' I said. 'But I promise I wasn't going to steal anything.'

By now he was putting on his clothes and giving me the distinct impression we were over. 'You shouldn't go through my things,' he said. 'They're private.'

The truth was, there wasn't much, if anything, private in his wallet. He had some cash, a debit card, a few receipts, a driving licence, his student ID, and that was about it. He was referring to the principle of privacy rather than the actuality of what I'd seen. He saw what I'd done as an intrusion. I can't say I blame him – I'd have acted the same in his position. He was in such a rush to leave that he began walking out the bedroom while still pulling on his jacket.

'I'm going,' he said at the top of the stairs, delivering the words with a dramatic finality.

So I'd lost my boyfriend, if that's what he was, and managed to deeply offend him in the process. Yet another weight on my conscience, but a relatively small one in the grand scheme of things. I wasn't in love with him so our final parting didn't come as a shattering blow, but I did feel I'd miss him. He'd been good for me when I needed cheering up. I didn't doubt I'd need cheering up again in the near future. But who would be there for me?

'Call me,' I shouted as he descended the stairs.

'I'll let myself out!' he shouted back.

Then the house was silent and I was on my own, waiting for the sword of Damocles to fall on my unprotected head.

It was going to be a long day.

But I had an idea which would help me pass time constructively.

I'd decided to track down Joshua Hawkins and see what he was getting up to.

It was just possible I'd be able to get the jump on him.

15

WAY BACK WHEN

It soon became apparent that although I could make sounds – such sounds as were so quiet they could barely be heard – and move my fingers, I wasn't able to communicate. I lacked the co-ordination to blink once for yes and twice for no, or do anything else with a consistency which might have allowed me to air my views to the world at large. I was trapped in the den of my own head. I made it bearable by transforming it, over time, into a place of peace.

One of my best days was the first day I was aware of Joshua visiting me. He was introduced as 'your brother' and no doubt the nursing staff had been told this was his relationship to me.

I was grateful for his company even though we couldn't have a conversation together. He sat near me while my mother rabbited on, doing her best to lift our spirits. I don't know how old he was at the time – two or three, I suppose.

A breakthrough came some years later. Joshua began, bit-by-tortuous-bit, to understand fragments of what I was saying. He was the only one of my visitors who did, perhaps because there is a special bond between mother and son. He never told anyone he was getting to grips with the odd language I'd begun to use. It became our secret, the biggest secret either of us had.

As he grew older I let him in on the other things I was keeping to myself. I explained that he wasn't my brother, he was my son. I got him to swear he wouldn't let anyone know before telling him. I didn't want him causing distress to our mum and dad.

The news came as a shock to him but he kept it to himself so I felt confident I could trust him with another big secret. He'd often asked me what had happened to me but I'd never disclosed the truth. I'd just said I couldn't remember exactly.

But the day came when I gave him a blow-by-blow account of what had gone on in the park when me and Tony were attacked. Once again, I made him swear to keep quiet before telling him who was responsible for my condition.

'I have to go to the police about this,' he said.

His words horrified me. 'You can't. You promised to keep it to yourself.'

'But why? They ought to be brought to justice.'

He was young and naïve – just as I had been at his age. I couldn't explain that I'd long ago given up my thirst for vengeance. However, there was another reason to keep the matter quiet – a far more pressing reason.

'You don't know what these people are like, Joshua. They'll kill us both if they have to, and the police won't be able to protect either of us. Don't take that risk.'

'You know who did this. They ought to face a trial and pay.'

'Even if you tell the police and get them in court, it won't get you what you want. You want the court to find them guilty, but what evidence is there apart from me? If I was somehow able to speak out in a court, would I be believed without corroborative evidence? No.'

'But it's so unjust. Why should they get off?'

A mother sometimes has the hard task of explaining to her child how the world really works. 'Because life is an unfair lottery, Joshua, and they've stolen a winning ticket.'

His reply made my insides turn to ice.

'Maybe I don't need to go to the police. Maybe I can go it alone.'

Those words made me worry he'd get himself killed in spite of the warning I'd given him. 'Whatever you're thinking, don't do it, Josh. One way or another it'll come back to bite you, and me as well. I'll be killed here in my hospital bed with no chance of escape. You wouldn't want that on your conscience, would you?'

'No, of course not,' he said.

I can only hope he meant it.

HERE AND NOW

Why me? I wondered. Why has Joshua included me on his death list? I didn't even do anything. I was just a bystander.

But then, I reflected, I'd given him compelling reasons for wanting me dead.

When Charlotte had needed help, I hadn't stirred myself to call an ambulance. It was the least I could've done, and it wouldn't have cost me much to do it.

If he'd been minded to give me a break because I hadn't taken an active part in the attack which disabled her and killed her boyfriend, he would've changed his mind the instant he found out what I did for a living.

I was the best friend to all the criminals in Crystal Palace. Any lesson I might have learnt the fateful day when Charlotte had been reduced to a quadriplegic had been wasted on me. And now Joshua was going to teach me what my own experiences should have drilled into me. It was to be a lethal lesson.

Only minutes before I'd been planning to get the drop on Joshua but now a sort of fatalistic depression hit me in the face like a sock full of wet gravel. I lay on my bed hardly able to move and listened to the clock ticking, wondering when the whetted blade of the axe was going to fall.

I've been anxious many times. Most of my life has been lived in a state of anxiety excepting those periods I've been drunk enough to forget my woes. That period lying on my bed helpless was my first and only taste of genuine depression. At least I think it was. I couldn't stir myself but there was no physical reason I couldn't move. I certainly hadn't been poisoned, not by Jake or anyone else. There was this black cloud hanging about a foot above my head and I couldn't shift it.

My situation felt like being in a Greek tragedy. All along, right from the very beginning, I'd known what the ending was going to be. It was pre-ordained and there was no escaping it. I couldn't change it, so there was no point in doing anything other than wait for it to happen. I found myself actually wanting it to come and deliver me from my self-inflicted hell.

After about two hours I said to myself, *Come on, Jaz, you can't carry on like this. You have to fight it. You have to force yourself to be positive.*

I pushed myself up into a sitting position and grabbed my mobile off the bedside table. If I was serious about tracking Joshua down and stopping him it would be good to have some help. I called Kylie but she didn't answer. Her mobile went straight to voicemail.

The cloud of depression grew thicker and darker. Somehow I rallied myself and pushed it out of my way.

This is it, Jaz, I told myself, *you're getting to the bottom of things even if you kill yourself doing it.*

Then I texted her:

Kylie, I think I know who's behind all this. I reckon it's Joshua – Charlotte's brother. It's some sort of revenge thing. I could do with your help to stop him. Please call back ASAP. Jaz.

I put my mobile on a chest of drawers and took a cold shower in the hope it'd put some life into me. All it did was make me shiver and gasp so I turned the tap to warm and stood under the steaming jet for about five minutes. I got out, towelled off, and put on a pair of skinny jeans with a soft wool top. Then I fortified myself with a strong black coffee, drank two more for good measure, and sat on the sofa with my tablet doing searches on Joshua Hawkins and making notes.

He had a Facebook account which was restricted so I couldn't see much of it and what I could see wasn't very informative. His profile picture was the standard blank silhouette you get when you haven't uploaded a photo.

By searching other social media I was able to discover he'd left college the previous June and was taking a year out. Doing what? Travelling or killing people? He planned to study medicine at King's College starting in September. I wondered if his urge to become a doctor was the result of having a sister who was severely disabled and he was hoping to find a cure for her condition. But, pending that, he was eliminating the cause of it.

If I could find out where he was living, I could stake the place out, find out what he looked like, follow him, and get a feel for what he was up to and how he aimed to get shot of me.

I glanced at my mobile. It was half an hour since I'd sent Kylie the text and she hadn't replied. It could mean she'd carried out her threat to leave and didn't want to communicate with me for fear of giving away too much about where she'd gone, or it could mean she was Joshua's latest victim. Either way, things were shaping up to pit me and Joshua against one another in a final face-off. I felt tired, too tired to fight. That was the depression getting to me again. I'd been too stressed out for too long, and my body and mind were in danger of caving in under the pressure. I fought back.

Be strong, Jaz. If you can only keep going a few more days you might be able to save yourself. Your life is crappy but it's worth living. Think of Mum and Dad, and Karl. Do it for them, as well as for yourself.

I searched for clues as to Joshua's whereabouts. I couldn't find out where he lived but I discovered via a tweet he had a friend called Gareth Sumner who worked as an operating theatre porter at the Royal London Hospital.

Joshua's address was the thing I most needed. I decided on a plan of action to get it. The plan involved visiting The Royal London Hospital on Whitechapel Road. I could have telephoned but I reckoned I'd be more likely to be taken notice of in person.

It took me half an hour to get there by train and a further twenty minutes to walk to the entrance. I went inside, made my way to reception, and spoke to the hangdog man who was on duty that day. He was balding and middle-aged and looked as if he'd rather be doing any other job than the one he had.

'I need to speak to one of your porters,' I said. 'Gareth Sumner – he's a theatre porter. It's urgent. Would you be able to get him on your internal line for me please?'

He shook his head. 'It's not so simple,' he said. 'This is a big place.'

I adopted the look of a helpless female. It's a pose I hate and don't normally go for, but desperate times call for desperate measures.

'Please help me,' I said, giving him a full-on sad puppy dog look. 'It means so much to me.'

'All right,' he said with resignation in his voice. 'I'll do my best. What was the name again?'

'Gareth Sumner.'

He keyed it into a PC on his desk. 'And who wants to talk to him?'

'My name is Amy Foster. He doesn't know me. I'm a relative and I'm only here for the day.'

'I'll do my best.'

He looked at the screen of his PC then dialled a number on his telephone and spoke into it. He smiled, gave me the thumbs-up, and passed the receiver to me. I turned away so he wouldn't hear too much of my conversation.

'Gareth?' I said.

'Yes, who is this?'

'My name is Amy Foster. I'm a cousin of a friend of yours – Joshua Hawkins. I have some confidential news about his uncle and I need to tell him about it in person. It's not the sort of thing you discuss on the telephone. Unfortunately my mobile was stolen and I've lost my contact details for him. Can you give me his address, please?'

'Sorry, I can't remember it, I'll have to look it up. Is there any way I can contact you?'

I turned to the receptionist.

'Could you let me have a piece of paper and a pen please?'

With a wry smile he reached down, fished a ballpoint pen and a compliments slip from his desk, and put them in front of me.

'Thank you,' I said to him, then I turned my attentions back to Gareth Sumner. 'I'm afraid not. Please give me your mobile number and I'll give you a call or text you later.'

I was planning to get a cheap pay-as-you-go mobile phone which couldn't be traced back to me, and use that to contact Gareth, so as not to risk having him give Joshua my mobile phone number.

'Okay,' he replied, and gave me his number. I wrote it down on the compliments slip as he spoke.

'I'll be in touch.'

'I'll wait to hear from you. I have to go now. My break's just finished.'

I handed the receiver and pen back to hangdog man, put the compliments slip in my bag, and left the hospital feeling that I was, if nothing else, spending my time constructively rather than merely waiting for the worst to happen. I didn't yet have Joshua's address and nor did I know what he looked like, but with luck and a following wind, I soon would.

Now what? I thought.

The answer seemed obvious: get a pay-as-you-go mobile phone, get Joshua's address from Gareth, then stake out Joshua's place, identify him, follow him, and see what he got up to. If he was the poisoner, what then? Would I be able to scare him off? Probably not, so what could I do? Tell the police? If Joshua had killed all the other witnesses to the incident I might be able to do it without risking my own freedom. But what if the police couldn't pin the murders on him? He'd still be out to get me. Did that mean I'd have to kill him before he killed me?

I couldn't see myself killing anyone again – not on purpose anyway – and decided to cross that bridge when I got to it.

I bought a mobile phone from a nearby supermarket and took it to Crystal Palace on the train, intending to activate it when I got home. After following the instructions to set it up, I texted Gareth and grabbed a bite to eat – a Heinz all-day breakfast. I was busy eating it when my mobile – my real mobile – interrupted me. A quick glance at the screen told me it was Jake. Presumably he was ringing to say he'd overreacted this morning, he wanted to apologise, and hoped I was willing to see him again. I was still in two minds about whether I should be dating a nineteen-year-old so I let it ring a few times, which gave me the opportunity to consider what my take on the call was going to be. Was I going to finish with him? Or would I be weak and prolong the life of the sick animal that our relationship surely was for a few more days? I didn't know, couldn't decide, and on the fifth ring I picked up.

'Hi, Jake, how are you doing?'

He didn't answer right away which was unlike him. When he did reply he sounded out of sorts.

'I've come down with something and I can't get the doctor to give me an appointment,' he said. His teeth sounded to be chattering so I guessed he had quite a temperature. 'Could you come round here and help me, please, Jaz?'

The thought of tending a sick person didn't do wonders for me. I had pressing things to do. What's more, Jake had just inadvertently made clear one of the reasons I had for not wanting to date a young person – his lack of the savvy which comes with age. He had no idea how to do the basic task of getting an appointment to see a doctor on the NHS. I was willing to bet he lacked a lot of similar life skills and when he'd lived at home his mummy had always done that kind of thing for him.

'Just ring the surgery and tell them you're in pain, Jake,' I said. 'Be pushy about it and don't let them fob you off.'

He sobbed. He actually sobbed. 'Please help me, Jaz, I think I'm dying,' he said. 'I think I've got meningitis and I'm too ill to leave the house without help.'

His melodramatic outburst shocked me. I hadn't got him taped as a hypochondriac. I felt myself going right off him. I never have cared for snivelling types. I was about to say goodbye and hang up when I thought, *Maybe he really does have meningitis.* I knew what the disease could do. There'd been a promising young solicitor called Alison who'd joined Womack and Brewer LLP some years previously. She was sharp and obviously destined to go on to bigger things than Womack and Brewer LLP were able to offer. However, she'd caught meningitis and hadn't received treatment in a timely manner. The doctors managed to save her life but she'd suffered brain damage and was left partially deaf, and unable to understand the legal documents she'd once effortlessly drafted. The firm had kept her on as a librarian and records-keeper, which was the most complex level of task she could carry out after her recovery.

I decided I didn't want that to happen to Jake and even though we'd fallen out. I was going to see to it he got treatment quickly, if it was needed. I'd never get over it if he died alone in his house and I could've helped him. So staking out Joshua's place would have to be put on hold for a while.

'All right, Jake,' I said. 'I'll be over as soon as I can. What's your address?'

I wrote it down in blue biro on the edge of a newspaper I had on the kitchen table. 58B Cranella Street. I knew the area vaguely. At one time or another I'd probably helped a felon who lived near him to escape justice.

'Please hurry,' he blubbed. That did it for me. I made up my mind to finish with him as soon as I'd made sure he wasn't in danger of dying any time soon.

'I will,' I said, barely able to supress my irritation at his whining. 'I'll be there in half an hour, tops.'

Almost as soon as I'd hung up my mobile pinged. When I checked it, I saw that Jake had texted his address, presumably to make doubly sure I'd got it. He'd also helpfully pointed out that his door was unlocked and said I should walk right in without ringing the bell. He must've been desperate. He'd ended his text with a line of x's – kiss kiss kiss kiss kiss – sweet but cloying. If his rampant hypochondria and self-pity hadn't put me off him, the line of x's surely would have done.

I finished my meal and put the bowl in the sink, then got in my car, hoping that by this time the drinks from my last session had worn off.

Cranella Street had modest terraced houses at one end, large detached homes at the other, and medium sized semis in the middle. Jake lived in a maisonette carved out of the basement of one of the semis. I guessed his rent was costing him more money than my mortgage, as the road didn't look remotely like it belonged in student-land. It was well-maintained, so much so that it made a good impression on me in spite of the annoying drizzle which was falling from a grey April sky. Expensive cars were parked in the street, and a casually well-dressed couple were emerging from a house with their child in an expensive buggy.

All-in-all it looked like hipster-land, the sort of place you came to live when you had money but not enough – yet – to buy or rent in the most affluent suburbs. I surmised that Jake's parents were paying his way and were not short of a bob or two.

Due to the number of four-by-fours and big Mercs taking up the available parking I was obliged to put my car a couple of hundred yards away from number fifty-eight in a space I could barely squeeze it into. After a deal of sweaty manoeuvring I got parked up and headed for Jake's maisonette wishing I'd brought an umbrella. The rain wasn't heavy but it was relentless and by the time I got to fifty-eight I was dripping wet and my hair was a complete mess. Still, I wasn't visiting to impress him with my looks. I walked around the property looking for 58B and found a set of concrete steps at the side leading below ground. A brass sign on the wall above them said '58B'. An arrow beneath the sign was angled downwards.

I descended the steps to a grey cement path. On my left was a window; dead ahead there was a porch over a grey door with a large door knocker on it. At the side of the door a brass doorbell was set into the stonework. Someone disabled must've lived there once because adjacent to the door there was a lift back up to ground level, big enough to accommodate a wheelchair.

I chose the knocker over the doorbell and gave it three loud knocks. I waited but Jake didn't answer and I remembered I was meant to just walk right in.

I glanced back at the window – the curtains were drawn. *That is a touch melodramatic,* I thought. I pointlessly knocked again, the result of years of having it drummed into me during my childhood that you're meant to knock before entering someone's house, turned the brass handle, and pushed open the door.

The hall was exactly how I expected it to be: small and square with a tiled floor and a door to my left giving access to the front room. I shut the outside door and pushed open the door to the front room. The place was dark because the curtains were closed. I fumbled on the wall for a light switch, found one, and pressed it down. Nothing happened. The bulb must've gone. After my eyes had adjusted to the conditions I could see a little way into the room.

'Jake,' I called, wondering if he might be in bed.

There was no reply. He must've taken a turn for the worse. It was looking like he really was ill and I might end up having to call an ambulance. I took a couple of uncertain steps forward into the gloom intending to open the curtains.

That was when I saw something unnerving – a figure sitting upright in a chair. He mumbled incoherently and my heart began to beat like crazy against my ribs. I stopped dead. What was going on?

As my eyes grew more accustomed to the gloom I was able to identify the figure as Jake and I could tell he was tied to an old-fashioned bentwood kitchen chair. He was gagged and so scared his eyes were like truck headlights.

Fear gripped my insides. I had to get out, fast, but the door I'd just come through closed behind me and an arm reached from behind around my neck while another arm reached slightly higher, the hand clamping a piece of damp fabric over my nose and mouth.

Someone was trying to put me under with chloroform or something similar. In desperation I lashed out, tried to wriggle free, and at the same time tried to hold my breath. It wasn't long before shapes swirled before my eyes, I felt weak, and an inner darkness began to swallow me up. I fought hard as I could to stop myself from falling into it.

My efforts were to no avail.

The darkness won.

When I woke up I felt as if I was still asleep. I tried to open my eyes but couldn't, tried to move my arms and legs but couldn't. Then after a long struggle I managed to force my eyelids open. Above me was a white ceiling with an ornate pendant light dangling from it which was missing a bulb. By rolling my eyes to the side I could see curtains half-open and behind them a window. To the other side of me there was a charcoal grey door set in a light grey wall.

Where was I? How had I got here? At first I couldn't remember what'd happened. Then it all came back. Jake had called me, he'd told me he was ill, and when I'd gone to help I'd found him tied up and someone had attacked me. Hopefully my attacker hadn't injured me too badly – I wasn't in pain. As I came to my senses I discovered my hands were tied behind my back and my ankles were bound together. I was lying on the floor on a beige carpet. Whatever drug had been used on me, it was beginning to wear off. I was able to move a little.

It occurred to me I ought to make an attempt to escape from whatever peril I was in, but I was too drowsy to do much. I shook my head as best I could to bring myself around and wriggled my wrists, trying to slip my hands from their bonds. It was no use. They were tied too well. In fact they were tied so tight that as the effects of the drug wore off my wrists began to hurt. So did my ankles. I looked around for something to cut my bonds with but there was nothing which looked promising.

Turning my head as much as I was able I saw I was in Jake's front room. He was still tied to a chair, unable to speak because of the gag over his mouth. Behind him was a sofa. I tried to call out to him and found I was similarly gagged.

A hissing sound emanated from an adjacent room. Someone was making coffee. The grey door creaked open and a woman walked in holding a steaming mug in one hand.

She had dark auburn hair cut to just short of shoulder length. It got thicker as it got longer making it stick out from the bottom of her head in an 'A' shape. Her lips were emphasised with a bold red slash of lipstick, her cheekbones with a shadow of expertly-applied blusher. Somewhat incongruously she was wearing sunglasses, expensive ones by the looks of them. Who was this strange woman? What part did she have to play in all this?

She sat on the sofa and removed the sunglasses. Only then did she speak. 'I don't think much of your boyfriend,' she said. 'It didn't take much to get him to let me into his home on the understanding we'd have sex when he got me here. Too bad it didn't work out for him the way he expected.'

I knew that voice and now I recognised the face. It was Kylie. She was wearing a wig. She had great hair. Why hide it under an ugly wig?

'I didn't want it to end this way, messy and painful,' she continued. 'I wanted you to fall asleep without knowing what was going on, just like the others. But you somehow got lucky, or unlucky, depending on which way you look at it. That's why it's come to this.'

I tried to reply but couldn't. She came over and took the gag from my mouth. 'Yes?' she said.

I considered screaming to get attention but knew it was unlikely to bring anyone running to help me. I figured my best course of action would be to keep her talking and hope some sort of opportunity to escape presented itself. Failing that, I'd scream for help. 'Why are you doing this?' I asked, hoping it'd buy me time.

She returned to her perch on the sofa before answering. 'I got fed up of worrying that someone would crack and I'd get sent down for a murder I was involved with a long time ago,' she said. 'I didn't see why I should carry on living in fear for the rest of my life. And I was sick of kowtowing to Seth. I realised if everyone who knew our secret was out of the way, I could lead a normal life. It's that simple.'

My mind went into overdrive. How had I not worked all this out? How had I been so blind? How could I keep her talking longer and what would it gain me other than a few more minutes?

'What are you planning on doing to me – to us?'

She took a sip of her coffee. 'Wait and see,' she said.

'Tell me,' I said, 'I need to know.'

Jake's eyes were wide open with fear. I couldn't say I blamed him. Mine were probably the same.

'No you don't,' she said. 'But as you ask, you and your boyfriend are never going to be seen or heard from again. You're going to disappear like so many people do.'

I guessed we'd both be poisoned in some way, taken to a remote spot, and buried in a shallow grave. Maybe she had other plans for us, but that's the way I saw it panning out. My fear reached epic levels even I had never known before. *When all else fails, plead for your life, Jaz,* I thought.

'Don't do this, Kylie. You don't have to. I'll keep our secret. I've kept it all this time, haven't I?'

I was clutching at the most inadequate straws going, which is what drowning men and women have always done.

'You don't understand,' she said. 'I need to free myself of the paranoia I've had to endure all my adult life. I can't put up with it any longer and I won't be rid of it until every last witness who could testify against me is dead. Unfortunately your boyfriend has been drawn into things. Collateral damage you might say. But that's war for you.'

I clutched at an even smaller straw. 'What about Seth?'

She smirked. 'What about him?'

'You were in love with him. How could you do it to him?'

She took another sip of her coffee then held the mug in both hands, leaning forward. 'Yes I was in love with him, *was* being the operative word,' she corrected me. 'You wouldn't believe the things I did for that man in the name of love. But he cheated on me in spite of the loyalty I showed him, so I decided I'd be happier without him than with him. I was right. Killing him was an unexpected pleasure. By the way, he was the easiest of the lot of you to get rid of, because he thought he was untouchable – and because I was the one person he never suspected.' She put the mug down on the floor, walked over to me and crouched low so her face was above mine.

'What'll it take to make you change your mind?' I asked.

'If you could give me a time machine so that I could go back into the past and erase our mistakes, that would just about cover it. Have you got a time machine? No? I didn't think so.'

I began to yell as loud as I could but she quickly put the gag back on me so I only managed about two seconds. No-one came running to my rescue.

'I'm going to leave you two lovebirds for a few minutes. I need to get some things to help me tidy up,' she said, then she left and I heard the outside door slamming behind her.

The words 'tidy up' scared me. I didn't think they referred to getting Jake's maisonette straight. I was still groggy from whatever she'd used on me so I shook my head to clear a little of the fog from it. I thought I might have a chance of standing up if I got on my belly so I tried to roll over but couldn't manage it. I tried wriggling like a caterpillar but found any form of locomotion impossible. It didn't help that my ankles and wrists were throbbing.

I somehow rolled on my side and in desperation got myself into a foetal position by drawing my knees up to my chest, and then with a huge effort born of adrenaline fuelled fear, I forced my hands, which were bound behind my back, down my butt. Then by pulling my knees up even higher I got my hands over my feet. Until that moment I'd had no idea I was capable of such a manoeuvre. It's amazing what a body can do when you're knocking at death's door.

With my hands now in front of me I was able to get into a crawling position and push myself to my feet. I then made a series of awkward jumps towards the small kitchen at the back of the maisonette but lost my balance and fell heavily. When I landed it hurt like hell and felt as if I'd put my shoulder out.

Almost there, Jaz, I said to myself. *Don't quit now.*

I didn't think I could risk standing up again so I got on my hands and knees and did a cross between a crawl and a shuffle the rest of the way. Once in the kitchen I stood up and immediately staggered. I couldn't afford another fall – not onto the tiled kitchen floor. Somehow I managed to clutch the worktop for support.

I pulled open a drawer and found a small knife. It was a dinner knife rather than a cutting knife, but it seemed to have enough of a blade to cut my bonds, so I bent over and sawed my ankles free. It took some doing with a blunt dinner knife.

It was impossible for me to turn the knife around and use it to sever the cords binding my wrists so I cut the gag from my mouth, slashing my face in the process, and felt my own blood running down my face, saw it dripping onto the tiles I was standing on. It made a plip-plip noise and the sight of so much of my own blood would've scared me shitless if not for the fact I had bigger things scaring me right then.

With the handle of the knife between my teeth I was able – just – to saw the cord tying my wrists together. My jaws were aching by the time the strands were coming loose – and at that point, I heard the front door open.

This is it, Jaz, it's fight time, I whispered.

The sedative Kylie had administered to me was still in my system and although I'd been able to untie myself I was unsteady on my feet and knew I'd have no chance against her unarmed. I had the knife but it was pitifully small.

Think, Jaz, find a weapon.

I could've used the knife and would have done if it'd come down to it, but a dinner knife didn't seem threatening enough somehow, so I rummaged around in the drawer again and found a rolling pin. *That'd be better,* I thought. I grabbed it in my right hand and immediately had to put it down. My shoulder was hurting so much I couldn't pick it up. I used my left hand and rushed into the lounge just as Kylie entered it from the lobby, leading with her left shoulder, her right arm being occupied with dragging something. She glanced down and saw I was no longer on the floor then turned her head to look my way. By that time I was nearly on her. She looked on in horror as I brought the rolling pin down as hard as I could in a deadly arc.

What happens when you hit someone on the head with a hard object? Do they fall unconscious and wake up an hour later none the worse for wear, like they do in old movies? Or do they get a fractured skull, brain haemorrhage, and death or permanent disability from such a blow?

These thoughts ran through my mind in the instant I delivered the blow. They must have had some subconscious effect on my actions because when the rolling pin hit her, it didn't strike where I'd aimed on the crown of her head; it just missed her ear and landed near her right shoulder.

She let go of whatever she was dragging and fell against the wall. With a look of disbelief on her face she slid down it until she was sitting on the floor, back against the wall, knees drawn up into her chest.

Her right shoulder looked to be about two inches lower than her left one. She reached across her body with her left hand and gingerly ran her fingers along it towards her neck. Afterwards she looked up at me with sad eyes.

'You've broken my collarbone,' she said, in the voice of a small child. Still speaking in a small child's voice, she added: 'You shouldn't have done that. You've upset me now. I thought you were a nice girl, Jaz.'

She burst into tears. That's when I realised she was unhinged. She'd been carrying a bigger burden of guilt around than I had, and it'd fucked her up more than mine had fucked me up. I should've spotted the signs years before, I suppose, but I'd been too preoccupied with myself to take any notice of what might be going on in Kylie's head.

Fearing she might attack me, I was still holding the rolling pin aloft ready to defend myself. I realised it wasn't needed, as the one blow had knocked all the fight out of her, and I lowered my hand to my side, dropping my makeshift weapon to the floor. My handbag was on the sofa. I rooted in it and got out my mobile. Jake was making urgent noises through his gag. I glanced in his direction.

'Don't worry, Jake, I'll untie you in a minute,' I assured him.

Then I did something I should've done eighteen years earlier: I called the police.

When I'd finished speaking to them Kylie looked up at me again. By this time her blubbing had subsided to sniffling. Wiping the tears from her eyes with her good hand, she said, 'Was the baseball bat a nice touch?'

'Yes, Kylie,' I replied. 'It got me barking up all kinds of trees, none of them the right sort.'

She looked pleased with herself. 'I knew it would.'

Jake made some more anxious noises from under his gag to get my attention so I set him loose.

'Thanks,' he said. 'She made me lure you here by holding a knife to my throat. I was convinced she was going to use it.'

'You were right. She would have used it.'

When the police arrived I told them everything that had happened eighteen years ago, and I even fessed up to my more recent crime of killing poor Sean Price. I explained I'd been drugged when I'd run him over.

Kylie confirmed my version of events. She's since been charged, tried, and sent to Broadmoor – the prison for the criminally insane.

The newspapers and TV reported her trial and the sensational background to it, portraying me as almost as much of a victim as Charlotte. Charlotte's brother Joshua subsequently broke the news he'd been able to talk to her for some time but hadn't let on for fear of the criminal gang coming back to finish the job on his sister they'd started almost two decades before. Now the gang was finished he felt he could reveal all.

The police didn't take any action over the part I'd played in ruining Charlotte's life because she refused to give them any evidence against me. I've never been able to figure out why she did that, but I'm deeply grateful to her. The police did charge me for leaving the scene of the accident in which I killed Sean Price. My solicitor put forward a terrific plea in mitigation, arguing that being drugged and stressed had affected my reasoning, and so on, and I got off with four penalty points and a £2,000 fine.

The thing Kylie had been dragging into the room when I'd hit her was a wheelie case. She had a second one in her car. I don't know what she was planning on doing with them. One of the newspapers speculated she was going to shut me and Jake up in them and leave us in the house, like the poor spy who was found dead in a holdall in his own apartment. Another suggested she'd wheel us out one at a time and dump us in the canal, or on a railway siding. Either way, it wouldn't have been a good end for us.

Danny Scott didn't go to ground after all – he died in his own cellar. He'd gone down there to get a few items he needed but he never made it back up. He breathed his last at the bottom of the cellar steps, another of Kylie's victims.

I've given up my legal job and gotten a low-paying admin job working for Bromley Council. I make ends meet by letting out a room to a lodger. I guess one day I'll retrain and get back to earning a half-decent income. In the meantime I have the satisfaction of knowing I'm no longer helping criminals escape their just desserts and I'll never return to that line of work.

Me and Jake didn't get back together, of course.

I doubt I'll ever visit Charlotte again, or speak to any other member of her family. It'd be too traumatic for them and for me.

Right now I'm shaking like a leaf in a force-twelve hurricane because I'm desperate for a drink. I'm not going to have one, though. I spoke to Bernie – my AA counsellor – earlier today, and tonight I'm going to my first AA meeting in months. I'm determined to stay off the sauce for good.

This time I really mean it.

The End

ACKNOWLEDGMENTS

I would like to thank the team at Bloodhound Books for doing such a great job of producing my book and bringing it to the attention of readers.

I'd also like to thank Clare Law for her great edit.

Finally, I owe a big thank-you to all the friends I have who've encouraged me with my writing. In no particular order, they are: Paul D, Denis, Pearl, Martin, Melinda, Paul M, Owen, Debbie, Marc, Julian, Sean, Phil, and Ted. (I hope I haven't left anybody out – if I have, I'm very sorry!)

Printed by Amazon Italia Logistica S.r.l.
Torrazza Piemonte (TO), Italy